# PRETTIES

## SCOTT WESTERFELD

SIMON AND SCHUSTER

SIMON AND SCHUSTER
First published in Great Britain in 2006 by Simon & Schuster UK Ltd,
1st Floor, 222 Gray's Inn Road, London WC1X 8HB

This edition published in 2014

Originally published in the USA in 2005 by Simon Pulse,
an imprint of Simon & Schuster Children's Division, New York.



A CIP catalogue record for this book is available from the British Library

ISBN: 978-1-47112-395-5

10 9 8 7 6 5 4 3



Printed and bound by CPI Group (UK) Ltd, Croydon, CR0 4YY

www.simonandschuster.co.uk

www.scottwesterfeld.com

# PRETTIES

**Also by Scott Westerfeld:**

**UGLIES**
**SPECIALS**
**EXTRAS**

**LEVIATHAN**
**BEHEMOTH**
**GOLIATH**

To the Australian SF community for all your acceptance and support

# Part 1

## SLEEPING BEAUTY

Remember that the most beautiful
things in the world are the most useless.
—John Ruskin, *The Stones of Venice, I*

# CRIMINAL

Getting dressed was always the hardest part of the afternoon.

The invitation to Valentino Mansion said semiformal, but it was the semi part that was tricky. Like a night without a party, "semi" opened up too many possibilities. Bad enough for boys, for whom it could mean jacket and tie (skipping the tie with certain kinds of collars), or all white and shirtsleeves (but only on summer afternoons), or any number of longcoats, waistcoats, tailcoats, kilts, or really nice sweaters. For girls, though, the definition simply exploded, as definitions usually did here in New Pretty Town.

Tally almost preferred formal white-tie or black-tie parties. The clothes were less comfortable and the parties no fun until everyone got drunk, but at least you didn't have to think so hard about getting dressed.

"Semiformal, semiformal," she said, her eyes drifting over the expanse of her open closet, the carousel stuttering back and forth as it tried to keep up with Tally's random eyemouse clicks, setting clothes swaying on their hangers. Yes, "semi" was definitely a bogus word.

"Is it even a word?" Tally asked aloud. "'Semi'?" It felt strange in her mouth, which was dry as cotton because of last night.

"Only half of one," the room said, probably thinking it was clever.

"Figures," Tally muttered.

She collapsed back onto her bed and stared up at the ceiling, feeling the room threaten to spin a little. It didn't seem fair, having to get worked up over half a word. "Make it go away," she said.

The room misunderstood, and slid shut the wall over her closet. Tally didn't have the strength to explain that she'd really meant her hangover, which was sprawled in her head like an overweight cat, sullen and squishy and disinclined to budge.

Last night, she and Peris had gone skating with a bunch of other Crims, trying out the new rink hovering over Nefertiti Stadium. The sheet of ice, held aloft by a grid of lifters, was thin enough to see through, and was kept transparent by a horde of little Zambonies darting among the skaters like nervous water bugs. The fireworks exploding in the stadium below made it glow like some kind of schizoid stained glass that changed colors every few seconds.

They all had to wear bungee jackets in case anyone broke through. No one ever did, of course, but the thought that at any moment the world could fall away with a sudden crack kept Tally drinking plenty of champagne.

Zane, who was pretty much the leader of the Crims, got bored and tipped a whole bottle onto the ice. He said that alcohol had a lower freezing point than water, so it might send someone tumbling down into the fireworks. But he hadn't poured out enough to save Tally's head this morning.

The room made the special sound that meant another Crim was calling.

"Hey."

"Hey, Tally."

"Shay-la!" Tally struggled up onto one elbow. "I need help!"

"The party? I know."

"What's the deal with semiformal, anyway?"

Shay laughed. "Tally-wa, you are so missing. Didn't you get the ping?"

"What ping?"

"It went out hours ago."

Tally glanced at her interface ring, still on her bedside table. She never wore it at night, an old habit from when she'd been an ugly, sneaking out all the time. It sat there softly pulsing, still muted for sleeptime. "Oh. Just woke up."

"Well forget semi anything. They changed the bash to fancy dress. We have to come up with costumes!"

Tally checked the time: just before five in the afternoon. "What, in three hours?"

"Yeah, I know. I'm all over the place with mine. It's so shaming. Can I come down?"

"Please."

"In five?"

"Sure. Bring breakfast. Bye."

Tally let her head fall back onto the pillow. The bed was spinning like a hoverboard now, the day just starting and already wiping out.

She slipped on her interface ring and listened angrily as the ping played, saying that no one would be admitted tonight without a really bubbly costume. Three hours to come up with something decent, and everyone else had a huge head start.

Sometimes, it felt like being a real criminal had been much, much simpler.

*

Shay had breakfast in tow: lobster omelettes, toast, hash browns, corn fritters, grapes, chocolate muffins, and Bloodies—more food than a whole packet of calorie purgers could erase. The overburdened tray shivered in the air, its lifters trembling like a littlie arriving at school, first day ever.

"Um, Shay? Are we going as blimps or something?"

Shay giggled. "No, but you sounded bad. And you have to be bubbly tonight. All the Crims are coming to vote you in."

"Great, bubbly." Tally sighed, relieving the tray of a Bloody Mary. She frowned at the first sip. "Not salty enough."

"No problem," Shay said, scraping off the caviar decorating an omelette and stirring it in.

"Ew, fishy!"

"Caviar is good with anything." Shay took another spoonful and put it straight into her mouth, closing her eyes to chew the little fish eggs. She twisted her ring to start some music.

Tally swallowed and drank more Bloody, which at least stopped the room from spinning. The chocolate muffins were starting to smell good. Then she'd move on to the hash browns. Then the omelette; she might even try the caviar. Breakfast was the meal when Tally most felt like she had to make up for the time she'd lost out in the wild. A good breakfast binge made her feel in control, as if a storm of city-made tastes could erase the months of stews and SpagBol.

The music was new and made her heart beat faster. "Thanks, Shay-la. You are totally life-saving."

"No problem, Tally-wa."

"So where were you last night, anyway?"

Shay just smiled, like she'd done something bad.

"What? New boy?"

Shay shook her head. Batted her eyes.

"You didn't surge again, did you?" Tally asked, and Shay giggled. "You did. You're not supposed to more than once a week. Could you be any more missing?"

"It's okay, Tally-wa. Just local."

"Where?" Shay's face didn't look any different. Was the surgery hidden under her pajamas?

"Look closer." Shay's long lashes fluttered again.

Tally leaned forward, staring into the perfect copper eyes, wide and speckled with jewel dust, and her heart beat still faster. A month after coming to New Pretty Town, Tally was still awestruck by other pretties' eyes. They were so huge and welcoming, bright with interest. Shay's lush pupils seemed to murmur, I'm listening to you. You fascinate me. They narrowed down the world to only Tally, all alone in the radiance of Shay's attention.

It was even weirder with Shay, because Tally had known her back in ugly days, before the operation had made her this way.

"Closer."

Tally took a steadying breath, the room spinning again, but in a good way. She gestured for the windows to transpare a little more, and in the sunlight she saw the new additions. "Ooh, pretty-making."

Bolder than all the other implanted glitter, twelve tiny rubies ringed each of Shay's pupils, glowing softly red against emerald irises.

"Bubbly, huh?"

"Yeah. But hang on . . . are the bottom-left ones different?" Tally squinted harder. One jewel in each eye seemed to be flickering, a tiny white candle in the coppery depths.

"It's five o'clock!" Shay said. "Get it?"

It took Tally a second to remember how to read the big

clock tower in the center of town. "Um, but that's seven. Wouldn't bottom-right be five o'clock?"

Shay snorted. "They run counterclockwise, silly. I mean, so boring otherwise."

A laugh bubbled up in Tally. "So wait. You have jewels in your eyes? And they tell time? And they go backward? Isn't that maybe one thing too many, Shay?"

Tally immediately regretted what she'd said. The expression that clouded Shay's face was tragic, sucking away the radiance of a moment before. She looked about to cry, except without puffy eyes or a red nose. New surge was always a delicate topic, like a new hairstyle, almost.

"You hate them," Shay softly accused.

"Of course I don't. Like I said: totally pretty-making."

"Really?"

"Very. And it's good they go backward."

Shay's smile returned, and Tally breathed a sigh of relief, still not believing herself. It was the kind of mistake only brand-new pretties made, and she'd had the operation over a month ago. Why was she still saying bogus things? If she made a comment like that tonight, one of the Crims might vote against her. It only took one veto to shut you out.

And then she'd be alone, almost like running away again.

Shay said, "Maybe we should go as clock towers tonight, in honor of my new eyeballs."

Tally laughed, knowing the lame joke meant she was forgiven. She and Shay had been through a lot together, after all. "Have you talked to Peris and Fausto?"

Shay nodded. "They said we're all supposed to dress criminal. They've got an idea already, but it's secret."

"That's so bogus. Like they were such bad boys. All

they ever did in the ugly days was sneak out and maybe cross the river a few times. They never even made it to the Smoke."

The song ended just then, and Tally's last word fell into sudden silence. She tried to think of what to say, but the conversation just faded out, like fireworks in a dark sky. The next song seemed to take a long time to start.

When it did, she was relieved and said, "Crim costumes should be easy, Shay-la. We're the two biggest criminals in town."

Shay and Tally tried for two hours, making the hole in the wall spit out costumes and trying them on. They thought of bandits, but didn't really know what one looked like—in all the old bandit movies in the wallscreen, the bad guys didn't look Crim, just retarded. Pirates were much better dressing, but Shay didn't want to wear a patch over one of her new eyeballs. Going as hunters was another idea, but the hole in the wall had this thing about guns, even fake ones. Tally thought of famous dictators from history, but most of them turned out to be men and fashion-missing.

"Maybe we should be Rusties!" Shay said. "In school, they were always the bad guys."

"But they mostly looked like us, I thought. Except ugly."

"I don't know, we could cut down trees or burn oil or something."

Tally laughed. "This is a costume, Shay-la, not a lifestyle."

Shay spread her arms and said more things, trying to be bubbly. "We could smoke tobacco? Or drive cars?"

But the hole in the wall wouldn't give them cigarettes or cars.

It was fun, though, hanging out with Shay and trying

things on, then snorting and giggling and tossing the costumes back into the recycler. Tally loved seeing how she looked in new clothes, even silly ones. Part of her could still remember back before, when looking in the mirror had been painful, her eyes too close together and nose too small, hair frizzy all the time. Now it was like someone gorgeous stood across from Tally, following her every move—someone whose face was in perfect balance, whose skin glowed even with a total hangover, whose body was beautifully proportioned and muscled. Someone whose silvery eyes matched anything she wore.

But someone with bogus taste in costumes.

After two hours they were lying on the bed, which was spinning again.

"Everything sucks, Shay-la. Why does everything suck? They'll never vote me in if I can't even come up with a non-bogus costume."

Shay took her hand. "Don't worry, Tally-wa. You're already famous. There's no reason to be nervous."

"That's easy for you to say." Even though they'd been born on the same day, Shay had become pretty weeks and weeks before Tally. She'd been a full-fledged Crim for almost a month now.

"It's not going to be a problem," Shay said. "Anyone who used to hang out with Special Circumstances is a natural Crim."

A feeling went through Tally when Shay said that, like a ping, but hurting. "Still. I hate not being bubbly."

"It's Peris's and Fausto's fault for not telling us what they're wearing."

"Let's just wait till they get here. And copy them."

"They deserve it," Shay agreed. "Want a drink?"

"I think so."

Tally was too spinning to go anywhere, so Shay told the breakfast tray to go and get some champagne.

When Peris and Fausto came in, they were on fire.

It was really just sparklers wound into their hair and stuck onto their clothes, making safety flames flicker all over them. Fausto kept laughing because it tickled. They were both wearing bungee jackets—their costume was that they'd just jumped from the roof of a burning building.

"Fantastic!" Shay said.

"Hysterical," Tally agreed, but then asked, "but how is that Crim?"

"Don't you remember?" Peris said. "When you crashed a party last summer, and got away by stealing a bungee jacket and jumping off the roof? Best ugly trick in history!"

"Sure . . . but why are you on fire?" Tally asked. "I mean, it's not Crim if the building's really on fire."

Shay was giving Tally a look like she was saying something bogus again.

"We couldn't just wear bungee jackets," Fausto said. "Being on fire is much bubblier."

"Yeah," Peris said, but Tally could tell he saw what she meant, and was sad now. She wished she hadn't mentioned it. Stupid Tally. The costumes really were bubbly.

They put the sparklers out to save them for the party, and Shay told the hole in the wall to make two more jackets.

"Hey, that's copying!" Fausto complained, but it turned out not to matter. The hole wouldn't do costume bungee jackets, in case someone forgot and jumped off something and splatted. It couldn't make a real jacket; you had to ask Requisition for anything complicated or permanent. And Requisition wouldn't send any up because there wasn't a fire.

Shay snorted. "The mansion is being totally bogus today."

"So where'd you get those?" Tally asked.

"They're real." Peris smiled, fingering his jacket. "We stole them from the roof."

"So they are Crim," Tally said, and jumped off the bed to hug him.

With Peris in her arms, it didn't feel like the party was going to suck, or that anyone was going to vote against her. His big brown eyes beamed down into hers, and he lifted her up and squeezed her hard. She'd always felt this close to Peris back in ugly days, playing tricks and growing up together. It was bubbly to feel this way right now.

All those weeks that Tally had been lost in the wild, all she'd ever wanted was to be back here with Peris, pretty in New Pretty Town. It was totally stupid being unhappy today, or any day. Probably just too much champagne. "Best friends forever," she whispered to him, as he set her down.

"Hey, what's this thing?" Shay said. She was deep in Tally's closet, poking around for ideas. She held up a shapeless mass of wool.

"Oh, that." Tally let her arms fall from around Peris. "That's my sweater from the Smoke, remember?" The sweater looked strange, not like she remembered. It was messy, and you could see where human hands had knitted the different pieces together. People in the Smoke didn't have holes in the wall—they had to make their own things, and people, it turned out, weren't very good at making things.

"You didn't recycle it?"

"No. I think it's made of weird stuff. Like, the hole can't use it."

Shay held the sweater to her nose and inhaled. "Wow.

It still smells like the Smoke. Campfires and that stew we always ate. Remember?"

Peris and Fausto went over to smell it. They'd never been out of the city, except for school trips to the Rusty Ruins. They certainly hadn't gotten as far as the Smoke, where everyone had to work all day making stuff, and growing (or even killing) their own food, and everyone stayed ugly after their sixteenth birthday. Ugly until they died, even.

Of course, the Smoke didn't exist anymore, thanks to Tally and Special Circumstances.

"Hey, I know, Tally!" Shay said. "Let's go as Smokies tonight!"

"That would be totally criminal!" Fausto said, his eyes full of admiration.

The three looked at Tally, all of them thrilled with the idea, and even though another nasty ping went through her, she knew it would be bogus not to agree. And that with a totally bubbly costume like a real-life Smokey sweater to wear, there was no way anyone would vote against her, because Tally Youngblood was a natural Crim.

## BASH

The bash was in Valentino Mansion, the oldest building in New Pretty Town. It sprawled along the river only a few stories high, but was topped by a transmission tower visible halfway across the island. Inside, the walls were made of real stone, so the rooms couldn't talk, but the mansion had a long history of giant and fabulous bashes. The wait to become a Valentino resident was at least forever.

Peris, Fausto, Shay, and Tally walked down through the pleasure gardens, which were already bubbling with people headed to the bash. Tally saw an angel with beautiful feathered wings that must have been requisitioned months ago, which was so cheating, and a bunch of new pretties wearing fat-suits and masks that gave them triple chins. A mostly naked clique of Bashers were pretending to be pre-Rusties, building bonfires and drumming, establishing their own little satellite party, which was what Bashers always did.

Peris and Fausto kept arguing about exactly when to light themselves on fire again. They wanted to make an entrance but also save their sparklers for the other Crims. As they got closer to the mansion's noise and glimmer, Tally's nerves started to jump. The Smokey costumes didn't look like much. Tally wore her old sweater and Shay a copy, along with rough pants, knapsacks, and handmade-looking shoes that Tally had described to the hole in the wall, remembering someone wearing them in the Smoke. For unbathed authenticity they had rubbed dirt into their clothes and faces, which had seemed bubbly during the walk down, but now just felt dirty.

At the door were two Valentinos dressed up as wardens, making sure no one got inside without a costume. They stopped Fausto and Peris at first, but laughed when the two set themselves on fire, waving them through. They just shrugged at Shay and Tally, but let them in.

"Wait till the other Crims see us," Shay said. "They'll get it."

The four pushed through the crowds and into a total confusion of costumes. Tally saw snowmen, soldiers, thumb-game characters, and a whole Pretty Committee of scientists carrying facegraphs. Historical figures were everywhere in crazy clothes from all over the world, which reminded Tally how different from one another everyone used to look back when there were way too many people. A lot of the older new pretties were dressed in modern costumes: doctors, wardens, builders, or politicians—whatever they hoped to become after having the middle-pretty operation. A bunch of firefighters laughingly tried to extinguish Peris's and Fausto's flames, but only succeeded in annoying them.

"Where are they?" Shay kept asking, but the stone walls didn't answer. "This is so missing. How do people live here?"

"I think they carry handphones all the time," Fausto said. "We should have requed one."

The problem was that in Valentino Mansion you couldn't just call people by asking—the rooms were old and dumb, so it was like being outside. Tally placed one palm against the wall as they walked, liking how cool the ancient stones felt. For a moment, they reminded her of things out in the wild, rough and silent and unchanging. She wasn't really dying to find the other Crims; they'd all be looking at her and wondering how to vote.

They wandered the crowded hallways, peeking into rooms full of old-timey astronauts and explorers. Tally counted five Cleopatras and two Lillian Russells. There were even a few Rudolph Valentinos; it turned out the mansion was named after a natural pretty from back in the Rusty days.

Other cliques had organized theme costumes—teams of Jocks carrying hockey sticks and wobbly on hoverskates, Twisters as sick puppies wearing big cone-shaped plastic collars. And of course the Swarm was everywhere, all jabbering to one another on their interface rings. Swarmers had skintennas surged into them so they could call one another from anywhere, even inside Valentino Mansion's dumb walls. The other cliques always made fun of the

Swarm, who were afraid to go anywhere except in giant groups. They were all dressed as houseflies with big bug eyes, which at least was sense-making.

No other Crims appeared among the tumult of costumes, and Tally began to wonder if they'd all ditched the party rather than vote for her. Paranoid thoughts began to plague her, and she kept catching glimpses of someone lurking in the shadows, half-hidden by the crowds, but always there. Every time she turned around, though, the gray silk costume slipped out of sight.

Tally couldn't tell whether it was a boy or a girl. The figure wore a mask, scary but also beautiful, its cruel wolf eyes glinting in the low, flickering party lights. The plastic face jarred something in Tally, a painful memory that took a moment to gel.

Then she realized what the costume was supposed to be: an agent of Special Circumstances.

Tally leaned back against one of the cool stone walls, remembering the gray silk coveralls that Specials wore and the cruel pretty faces they were given. The sight made her head spin, which was the way Tally always felt when she thought back to her days in the wild.

Seeing the costume here in New Pretty Town didn't make any sense. Besides herself and Shay, hardly anyone had ever seen a Special. To most people they were just rumors and urban legends, blamed whenever anything weird happened. Specials kept themselves well hidden. Their job was to protect the city from outside threats, like soldiers and spies back in the days of the Rusties, but only total criminals like Tally Youngblood ever met them in person.

Still, someone had done a pretty good job on the costume. He or she must have seen a real Special at some point. But why was the figure following her? Every time

Tally turned, it was there, moving with the terrible and predatory grace she remembered from being hunted through the ruins of the Smoke on that awful day when they had come to take her back to the city.

She shook her head. Thinking of those days always brought up bogus memories that didn't fit together. The Specials hadn't hunted Tally, of course. Why would they? They'd rescued her, bringing her home after she'd left the city to track down Shay. The thought of Specials always left her spinning, but that was just because their cruel faces were designed to freak you out, the same way that looking at regular pretties made you feel good.

Maybe the figure wasn't following her at all; maybe it was more than one person, some clique all dressed the same and spread out across the party, which made it feel like one of them was lurking her. That idea was a lot less crazy-making.

She caught up with the others, and joked with them as they searched for the rest of the Crims. But as Tally kept one eye out for figures in the shadows, she slowly became sure that it wasn't a clique. There was always exactly one, not talking to anybody, totally lurking. And the way the figure moved, so gracefully . . .

Tally told herself to calm down. Special Circumstances had no reason to follow her. And it made no sense for a Special to come to a costume party dressed as a Special.

She forced a laugh from herself. It was probably one of the other Crims playing a joke on her, one who'd heard Shay's and Tally's stories a hundred times and knew all about Special Circumstances. If so, it would be totally bogus to go all brain-missing in front of everyone. Better to ignore the fake Special altogether.

Tally looked down at her own costume, and wondered

if the Smokey clothes were helping to freak her out. Shay had been right: The smell of the old, handmade sweater brought back their time outside the city, days of back-breaking work and nights staying warm by the campfire, mingled with memories of the aging ugly faces that still brought her awake screaming sometimes.

Living in the Smoke had totally done a job on Tally's head.

No one else mentioned the figure. Were they all in on the joke? Fausto kept worrying that his sparklers were going to run out before any of the other Crims saw them. "Let's see if they're in one of the spires," he said.

"At least we can call them from a real building," Peris agreed.

Shay snorted and headed toward the nearest door. "Anything to get out of this bogus pile of rocks."

The party was spilling outside, anyway, expanding beyond the ancient stone walls. Shay led them toward a party spire at random, through a cluster of Hairdos with beehive wigs, each with its own swarm of bumblebees, which were really micro-lifters painted yellow and black in holding patterns around their heads.

"They didn't get the buzzing sound right," Fausto said, but Tally could tell he was impressed by the costumes. The sparklers in his hair were sputtering out, and people were looking at him like, huh?

From inside the party tower, Peris called Zane, who said the Crims were all right upstairs. "Good guess, Shay."

The four of them crammed into the elevator with a surgeon, a trilobite, and two drunken hockey players struggling to stay upright on hoverskates.

"Get that nervous look off your face, Tally-wa," said Shay, squeezing her shoulder. "You'll be in, no problem. Zane likes you."

Tally managed a smile, wondering if that was really true. Zane was always asking her about ugly days, but he did that with everyone, sucking up the Crims' stories with his gold-flecked eyes. Did he really think that Tally Youngblood was anything special?

It was clear that someone did—as the elevator doors closed, Tally glimpsed gray silk slipping gracefully through the crowd.

## LURKER

Most of the other Crims had come as lumberjacks, dressed in plaid and grotesquely muscle-padded, holding big fake chainsaws and glasses of champagne. There were also butchers, a few smokers who'd made their own fake cigarettes, and a hangman with a long noose draped over her shoulder. Zane, who knew a lot about history, had come as some dictator's assistant who wasn't totally fashion-missing, all in tight black with a bubbly red armband. He'd done costume surge to make his lips thin and cheeks sunken, which made him look kind of like a Special.

They all laughed at Peris's costume, and tried to relight Fausto, but only managed to burn a few wisps of his hair, which was totally bogus-smelling. It took an anxious moment for them to figure out Tally's and Shay's costumes, but soon the other Crims were crowding in to touch the rough fibers of the handmade sweater and asking if it was itchy. (It was, but Tally shook her head.)

Shay stood close to Zane and got him to notice her new eye surge.

"Think they're pretty-making?" she asked.

"I give them fifty milli-Helens," he said.

This went totally missing on everyone.

"A milli-Helen is enough beauty to launch exactly one ship," Zane explained, and the older Crims all laughed. "Fifty's pretty good."

Shay smiled, Zane's praise lighting her face up like champagne.

Tally tried to be bubbly, but the thought of the costumed Special lurking her was too dizzy-making. After a few minutes, she escaped onto the party spire's balcony to fill her lungs with cold, fresh air.

A few hot-air balloons were tethered to the spire, hovering like huge black moons in the sky. The Hot-airs riding in one gondola were shooting roman candles at the others, laughing as the safety flames roared across the darkness. Then one of the balloons began to rise, the roar of its burner audible above the party noise, its tether dropping to slap against the spire. It lifted on a tiny finger of flame, finally disappearing into the distance. If Shay hadn't introduced her to the Crims, Tally figured she would have been a Hot-air. They were always drifting off into the night and landing at random places, calling a hovercar to pick them up from some distant suburb or even past the city limits.

Staring out over the river toward the darkness of Uglyville made Tally's brain much less spinning. It was strange. Her time in the wild was so fuzzy, but Tally could perfectly remember being a young ugly, watching the lights of New Pretty Town from her dorm window and dying to turn sixteen. She had always imagined herself here on this side, in some high tower, with fireworks going off around her, surrounded by pretties and pretty herself.

Of course, the Tally of those fantasies had usually been wearing a ball gown—not a woolen sweater and work pants, her face smeared with dirt. She fingered a thread working its way free of the weave, wishing that Shay hadn't found the sweater tonight. Tally wanted to leave the Smoke behind, to escape all the tangled memories of running and hiding and feeling like a betrayer. She hated glancing every minute at the elevator door, wondering if the costumed Special had followed her up here. She wanted to feel totally belonging somewhere, not waiting for the next disaster to strike.

Maybe what Shay kept saying was right, and tonight's vote would fix all that. The Crims were one of the tightest cliques in New Pretty Town. You had to be voted in, and once you were a Crim, you could always depend on friends and parties and bubbly conversation. No more running for Tally.

The only catch was, no one could join who hadn't been totally tricky in their ugly days, with good stories to tell about sneaking out and hoverboarding all night and running away. Crims were pretties who hadn't forgotten being uglies, who still enjoyed the practical jokes and criminal tricks that made Uglyville, in its own way, bubbly.

"What would you give the view?" It was Zane, suddenly next to her, looking all of his two-meter maximum pretty height in the ancient black uniform.

"Give it?"

"A hundred milli-Helens? Five hundred? Maybe a whole Helen?"

Tally took a steadying breath, looking down at the dark river. "I'd give it none. It's Uglyville, after all."

Zane chuckled. "Now, Tally-wa, there's no reason to be nasty about our ugly little brothers and sisters. It's not their fault they aren't as pretty as you." He pushed a stray lock of Tally's hair back around her ear.

"Not them, the place. Uglyville is a prison." The words felt wrong in her mouth, too serious for a bash.

But Zane didn't seem to mind. "You escaped, didn't you?" He stroked the sweater's strange fibers, like the rest of them kept doing. "Was the Smoke any better?"

Tally wondered if he wanted a real answer. She was nervous about saying something bogus. If Zane thought Tally was missing, vetoes would rain down no matter what Shay and Peris had promised.

She looked up into his eyes. They were a shimmering metallic gold, reflecting the fireworks like tiny mirrors, and something behind them seemed to pull at Tally. Not just the usual pretty magic, but something that felt serious, as if the bash around them had disappeared. Zane always listened raptly to her Smoke stories. He'd heard them all by now, but maybe there was something more he wanted to know.

"I left the night before my sixteenth birthday," she said. "So I wasn't exactly escaping Uglyville."

"That's right." Zane released her from his gaze and looked out across the river. "You were running from the operation."

"I was following Shay. I had to stay ugly to find her."

"To rescue her," he said, then trained his golden eyes on her again. "Was that really it?"

Tally nodded carefully, last night's champagne spinning her head. Or maybe tonight's. She looked at the empty glass in her hand and wondered how many she'd had.

"It was just a thing I had to do." As she said the words, Tally knew that they sounded bogus.

"A special circumstance?" Zane asked, his smile wry.

Tally's eyebrows lifted. She wondered what tricks Zane

had pulled back when he was an ugly. He didn't tell that many stories himself. Though he wasn't that much older than her, Zane never seemed to have to prove that he was a real Crim, he just was.

Even with his lips thinned by costume surge, he was beautiful. His face had been sculpted into more extreme shapes than most, as if the doctors had wanted to push the Pretty Committee's specs to the limit. His cheekbones were as sharp as arrowheads underneath his flesh, and his eyebrows arched absurdly high when he was amused. Tally saw with sudden clarity that if any of his features were shifted a few millimeters he would look terrible, and yet at the same time it was impossible to imagine that he had ever been an ugly.

"Did you ever go to the Rusty Ruins?" she asked. "Back when you were . . . young?"

"Almost every night, last winter."

"In winter?"

"I love the ruins covered with snow," he said. "It makes the edges softer, adding mega-Helens to the view."

"Oh." Tally remembered traveling across the wild in early autumn, how cold it had been. "Sounds totally . . . freezing."

"I could never get anyone else to come with me." His eyes narrowed. "When you talk about the ruins, you never mention meeting anyone there."

"Meeting someone?" Tally closed her eyes, finding herself suddenly balance-missing. She leaned against the balcony rail and took a deep breath.

"Yeah," he said. "Did you ever?"

The empty champagne glass slipped from her hand and tumbled into the blackness.

"Look out below," Zane murmured, a smile on his lips.

A tinkling crash rose up from the darkness, surprised laughter spreading from it like ripples from a stone in water. It sounded a thousand kilometers away.

Tally took in more breaths of the cold night air, trying to regain her composure. Her stomach was doing flip-flops. It was so shaming to be like this, about to throw breakfast after a few lousy glasses of champagne.

"It's okay, Tally," Zane whispered. "Just let yourself be bubbly."

Tally realized how bogus that was, having to be told to stay bubbly. But even through his costume surge, Zane's gaze had softened, as if he really did want her to relax.

She turned away from the drop into emptiness, gripping the guardrail with both hands behind her. Shay and Peris were also out on the balcony now; she was surrounded by all her new Crim friends, protected and part of the group. But they were watching her carefully too. Maybe everyone was expecting something special from her tonight.

"I never saw anyone out there," Tally said. "Someone was supposed to come, but never did."

She didn't hear Zane's response.

The lurker had appeared again—across the crowded spire, standing still and staring straight at her. The mask's flashing eyes seemed to acknowledge her gaze for a moment, then the figure turned and slipped among the white coats of the costumed Pretty Committee, disappearing behind their giant facegraphs of every major pretty type. And even though Tally realized it was a bogus thing to do, she pushed away from Zane and through the crowd, because there was no way she could pull herself together tonight until she found out who this person was, Crim or Special or random new pretty. She had to know why someone was throwing Special Circumstances in her face.

Tally dodged between white coats and bounced like a pinball through a clique all dressed in fat-suits, their softly padded bellies spinning her in circles. She bowled over most of a hockey team, who wobbled on their slippy hover-skates like littlies. Glimpses of gray silk teased Tally from just ahead as she ran, but the crowd was thick and in frantic motion, and by the time she reached the central column of the spire, the figure had disappeared.

Glancing at the lights above the elevator door, she saw that it was on its way up, not down. The fake Special was still around, somewhere in the spire.

Then Tally noticed the door to the emergency stairs, bright red and plastered with warnings that an alarm would sound if you opened it. She looked around again—still no gray figure. Whoever it was had to have escaped down the stairs. Alarms could be switched off; she'd pulled that trick herself a million times as an ugly.

Tally reached out toward the door, her hand shaking. If a siren started blaring, everyone would be staring at her and whispering as the wardens arrived and evacuated the tower. It would be a really bubbly end to her career as a Crim.

Some Crim, she thought. She'd be a pretty bogus criminal if she couldn't set off an alarm every once in a while.

She pushed the door open. It didn't make a sound.

Tally stepped into the stairwell. The door closed behind her, muffling the tumult of the party. In the sudden quiet, she could feel her heart pounding in her chest and hear her own breath, still ragged from the chase. The beat of the music seemed to leak under the door, making the concrete floor shudder.

The figure sat on the stairs, a few steps up. "You made it." It was a boy's voice, indistinct behind the mask.

"Made it where? This party?"

"No, Tally. Through the door."

"It wasn't exactly locked." She tried to stare her way through the jeweled eyes of the mask. "Who are you?"

"You don't recognize me?" He sounded genuinely puzzled, as if he were an old friend, someone who wore a mask all the time. "What do I look like?"

Tally swallowed and said softly, "Special Circumstances."

"Good. You remember." Tally could hear the smile in his voice. He was talking slowly and carefully, as if she were some kind of idiot.

"Of course I remember. Are you one of them? Do I know you?" Tally couldn't recall any individual Specials; in her memory, their faces all ran together into one cruel and pretty blur.

"Why don't you take a look?" The figure didn't move to take off his mask. "Go ahead, Tally."

Suddenly, she realized what was going on here. Recognizing what the costume meant, chasing him across the party, braving the alarmed door—all of it had been a test. Some kind of recruitment. He was sitting there wondering if she would dare pull off his mask.

Tally was sick of tests. "Just stay away from me," she said.

"Tally—"

"I don't want to work for Special Circumstances. I just want to live here in New Pretty Town."

"I'm not—"

"Leave me alone!" she shouted, clenching her fists. The cry echoed off the concrete walls, leaving a moment of silence, as if it had surprised them both. The music from the party drifted through the stairwell, muffled and timid.

Finally, a sigh came through the mask, and he held up

a crude leather pouch. “I have something for you. If you’re ready for it. Do you want it, Tally?”

“I don’t want anything from . . .” Tally’s voice trailed off. Soft shuffling sounds came from below them. Not the party. Someone was coming up the stairs.

The two of them moved at the same time, peering over the handrail down the narrow stairwell shaft. A long way down, Tally saw flashes of gray silk and hands grasping the rails, half a dozen people climbing the stairs incredibly fast, their footsteps barely audible over the muffled music.

“See you later,” the figure said, standing.

Tally blinked. He pushed her aside, spooked by the sight of real Specials. So who was he? Before his fingers reached the doorknob, Tally snatched the mask from his face.

He was an ugly. A real ugly.

His face was nothing like the costumed fatties done up for the bash, with their big noses or squinty eyes. It wasn’t just exaggerated features that made him different; it was everything, as if he were made of some utterly different substance. In those seconds, Tally’s pretty-perfect eyesight caught every gaping pore, the random tangles in his hair, the crude imbalance of his disjointed face. Her skin crawled at his imperfections, the tufts of teenage beard, his unsurged teeth, the eruptions on his forehead screaming out disease. She wanted to pull away, to put distance between herself and his unlucky, unclean, unhealthy ugliness.

But somehow she knew his name. . . .

“Croy?” she said.

"Later, Tally," Croy said, snatching back his mask. He yanked open the door, and the noise of the party rushed into the stairwell as he darted through, the gray silk of his costume disappearing into the crowd.

Tally just stood there as the door swung closed again, too stunned to move. Like her old sweater, she'd remembered ugliness all wrong: Croy's face was much worse than her mental image of the Smokies. His crooked smile, his dull eyes, the way his sweating skin carried angry red marks where the mask had pressed against it . . .

But then the door slammed itself shut, and among the echoes Tally heard the footsteps still climbing toward her, real Specials on their way up, and for the first time all day, a clear thought went through her head.

Run.

She pulled open the door and plunged into the crowd.

The elevator was just spilling open, and Tally stumbled into a clique of Naturals plastered with brittle leaves, walking last days of autumn who shed yellows and reds as she shoved through them. She managed to keep her footing—the floor was sticky with spilled champagne—and caught another glimpse of the gray silk.

Croy was headed toward the balcony and the Crims.

She tore after him. Tally didn't want anyone lurking her, panicking her at parties, tangling her memories when she needed to be bubbly. She had to catch Croy and tell him never to follow her again.

This wasn't Uglyville or the Smoke—he had no right to be here. He had no business stepping out of her ugly past.

And there was another reason she was running: the Specials. It had only taken a glimpse of them to put every cell in her body on high alert. Their inhuman speed repelled her, like watching a cockroach skitter across a plate. Croy's movements might have seemed unusual, his Smokey confidence standing out in a party full of new pretties, but the Specials were another species altogether.

Tally burst out onto the balcony just in time to see Croy leap up onto the rail, waving his arms for a precarious moment. Then he got his balance, bent his knees, and pushed off into the night.

She ran to the spot and leaned over. Croy was tumbling downward out of sight, his form swallowed by the darkness below. After a sickening moment he reappeared, head over heels, gray silk catching the light of fireworks as he hover-bounced toward the river.

Zane stood beside her, looking down. "Hmm, the invitation didn't say 'bungee jackets required,'" he murmured. "Who was that, Tally?"

She opened her mouth, but an alarm began to howl.

Tally spun around and saw the crowd parting. The group of Specials were pouring through the stairwell door, slicing their way through confused new pretties. Their cruel faces weren't costumes any more than Croy's ugliness had been, and they were just as shocking to look at. The wolflike eyes sent a chill through Tally, and their advance, as purposeful and dangerous as a hunting cat's, made her body scream to keep running.

At the other end of the balcony she saw Peris, standing frozen next to the rail, awestruck by the spectacle. His safety sparklers were sputtering out at last, but the light on his bungee jacket collar glowed bright green.

Tally pushed toward him through the other Crims,

judging the angles, knowing exactly when to jump. For a moment, the world became strangely clear, as if the sight of Croy's ugliness and the cruel-pretty Specials had removed some barrier between her and the world. Everything was bright and harsh, the details so sharp that Tally squinted as if dashing into a freezing wind.

She hit Peris just right, her arms wrapping around his shoulders, her momentum lifting both of them up and over the balcony railing. They tumbled out of the light and into blackness, Peris's costume flaring up one last time in the wind of their descent, the safety sparks bouncing from her face as cool as snowflakes.

He was half-screaming and half-laughing, as if enduring an annoying but invigorating practical joke—cold water over the head.

Halfway down it occurred to Tally that the bungee jacket might not catch them both.

She squeezed harder, and heard Peris grunt as the lifters kicked in. The jacket pulled him upright, almost wrenching Tally's shoulders from their sockets. Her muscles were still powerful from their weeks of manual labor in the Smoke—if anything, the operation had tuned them up—but she barely kept her grip as the jacket absorbed the velocity of their fall. Her arms slipped farther down until they were wrapped around Peris's waist, her fingers painfully entangled in the jacket's straps.

As they came to a shuddering halt, Tally's feet brushed the grass, and she let go.

Peris shot back up into the air, his knee catching Tally's brow and sending her staggering back into the darkness. She lost her footing, landing on a drift of fallen leaves that crunched beneath her.

For a moment Tally lay still. The pile of leaves smelled

softly of earth and rot, like something old and tired. She blinked as something trickled into one eye. Maybe it was raining.

She looked up at the party tower and the distant hot-air balloons, blinking and catching her breath. She could make out a few figures peering down from the bright balcony ten stories above. Tally wondered if any of them were Specials.

Peris was nowhere to be seen. She remembered bungee jumping as an ugly, how a jacket would carry you down a slope. He must have bounced down toward the river after Croy.

Croy. She wanted to say something to him. . . .

Tally struggled to her feet and faced the river. Her head throbbed, but the clarity that had come over her as she'd thrown herself off the balcony hadn't faded. Her heart pounded as a burst of fireworks lit the sky, casting pink light and sudden shadows through the trees, every blade of grass in sharp relief.

Everything felt very real: her intense revulsion at Croy's ugly face, her fear of the Specials, the shapes and smells around her. It felt as if a thin plastic film had been peeled from her eyes, leaving the world with razored edges.

She ran downhill, toward the mirrored band of the river and the darkness of Uglyville. "Croy!" she cried.

The pink flower in the sky faded, and Tally tripped over the winding roots of an old tree. She stumbled to a halt.

Something was gliding up out of the darkness.

"Croy?" The fireworks had left green spots scattered across her vision.

"You don't give up, do you?"

He was on a hoverboard a meter off the ground, feet spread for balance, looking comfortable. His gray silks had been replaced with pitch-black, his cruel pretty mask discarded. Behind him, two other black-clad figures rode, younger uglies wearing dorm uniforms and nervous looks.

"I wanted . . ." Her voice trailed off. She'd followed him to say, Go away, leave me alone, never come back. To scream it at him. But everything had become so clear and intense . . . what she wanted now was to hold on to this bright focus. Croy's invasion of her world was a part of that, she somehow knew.

"Croy, they're coming," one of the younger uglies said.

"What did you want, Tally?" he asked calmly.

She blinked, uncertain, worried that if she said the wrong thing, the clarity might go away—the barrier would close again.

She remembered what he'd offered in the stairwell. "You had something to give me?"

He smiled, and pulled the old leather pouch from his belt. "This? Yeah, I think you're ready for it. Only one problem: You'd better not take it from me right now. Wardens are coming. Maybe Specials."

"Yeah, in about ten seconds," the nervous ugly complained.

Croy ignored him. "But we'll leave it for you at Valentino 317. Can you remember that? Valentino 317."

She nodded, then blinked again. Her head felt light.

Croy frowned. "I hope so." He spun his board around in one graceful movement, and the other two uglies followed suit. "Later. And sorry about your eye."

They darted away toward the river, veering off in three different directions as they disappeared into the darkness.

"Sorry about my what?" she asked softly.

Then Tally found herself blinking again, her vision blurring. She reached up to touch her forehead. Her fingers came away sticky, and more dark blotches dripped into her palm as she stared at it dumbfounded.

She finally felt the pain, her head throbbing in time with her heartbeat. The collision with Peris's knee must have opened up her forehead. Her fingers traced a line of blood that dripped around her brow and down one cheek, as hot as tears.

Tally sat down on the grass, suddenly shaking all over.

Fireworks lit the sky again, turning the blood on her hand bright red, each drop a little mirror reflecting the explosion overhead. There were hovercars in the sky now, lots of them.

Tally felt something slipping away as she bled, something she'd wanted to keep hold of . . .

"Tally!"

Looking up, she saw Peris, chuckling as he climbed the hill.

"Now that was not a bubbly move, Tally-wa. I almost wound up in the river!" He mimed drowning, grasping at water and slipping under.

She found herself giggling at his performance, her weird shakiness turning bubbly now that Peris was here. "What's the matter? Can't you swim?"

He laughed and sank to the grass beside her, fighting with the straps of the bungee jacket. "I'm not dressed for it." He rubbed one shoulder. "Also . . . ow on the clinginess."

Tally tried to remember why jumping off the tower had seemed like such a good idea, but the sight of her own blood had left her brain-missing, and she just wanted to sleep. Everything was harsh and shiny. "Sorry."

"Just warn me next time." Fireworks exploded overhead, and Peris squinted at her, his face beautifully puzzled. "What's with the blood?"

"Oh, yeah. Your knee whacked into me when you bounced. Isn't it bogus?"

"Not very pretty-making." He reached out and squeezed her arm softly. "Don't worry, Tally. I'll ping a warden car. There's tons out tonight."

But one was already coming. It passed silently overhead, running lights casting a red tinge on the grass around them. A spotlight picked them out. Tally sighed, letting the uncomfortable shininess of everything slip away. She realized now why it had been such a bogus day. She'd been trying way too hard, worrying about how the Crims would vote and what to wear, more serious than bubbly. No wonder the party-crashers had driven her over the edge.

She giggled. Literally over the edge.

But everything was okay now. With the uglies and cruel pretties gone and Peris here to take care of her, a restful feeling settled over Tally. Funny how that kick to the head had left her brain-missing for a moment, actually talking to those uglies like they mattered.

The hovercar landed nearby, and two wardens jumped out and headed over, one with a first-aid kit in hand. Maybe while they were fixing her head, Tally thought, she could get some eye surge like Shay's. Not exactly the same, which would be bogus, but sort of matching.

She looked up into the wardens' middle-pretty faces, calm and wise and knowing what to do. The look of concern on their faces made the blood all over her face feel less shaming.

They gently led her to the car and sprayed new skin onto the wound, giving her a pill to stop the swelling. When she asked about bruises, they laughed and said the operation took care of that. No more bruises ever.

Because it was a head wound, they gave Tally a neural exam, waving a glowing red pointer back and forth while they tracked her eyemouse. The test seemed pretty retarded, but the wardens said it proved she didn't have a concussion or brain damage. Peris told a story about when he'd walked into a glass door at Lillian Russell Mansion and had to stay awake or die, and they all laughed.

Then the wardens asked a few questions about the tricking uglies who'd come across the river that night and caused all the trouble. "Did you know any of them?"

Tally sighed, not really wanting to get into it. It was totally shaming to be the cause of the uglies' party-crashing. But it was middle pretties asking, and you couldn't blow them off. They always knew what they were doing, and it would be bogus to tell a lie straight to their calm, authoritative faces.

"Yeah. I kind of remembered one of them. Croy."

"He was from the Smoke, wasn't he, Tally?"

She nodded, feeling stupid wearing the Smokey sweater with dirt and blood all over it. It was all Valentino Mansion's fault for switching the dress code: There was nothing more bogus than still being in a costume after you'd left a party.

"Do you know what he wanted, Tally? Why he was here?"

She looked at Peris for help. He was hanging on every word, his luminous eyes bugging wide. It made her feel important.

She shrugged. "Just ugly tricks, that's all. Showing off in front of his friends, probably." Which sounded bogus. Croy didn't live in Uglyville, after all. He was a Smokey, from out in the wild between cities. The two with him might have been city kids just tricking, but Croy had definitely had a plan.

But the wardens only smiled and nodded, believing her. "Don't worry, it won't happen again. We'll be keeping an eye on you to make sure it doesn't."

She smiled back at them, and they took her home.

*

When Tally made it to her room, there was a ping from Peris, who'd gone back to the party.

"Guess what?" he yelled. Crowd sounds and music bled in around the words, making Tally wish she'd gone back to the bash, even with sprayed-on skin all over her forehead.

She frowned and flopped onto her bed as the message continued: "When I got back, the Crims had already voted! They thought it was totally bubbly that real-life Specials were at the party, and our dive off the tower got six hundred milli-Helens from Zane! You are so Crim! See you tomorrow. Oh yeah, and don't get that scar erased until everyone's seen it. Best friends forever!"

As the message ended, Tally felt the bed spin a little. She closed her eyes and let out a long, slow sigh of relief. Finally, she was a full-fledged Crim. Everything she'd ever wanted had come to her at last. She was beautiful, and she lived in New Pretty Town with Peris and Shay and tons of new friends. All the disasters and terrors of the last year—running away to the Smoke, living there in pre-Rusty squalor, traveling back to the city through the wilds—somehow all of it had worked out.

It was so wonderful, and Tally was so exhausted, that belief took a while to settle over her. She replayed Peris's message a few times, then pulled off the smelly Smokey sweater with shaking hands and threw it into the corner. Tomorrow, she would make the hole in the wall recycle it.

Tally lay back and stared at the ceiling for a while. A ping from Shay came, but she ignored it, setting her interface ring to sleeptime. With everything so perfect, reality seemed somehow fragile, as if the slightest interruption could imperil her pretty future. The bed beneath her, Komachi Mansion, and even the city around her—all of it felt as tenuous as a soap bubble, shivering and empty.

It was probably just the knock to her head causing the weird missingness that underlay her joy. She only needed a good night's sleep—and hopefully no hangover tomorrow—and everything would feel solid again, as perfect as it really was.

Tally fell asleep a few minutes later, happy to be a Crim at last.

But her dreams were totally bogus.

# ZANE

So, there was this beautiful princess.

She was locked in a high tower, one with stone walls and cold, empty rooms that couldn't talk. There was no elevator or even fire stairs, so Tally wondered how the princess had gotten up there.

But there she was, at the top. No bungee jacket and fast asleep.

The tower was guarded by a dragon. It had jeweled eyes and hungry, cruel features, and moved with a brutal suddenness that made Tally's stomach churn. Even dreaming, she recognized exactly what the dragon was. It was a cruel pretty, an agent of Special Circumstances, or maybe a bunch of them all rolled up into one gray and silk-scaled serpent.

And you couldn't have this dream without a prince.

He made it past the dragon, not so much slaying as creeping, finding chinks in the ancient stone wall to slip his fingers into, because it was old and crumbling. He climbed the tower's daunting height easily, sparing only an amused look down at the dragon, which had been distracted by a host of playful rats scurrying through its claws.

The prince made it in through the high stone window and swept the princess into a kiss, which woke her up, and that was the whole story. Getting back down and past the dragon didn't turn out to be an issue, because this was a dream and not a movie or even a fairy tale, and it was all over with one big kiss, a classic happy ending.

Except for one thing.

The prince was totally ugly.

Tally woke up with a throbbing head.

Catching her reflection in the mirror wall, she remembered that the headache wasn't just a hangover. And discovered that getting kicked in the head was not pretty-making. As the wardens last night had warned might happen, the sprayed-on skin above her eye had turned an angry red. She'd have to go to a surge office to get the scar completely erased.

But Tally decided not to fix it yet. Like Peris had said, it did look really criminal. She smiled, remembering her new status. The scar was perfect.

There was a mountain of pings from other Crims, drunken congratulations and reports of more wild behavior as the party had gone on (though nothing as bubbly as her dive off the tower with Peris). Tally listened to the messages with eyes closed, sinking into the crowd noises in the background, loving how connected she was to the others even though she'd come home early. That's what being voted into a clique meant: knowing you had friends whatever you did.

Zane had left three messages in all, the last one asking

if Tally wanted to have breakfast this morning. He didn't sound as drunk as the rest of them, so maybe he was already awake.

When she pinged him, he answered. "How are you?"

"Face-missing," she said. "Did Peris tell you how my head got bonked?"

"Yeah. You were actually bleeding?"

"Very."

"Whoa." Zane's voice was breathy in her ear, his usual cool overwhelmed. "Nice dive, though. Glad you didn't . . . you know, die."

Tally smiled. "Thanks."

"So, did you read the weirdness about the party?"

There'd been a news-ping among Tally's messages, but she hadn't felt up to reading. "What weirdness?"

"Someone hacked the mail yesterday and sent out that new invitation, the one that changed the dress code to costumes. Everyone on the Valentino Bash Committee thought it was someone else who'd done it, so they all just went along. But nobody knows who actually wrote it. Dizzying, huh?"

Tally blinked, the room suddenly out of focus. Dizzying was right. The world seemed to turn around her, as if she were inside the stomach of something big and out of control. Only uglies did stuff like hack mail. And she could only think of one person who would want the Valentino party turned into a costume bash: Croy with his cruel-pretty mask and weird offers.

Which meant it all had to do with Tally Youngblood.

"That is deeply bogus, Zane."

"Totally. You hungry?"

She nodded, feeling her head begin to throb again. Out the window, the Garbo Mansion party towers rose up, tall and spindly. Tally stared at them, as if fixing her gaze could make the world less spinning. She had to be overreacting; everything wasn't about her, after all. It could have just been pointlessly tricking uglies, or someone on the Valentino Bash Committee going brain-missing.

But even if it had been simply a mistake, Croy had to have been ready with that costume. In the Rusty Ruins and wilderness where Smokies hid, there weren't any holes in the wall; you had to make your own things, which took time and effort. And Croy hadn't chosen just any costume. . . . Tally remembered the cold, jeweled eyes and felt faint.

Maybe food would fix her.

"Yeah, deeply hungry. Let's have breakfast."

They met in Denzel Park, a pleasure garden that snaked from the center of New Pretty Town down to Valentino Mansion. The mansion itself was hidden by trees, but the transmission tower on top was visible, the old-fashioned Valentino flag whipping in the cold wind. In the garden, the damage from the night before was mostly cleared up, except for a few blackened patches left by the Bashers' bonfires. A maintenance robot hovered above one circle of ashes, turning the soil over with careful movements of its claws, spraying seeds into the scorched earth.

Zane's suggestion of a picnic had raised Tally's eyebrows (a motion that was totally ouch), but walking down in the fresh air did help clear her head. The pills the wardens had given her muted the pain of her wound, but had no effect on her general fuzziness. The rumor in New Pretty Town was that doctors knew how to fix hangovers, but kept the cure a secret on principle.

Zane arrived on time, breakfast bobbing softly behind him in the cool breeze. As he grew near, his eyes widened at the scar on her forehead. One of his hands reached out, almost as if he wanted to touch it.

"Pretty bogus, huh?" she said.

"Totally criminal-looking," he said, still wide-eyed.

"Not so many milli-Helens, though, is it?"

He looked thoughtful for a moment. "I wouldn't measure it in Helens. I'm not quite sure what I'd use instead, though. Something bubblier."

Tally smiled: Peris had been right about not fixing her face right away. In his fascination with the scar, Zane was extra beautiful, and his expression gave her a tingly feeling—like being at the center of everything, but without the spinning.

Zane's costume surge had worn off; his lips returned to normal pretty fullness. Still, he always looked extreme in daylight. His face was all contrasts, his chin and cheekbones sharp, his forehead high. His skin was the same olive as everyone's, but in the sun, against his dark hair, it somehow looked pale. The operation guidelines wouldn't let you have jet-black hair, which the Committee thought was too extreme, but Zane dyed his with calligraphy ink. On top of that, he didn't eat much, keeping his face gaunt, his stare intense. Of all the pretties Tally had met since her operation, he was the only one whose looks really stood out.

Maybe that was why he was the head Crim—you had to be different from everyone else to really be a criminal. His gold eyes flickered as they searched for a spot, coming to rest in the dappled shadow of a broad oak tree.

They sat down on the grass and leaves, and Tally breathed in the scent of dew and earth. Breakfast settled between them, giving off warmth from the glowing elements that kept the scrambled eggs and hash browns from going cold and slimy.

Tally piled up a heated plate with eggs and cheese and

slices of avocado, and shoved half a muffin into her mouth. Looking up at Zane, she saw that he held nothing but a cup of coffee, and she wondered if eating like a greedy pig was a bogus move.

But what did it matter? She was a Crim now, she reminded herself, all voted on and full-fledged. And Zane had asked her here, after all, wanting to hang out. It was time to stop worrying about being accepted and start enjoying herself. There were worse things than sitting in a perfect park, being closely watched by a beautiful boy.

Tally consumed the rest of the muffin, which was totally steaming inside and marbled with half-melted chocolate, and picked up her fork to attack the eggs. She hoped that the breakfast had some calorie-purgers packed with it. They worked better if you took them right after eating, and she was going to eat a lot. Maybe losing blood made you starving.

"So last night, who was that guy?" Zane asked.

Still chewing, Tally only shrugged, but he waited patiently for her to swallow.

"Just some crashing ugly," she finally said.

"Figured that. Who else would Specials be chasing? I mean, was he someone you knew?"

Tally looked away. It was embarrassing to have your ugly life follow you across the river, at least in person. But Peris had heard her telling the wardens about it last night, so lying to Zane would be bogus. "Yeah, I guess I knew him. From the Smoke. This guy called Croy."

An odd look passed over Zane's face. His gold eyes stared into the distance, searching for something. A moment later, he nodded. "I knew him too."

Tally froze, her fork halfway to her mouth. "You're kidding."

Zane shook his head.

"But I thought you never ran away," Tally said.

"No, I didn't." He pulled up his legs and hugged his knees with one long arm, taking a sip of coffee. "Not any farther than the Rusty Ruins, anyway. But Croy and I were friends back when we were littlies, and we lived in the same ugly dorm."

"That's . . . funny." Tally finally took the bite of eggs, chewing them slowly. The city had a million people in it, and Zane had known Croy. "What are the odds of that?" she said softly.

Zane shook his head again. "Not a coincidence, Tally-wa."

Tally stopped chewing, the eggs tasting funny in her mouth, like everything was going to get all spinning again. The world had gone totally missing on coincidences lately.

"How do you mean?"

Zane leaned forward. "Tally, you know that Shay lived in my dorm, right? Back when we were uglies?"

"Sure," she said. "That's how she hooked up with you guys after coming here." Tally paused a moment, then felt a realization starting to fall slowly into place. Memories from the Smoke always came back at a brain-missing pace, like bubbles rising up through some thick, viscous liquid.

"Out in the Smoke," she said carefully, "Shay introduced me to Croy. They were old friends. So you three all knew one another?"

"Yeah, we did." Zane grimaced, as if something rotten had crawled into his coffee.

Tally looked down at her food unhappily. As Zane continued, it was just like the night before, the whole bogus story of the past summer pushing uncomfortably back into her head.

"There were six of us in my dorm," he said. "We called ourselves Crims back then, too. We did all the usual ugly tricks: sneaking out at night, hacking the dorm minders, coming across the river to spy on new pretties."

Tally nodded, remembering Shay's stories about before the two of them had met. "And going out to the Rusty Ruins?"

"Yeah, after some older uglies showed us how." He looked up the hill at the towering center of New Pretty Town. "Being out there makes you realize how big the world is. I mean, twenty million people used to live in that old Rusty city. Compared with that, this place is tiny."

Tally closed her eyes and put her fork onto her plate, her appetite fading. After everything that had happened last night, maybe breakfast with Zane hadn't been such a good idea. Sometimes he seemed to think he was still an ugly, trying to stay bubbly, pushing back against the easy fun of being pretty. That was why he was great at leading the Crims, of course. But one-on-one, he could be dizzy-making.

"Yeah, but the Rusties all died," she said quietly. "There were too many of them, and they were totally stupid."

"I know, I know. They almost destroyed the world," he recited, then sighed. "But sneaking out to the ruins was the most exciting thing I'd ever done."

Zane's eyes flashed as he said this, and Tally remembered her own trips to the ruins, how the empty majesty of the ghost-city had kept every nerve in her body on high alert. The feeling that real danger might be lurking out there, unlike the harmless thrill of a hot-air ascent or a bungee jump.

She shivered, recalling some of that old excitement as she met Zane's stare. "I know what you mean."

"And I knew I'd never go there again after the operation. New pretties don't do anything that tricky. So when I got close to turning sixteen, I started thinking about leaving the city, going into the wilderness. At least for a while."

Tally nodded slowly. She remembered Shay saying the same things back when they'd met, the words that had started her down the path to the Smoke. "And you talked Shay and Croy and the rest of them into coming along?"

"I tried." He laughed. "At first they thought I was crazy, because you can't live in the wild. But then we met this guy out there who—"

"Stop," Tally said. Suddenly her heart was beating fast, like when you took a purger and your metabolism kicked up to burn the calories. She felt a dampness on her face, the breeze suddenly cold. She felt moisture on her cheeks, but pretty faces didn't sweat. . . .

Tally blinked, her fists clenching until fingernails drove into her palms. The world had changed somehow. Pinpoints of sunlight cut harshly through the leaves overhead as she tried to take deep, slow breaths. She remembered now that the same thing had happened last night, when she'd seen Croy.

"Tally?" Zane said.

She shook her head, not wanting him to say anything. Not about meeting someone in the Rusty Ruins. She found herself speaking quickly to keep him quiet, repeating what Shay had told her. "You heard about the Smoke, right? Where people lived like pre-Rusties and were ugly for life. So you all decided to go there. But when the time came to run, most of you chickened out. Shay told me about that night: She was all packed and everything, but in the end she got too scared to go."

Zane nodded, looking down into his coffee.

"So you bailed too, didn't you?" Tally said. "You were supposed to run away that time?"

"Yeah," he said flatly. "I didn't go, even though the whole

thing was my idea. And I became pretty, right on schedule."

Tally looked away, unable to keep herself from remembering that summer. Shay's friends had all run off to the Smoke or turned pretty, leaving her alone in Uglyville. That's when she and Tally had met, becoming best friends. And when Shay's second attempt at running away had succeeded, Tally had been sucked into the whole mess.

She let out a slow breath, telling herself to calm down. Last summer might have been a nightmare, but it was also why she was a Crim now, and not just some boring brand-new pretty trying to get into a lame non-bubbly clique. Maybe it had been worth it all to wind up here, pretty and popular.

She looked at Zane, his beautiful eyes still staring into the dregs of his coffee, and felt herself relax. She smiled. He looked so tragic sitting there, dark eyebrows arched in despair, still regretting that he'd bailed on running away to the Smoke. She reached out to take his hand.

"Hey, it's no big deal. It wasn't that great out there. Mostly it was getting sunburned and bitten by bugs."

His eyes rose to meet hers. "At least you took the chance, Tally. You were brave enough to find out for yourself."

"I didn't have a choice, really. I had to go find Shay." She shivered, pulling her hand away. "I'm just lucky I made it back."

Zane moved closer and reached out, his delicate fingers tracing the sprayed-on skin over her scar, his golden eyes wide. "I'm glad you did."

She smiled, touching the back of his hand. "Me too."

Zane's fingers slid into her hair, and he gently pulled her closer. She closed her eyes, letting his lips press against hers, reaching up to feel the smooth, flawless skin of his cheek.

Tally's heart was beating hard again, her mind racing

even as her lips parted. Reality was shifting around her once more, but this time she liked the feeling.

When she'd arrived in New Pretty Town, Peris had warned Tally about sex. Getting too close to other pretties could be overwhelming when you were brand new. It took time to get used to all the gorgeous faces, the perfect bodies, the luminous eyes. When everyone was beautiful, you could wind up falling in love with the first pretty you kissed.

But maybe it was time. She had been here a month, and Zane was special. Not just because he led the Crims and looked different from everyone else, but the way he tried to stay bubbly, to bend the rules. It made him even prettier than the others, somehow.

And of all the unexpected turns in the last twenty-four hours, this was the nicest. Kissing Zane was dizzy-making, but not like she was falling into darkness. His lips were warm and soft and perfect, and she felt safe.

After a long moment, the two pulled a little apart, Tally's eyes still closed. She felt his breath against her, his hand warm and soft on the back of her neck. "David," she whispered.

## BUBBLY-MAKING

Zane pulled back, his eyes narrowing.

"Oh, I'm sorry," Tally sputtered. "I don't know what . . ."

As she trailed off, Zane nodded slowly. "No, that's okay."

"I didn't mean to . . . ," Tally started again, but Zane waved her silent, a thoughtful look spreading across his beautiful features. He stared at the ground, pulling up blades of grass between two fingers.

"I remember now," he said.

"Remember what?"

"That was his name."

"Whose name?"

Zane spoke in quiet, even tones, as if trying not to wake someone sleeping nearby. "He was the one who was supposed to take us to the Smoke. David."

Tally heard herself gasp softly. Her eyes were squinting, as if the sun had been turned up a notch. She could still feel the ghost of Zane's lips on hers, the warmth where his hands had touched her, but suddenly she was shivering.

She took Zane's hand. "I didn't mean to say that."

"I know. But things come back sometimes." He looked up from the grass, his golden eyes flashing. "Tell me about David."

Tally swallowed and turned away.

David. She could see him now, his funny big nose and high forehead. The handmade shoes he wore, and a jacket made out of dead animal skins sewn together. David had grown up out in the Smoke, had never set foot in a city his whole life. His face was ugly from top to bottom, tanned imperfectly by the sun, with a scar that went through his eyebrow . . . but remembering him sparked something inside Tally.

She shook her head, amazed. Somehow, she'd forgotten David.

"You met him in the Rusty Ruins, right?" Zane pressed her.

"No," she said. "I'd heard about him from Shay, and she tried to signal him once. But he never showed up. He was the one who took Shay to the Smoke, though."

"He was supposed to take me, too." Zane sighed. "But you went to the Smoke on your own, didn't you?"

"Yeah. But when I got there, he and I . . ." Tally remembered now. It all seemed a million years ago, but she could see herself—her ugly self—kissing David, traveling with him across the wilderness for weeks alone. A weird ping of memory moved through her, how strong and never-ending being with him had felt back then.

And then, somehow, he'd disappeared.

"Where is he now?" Zane asked. "Did the Specials catch him when they took down the Smoke?"

She shook her head. Her other memories of David were tricky and faded, but the moment when they had parted was simply . . . gone. "I don't know."

Tally felt faint, the world growing unsteady for the hundredth time that day. She reached out toward the breakfast tray, but Zane took her hand. "No, don't eat."

"What?"

"Don't eat anything else, Tally. In fact, take a couple of these." He pulled a packet of calorie-purgers from his pocket—four had already been punched out.

"It helps if your heart's beating faster." He punched out two more, and bolted them down with a drink of coffee.

"Helps what?" she asked.

Zane pointed at his head. "Thinking. Hunger focuses your mind. Any kind of excitement works, actually." He grinned, and pressed the packet into her hand. "Like kissing someone new. That works really well."

Tally gazed down at the calorie-purgers, uncomprehending. The shiny foil glimmered painfully in the sun, and the packet's edges felt sharp as razors.

"But I've eaten hardly anything. Not enough to gain weight."

"It's not about losing weight. I need to talk to you, Tally. I need you with me for another minute. I've been waiting for someone like you for a long time. I need you . . . bubbly."

"Purgers are supposed to make me bubbly?"

"They help. I'll explain later. Just trust me, Tally-wa." His gaze remained on her, almost crazily intense, like when he explained some new trick idea to the Crims. It could be hard to resist Zane when he was like this, even if he wasn't making any sense.

"Okay, I guess." With clumsy fingers, she punched out two purgers and brought them to her mouth, but hesitated. You weren't supposed to take them if you hadn't eaten. It was dangerous. Back in the Rusty days—before the operation, when everyone had been ugly—there had been a disease where people deliberately didn't eat. They were so afraid of getting fat that they got way too skinny, sometimes even starving themselves to death in a world full of food. It was one of the scary things the operation had gotten rid of.

But a couple of purgers wouldn't kill her. When Zane handed Tally his coffee, she washed them down, then grimaced at the acid taste.

"Strong coffee, huh?" he said, grinning.

After a moment, her heart started beating fast, her metabolism kicking up. Her vision stayed sharp. Like the night before, she felt as if a thin film of plastic between her and the rest of the world were being peeled away. She squinted harder in the bright sunlight.

"Okay," Zane said. "What's the last thing you remember about David?"

Tally tried to steady her shaking hands, ransacking her brain to fight through the fog around her ugly memories. "We were all out in the ruins," she said. "You remember Shay's story about how we kidnapped her?"

Zane nodded, though Shay had more than one way of telling that story. In some versions, Shay had been kidnapped by Tally and the Smokies right from Special Circumstances headquarters. In other versions, she left the city to rescue Tally from the Smokies, and the two of them escaped back to the city together. Of course, Shay's weren't the only stories that changed sometimes. Crims always exaggerated stuff about the old days, because making it bubbly was the point. But Tally had a feeling that Zane wanted the truth.

"The Specials had destroyed the Smoke," she continued. "But there were a few of us still hiding out in the ruins."

"The New Smoke. That's what the uglies were calling you."

"That's right. But how did you know about that? Weren't you pretty by then?"

Zane grinned. "You think you're the only brand-new pretty I ever got to tell me stories, Tally-wa?"

"Oh." Remembering the kiss of a moment before, Tally wondered exactly how Zane had gotten the others to remember their ugly days.

"But why did you come back to the city?" he asked. "Don't tell me Shay actually rescued you."

Tally shook her head. "I don't think so."

"Did the Specials catch you? Did they get David, too?"

"No." The word reached her lips without hesitation. However fuzzy her memories were, David was still out there somewhere, she knew. In her mind she could see him clearly now, hiding in the ruins.

"Tell me, Tally, why did you come back here and give yourself up?"

Zane still held her hand, was squeezing it hard as he

waited for an answer. His face was close again, gold eyes luminous in the dappled shade, drinking in everything she said. But somehow, the memories wouldn't come. Thinking about those times was like banging her head against a wall.

She chewed her lip. "How come I can't remember? What's wrong with me, Zane?"

"That's a good question. But whatever it is, it's wrong with all of us."

"Who? The Crims?"

He shook his head, glancing up at the party spires that loomed over them. "Not just us. Everyone. At least, everyone here in New Pretty Town. Most people won't even talk about when they were uglies. They say they don't want to discuss boring kid stuff."

Tally nodded. She had figured that out pretty quickly about New Pretty Town—outside the Crims, talking about ugly days was totally fashion-missing.

"But when you push them," Zane continued, "it turns out most of them can't remember."

Tally frowned. "But us Crims always talk about the old days."

"We were all troublemakers," Zane said. "So we have exciting stuff stored in our heads. But you have to keep telling those stories, listening to one another, and breaking the rules. You have to stay bubbly, or you'll gradually forget everything from back then. Permanently."

Returning his powerful gaze, she suddenly realized something. "That's what the Crims are for, isn't it?"

He nodded. "That's right, Tally—to keep from forgetting, and to help me figure out what's wrong with us."

"How did you . . . what makes you so different?"

"Another good question. Maybe I was just born this

way, or maybe it's because I made myself a promise after I chickened out that night last spring: One day I'm going to leave the city, pretty or not." Zane's voice faded on the last words, and he breathed out through his teeth. "It just turned out to be a lot harder than I thought. Things were getting seriously boring there for a while, and I was starting to forget." He brightened. "But then you showed up, with your screwy stories that don't make sense. Things are definitely bubbly now."

"I guess they are." Tally looked down at her hand in his. "One more question, Zane-la?"

"Sure." He smiled. "I like your questions."

Tally looked away, a little embarrassed. "When you kissed me just then, was that to help you stay bubbly and to make me remember better? Or was it . . ." She trailed off, looking nervously into his eyes.

Zane grinned. "What do you think?" But he didn't give her a chance to answer. He took her shoulders and pulled her close again, and kissed her deeper this time, the warmth of his lips mixing with the strength of his hands on her, the taste of coffee and the smell of his hair.

When it was done, Tally leaned back, breathing hard because the kiss had been totally oxygen-missing. But it had made her bubbly, more than the calorie-purging pills or even jumping off the party spire the night before. And she remembered another thing that should have been totally obvious to mention before now, but somehow hadn't been.

And it was going to make Zane totally happy.

"Last night," Tally said, "Croy told me they had something for me, but he didn't say what. He was going to leave it here in New Pretty Town, hidden so the wardens wouldn't find it."

"Something from the New Smoke?" His eyes grew wide. "Where?"

"Valentino 317."

## VALENTINO 317

"Wait a second," Zane said. He pulled off her interface ring and then his own, and led her deeper into the pleasure garden. "Better lose these," he said. "Don't want them following."

"Oh, right." Tally remembered ugly days, how easy it was to trick the dorm minders. "The wardens last night—they said they were going to keep an eye on me."

Zane chuckled. "They're always keeping an eye on me."

He threaded the rings onto two tall reeds, which bowed under the weight of the metal bands. "The wind will move them every now and then," he explained. "That way, it won't look like we took them off."

"But won't it look weird? Us staying in one place for so long?"

"It is a pleasure garden." Zane laughed. "I've spent my share of time in here."

A nasty ping went through Tally, but she didn't let it show. "What about finding them again?"

"I know this place. Quit worrying."

"Oh. Sorry."

He turned to her and laughed. "Nothing to be sorry for. This is the best breakfast I've had in ages."

They left the rings and headed down toward the river and Valentino Mansion, Tally wondering what they would discover in Room 317. In most mansions, each room had its own name—Tally's room in Komachi was called Etcetera; Shay's was Bluesky—but Valentino was so old that the rooms had numbers. Valentinos always made a big deal out of stuff like that, sticking to the ancient traditions of their crumbling home.

"Tricky place to hide it," Zane said as they approached the sprawling mansion. "Easier to keep secrets where the walls don't talk."

"That's probably why they hacked a Valentino bash and not one in some other mansion," Tally said.

"Except I had to go and screw everything up," Zane said.

Tally looked at him. "You?"

"We started off down in the stone mansion, but when we couldn't find you guys anywhere, I said we should go up into the new party spire so the smart walls would find you."

"We had the same idea," Tally said.

Zane shook his head. "Yeah, well, if we'd all stayed down in Valentino, the Specials wouldn't have spotted Croy so fast. He would have had time to talk to you."

"So they can listen through the walls?"

"Yeah." Zane grinned. "Why do you think I suggested a picnic on this bogusly cold day."

Tally nodded, thinking it through. The city interface brought you pings, answered your questions, reminded you of appointments, even turned the lights on and off in your room. If Special Circumstances wanted to watch you, they'd know everything you did and half of what you were thinking. She remembered talking to Croy up in the spire, her interface ring on her finger, the walls catching every word. . . . "Do they watch everybody?"

"No, they couldn't, and most people aren't worth

watching. But some of us get special treatment. As in Special Circumstances."

Tally swore. The Specials had shown up so quickly last night. She'd only had a few minutes with Croy, as if they'd been waiting close by. Maybe they'd already spotted that the party had been hacked. Or maybe they were never very far away from Tally Youngblood. . . .

She looked into the trees. Shadows shifted in the wind, and she imagined gray shapes flitting among them. "I don't think last night was because of you, Zane. It was my fault."

"How do you mean?"

"It's always my fault."

"That's bogus, Tally," Zane said softly. "There's nothing wrong with being special."

His voice trailed off as they passed through the main arch of Valentino Mansion. Within the cool stone walls, it was as silent as a tomb.

"The party was still going when we left," Zane whispered. "They probably all just went to bed."

Tally nodded. There weren't even any maintenance robots at work yet. Bits of torn costumes littered the hallways. Spilled drinks filled the air with a sickly sweet perfume, and the floor was sticky underfoot. The glamour of the party had been stripped away, like bubbliness turned into a hangover.

Her finger felt naked without an interface ring, bringing back memories of sneaking across the river as an ugly, the terror of being caught. But fear kept her bubbly, her senses sharp enough to hear stray party rubbish shifting in the drafty corridors, to separate the raisiny scent of spilled champagne from the stale funk of beer. Besides their own footsteps, the mansion was silent.

"Whoever lives in 317 is going to be asleep," Tally whispered.

"Then we'll wake them up," Zane said softly, eyes flashing in the semidarkness.

The ground-floor rooms were all numbered in the one hundreds, so they looked for a way up. New elevators had been added to the mansion at some point, but without interface rings, the doors wouldn't open for them. A set of stone stairs brought Tally and Zane to the third floor, across from 301. The numbers counted up as they walked down the hall, odds on one side and evens on the other. Zane squeezed her hand when they reached 315.

But the next room was numbered 319.

They retraced their steps, checking the other side of the hall, but found only doors numbered 316, 318, and 320. Searching the rest of the floor, they found more 320s and the 330s, odd and even, but no Valentino 317.

"This is a bubbly puzzle," Zane said, chuckling to himself.

Tally sighed. "Maybe it was all a joke."

"You think the New Smokies would hack a citywide invitation, sneak across the river, and crash a party just to waste our time?"

"Probably not," Tally admitted, but she felt something in her starting to fade. She found herself wondering if this whole expedition was kind of lame, looking for some big secret that uglies had left behind. Sneaking around in someone else's mansion was pretty bogus, after all. "You think breakfast is still warm?" she asked.

"Tally . . ." Zane turned his intense gaze on her. With trembling hands, he pushed her hair behind her ears. "Stay with me."

"I'm right here," she said.

He drew closer, until his lips almost brushed hers. "I mean, stay bubbly."

Tally kissed him, and with the pressure of his lips the world sharpened again. She pushed the hunger out of her mind and said, "Okay. What about the elevator?"

"Which one?"

She led him back to the space between Valentino 315 and 319. The long expanse of stone wall was interrupted by an elevator door.

"There used to be a room here," she said.

"But they got rid of it when they put in the elevator." Zane laughed. "Lazy pretties. Can't climb two flights of stairs."

"So maybe 317 is the elevator now."

"Well, that's bogus," Zane said. "We can't make it come without our rings."

"We could wait around until someone else calls the elevator, and slip in."

Zane looked up and down the empty hallway, piled with plastic cups and torn paper decorations. "Hours from now," he said, sighing. "When we won't be bubbly anymore."

"Yeah. Not bubbly." A layer of fuzziness was starting to sink across Tally's vision again, and her stomach growled in a food-missing way, which called up the mental image of a warm chocolate muffin. She shook her head to clear it, visualizing a Special Circumstances uniform instead. Last night the sight of gray silk had focused her mind, had propelled her after Croy and into the fire stairwell. The whole thing had been a test to see how well her brain was working. Maybe this was another test. A bubbly puzzle, as Zane had said.

She stared at the elevator door. There had to be a way inside.

Slowly, a memory came to her. It was from back in the

ugly days, but not so long ago. Tally remembered falling down a lightless shaft. It was one of the stories that Shay always liked to hear her tell, about how Tally and David had snuck into Special Circumstances headquarters. . . . "The roof," Tally said.

"What?"

"You can climb down into an elevator shaft from the roof. I've done it."

"Really?"

Instead of answering, Tally kissed him again. She couldn't remember exactly how, but knew that if she just stayed bubbly, it would come back to her. "Follow me."

Getting up to the roof wasn't as simple as she'd expected—the stairs they had taken up stopped at the third floor. Tally frowned, frustration deadening everything again. In Komachi Mansion, getting up to the roof was easy. "This is bogus. What do they do if there's a fire?"

"Stone doesn't burn," Zane said. He pointed at a small window at the end of the hall, sunlight streaming in through its stained-glass panels. "That's the way out." He strode toward it.

"What? Climb up the outside wall?"

Zane stuck his head out and looked down, letting out a long whistle. "Nothing like heights to keep you bubbly."

Tally frowned, unsure whether or not she wanted to be that bubbly.

Zane pulled himself up onto the sill and leaned out, grasping the top of the window. He stood carefully, slowly rising until Tally could see only his boots standing on the stone ledge outside. Her heart began to race again, until she could feel it beating in her fingertips. The world became as sharp as icicles.

For a long time his feet were motionless, then they shuffled closer to the edge, until only Zane's toes rested on the stone, precariously balanced.

"What are you doing up there?"

In answer, his boots lifted slowly into the air. Then Tally heard the muffled sound of soles scrabbling on stone. She stuck her head through and peered up.

Above her, Zane dangled from the edge of the roof, his feet swinging and scraping. Then one of his boots found purchase in a crack between the stones, and he hauled himself over and out of sight.

A moment later, his face appeared, grinning from ear to ear. "Come on up!"

Tally pulled her head in and took a deep breath, placing her hands on the ledge. The stone was rough and cold. The wind whistling through the window made the tiny hairs on her arms stand up.

"Stay bubbly," Tally said softly. She pulled herself up to sit in the window, the stone cold against her thighs, and took a quick glance at the ground. It was a long way down to the scattered leaves and tree roots that would break her fall. The wind picked up, making nearby branches wave, and Tally could see every twig. The smell of pine tree sharpened in her nostrils. Bubbly was not going to be a problem.

She slid one foot out onto the ledge, then the other.

Standing up was the scariest part. Tally clutched the window frame with one hand as she rose, the other feeling for a handhold on the outside wall. She didn't dare let herself look down again. The cool stone was pocked with holes and cracks, but none seemed large enough for more than fingertips.

When her legs had straightened all the way, Tally found herself paralyzed for a moment. She swayed slightly in the breeze, like an unsupported tower built too tall.

"Pretty bubbly-making, huh?" Zane's voice came from above. "Just grab the ledge."

She tore her gaze from the wall in front of her and looked up. The edge of the roof was just out of reach. "Hey, this isn't fair. You're taller than me."

"No problem." He lowered one hand.

"Are you sure you can hold me?"

"Come on, Tally-wa. What's the point of having all those new pretty muscles if you don't use them for anything."

"Like getting killed?" she said under her breath, but reached up to take his hand.

Her new muscles were stronger than she'd thought, though. With her fingers locked around Zane's wrist, Tally pulled herself easily up from the window ledge. Her free hand grasped the roof's edge, and one toe managed to get purchase in a crack in the mansion wall. With a grunt, Tally was up, rolling over the ledge and onto the roof. She sprawled on the reassuringly solid stone, giggling with the rush of relief that swept through her.

Zane grinned. "It's true, what I said before."

She looked up at him questioningly.

"I've been waiting for someone like you."

Pretties didn't blush—not in an ugly-making way, at least—but Tally rolled to her feet to hide her reaction. The bubbliness of their death-defying climb had made Zane's gaze too intense. She stood to take in the view.

From the roof, Tally could see the spires of New Pretty Town still towering over them, the green trails of pleasure gardens snaking up the central hill. Across the river, Uglyville was already awake. A soccer field full of just-turned-uglies swarmed around a black-and-white ball, and the wind carried to her ears the sound of a whistle being furiously blown. The view seemed terribly close and in focus, her nervous system still ringing, echoing from the moments she'd swung from Zane's hand.

The stone roof was flat, marked only by the spinning heads of three air vents, the towering transmission mast, and a metal shack no bigger than an ugly's closet. Tally pointed at the latter. "That's right above the elevator."

They crossed the roof. In the shack's ancient door, a rust-covered sheet of metal like those that littered the ruins, letters had been painstakingly scratched: VALENTINO 317.

"Very non-bogus, Tally," Zane said, grinning. He yanked at the door, but a shiny chain snapped taut with a screeched complaint. "Hmm."

Tally looked at the device that kept the chain from slipping, wracking her still-spinning brain. "That's called a . . . padlock, I think." She felt the smooth steel object between her fingers, trying to remember how they worked. "They had them in the Smoke, to secure stuff that people might steal."

"Great. All this and we still need our rings."

Tally shook her head. "Smokies don't use interface rings, Zane. To open a padlock, you need a . . ." She searched her memory for another old word, then found it. "There must be a key somewhere."

"A key? Like a password?"

"No. This kind of key is a little metal thing. You stick it in and turn, which makes the lock pop open."

"What does it look like?"

"A flat piece of steel, about as long as your thumb, with teeth."

Zane giggled at this image, but started looking around.

Tally stared at the door. The shack was obviously much older than the chain that held it shut. She wondered what it had been used for. Leaning close to the narrow gap Zane had opened, Tally sheltered her gaze with both hands and peered into the blackness. Her eyes adjusted slowly, until she could make out dark shapes within.

There seemed to be a huge pulley and a crude mechanical engine, like the kind they used out in the Smoke. The elevator had once moved up and down on a chain. This shack was old; it must have been abandoned after lifters had been invented, which was ages ago. Modern elevators ran on the same principle as hoverboards and bungee jackets. (Which was a lot safer than dangling from a chain. . . . Tally shivered at the thought.) When lifters had been added, the old mechanism must have been left up here on the roof to rust.

She yanked at the padlock again, but it held firm. Heavy and crude, the lock looked out of place here in the city. When wardens wanted to secure something, they stuck up a sensor that would tell you to keep out. Only New Smokies would have used a padlock made of metal.

Croy had told her to come here, so there had to be a key around somewhere.

"Another stupid test," she muttered.

"A what?" Zane asked. Looking for the key, he had climbed on top of the shack.

"Like Croy dressing up as a Special," she explained. "And making us find Valentino 317. The key has to be tricky to get hold of, because it's all a test. Their point is to make it hard to find this thing that Croy left for me. They don't want us to find it unless we're bubbly."

"Or maybe," Zane said, perching on one edge of the shack, "they want the search to make us bubbly, so we're thinking clearly when we find it."

"Whatever it is," Tally said, and sighed. She felt

annoyance rising in her, along with the feeling that this test would never end, that every solution would just lead to another level of problems, like some stupid thumbgame. Maybe the smartest move would be to blow it all off and just have breakfast. Why was she trying to prove herself to the New Smokies, anyway? They didn't matter. She was beautiful and they were ugly.

But Zane's brain was still spinning. "So they'd hide the key somewhere that would be extra tricky to get to. But what would be trickier than climbing up here?"

Tally's eyes swept the roof, until they found the spindly transmission tower. At its top, twenty stories above them, the Valentino flag whipped in the wind. At the sight of it, the world grew crisp again, and she smiled.

"Climbing up there."

## THE HIGH TOWER

The transmission tower was the newest piece of Valentino Mansion, made of steel painted over with white polymers to keep rust at bay. It was part of the system that tracked people's interface rings, supposedly to help find anyone who got lost or injured outside a smart building.

White struts loomed over Tally and Zane, crisscrossing like a cat's cradle, shining in the sun like porcelain. The tower didn't look hard to climb, except for the fact that it was five times as tall as Valentino Mansion, even taller than a party spire. As she stared up into its heights, a low rumble sounded in Tally's stomach. She was pretty sure it wasn't hunger. "At least there's no dragon guarding it," she said.

Zane lowered his anxious gaze from the tower. "Huh?"

Tally shook her head. "Just something from a dream I had."

"You really think the key's up there?"

"I'm afraid so."

"The New Smokies climbed all that way?"

Old memories came back. "No. They could've hoverboarded up the side. Boards can go that high if they stay close enough to a big piece of metal."

"You know, we could requisition a hoverboard . . . ," Zane said quietly.

She looked at him with surprise.

He muttered, "Of course, that wouldn't be very bubbly, would it?"

"It wouldn't. And anything that flies has a minder. Do you know how to trick a hoverboard's safety governor?"

"Used to, but I can't remember."

"Me either. Okay, then. We climb."

"Okay," he said. "But first . . ." He reached for Tally's hand, drew her to him, and they kissed again.

She blinked once, then felt a grin spreading on her face. "Just to keep us bubbly."

The first half was easy.

Tally and Zane stayed together, climbing opposite sides of the tower, finding ready handholds in the weave of struts and cables. The wind kicked up now and then, playfully tugging at Tally in a way that was nervous-making, but all it took was a quick glance downward to focus her mind.

Halfway up, she could already see the whole of Valentino Mansion, the pleasure gardens spread out in every direction, even the hovercar pads atop the central hospital where they did the operation. The river glittered as the sun climbed toward noon, and across the water, in Uglyville, Tally saw her old dorm hulking among the trees. On the soccer field, a few uglies were watching them and pointing, probably wondering who was climbing the tower.

Tally wondered how long it would be before someone on this side of the river noticed their ascent and pinged the wardens.

With her new muscles, the climb wasn't physically demanding. But as the two of them neared the top, the tower grew narrower, the handholds less sure. The polymer coating was slick, still wet in a few corners where the morning sun hadn't yet dried the dew. Microwave dishes and thick skeins of braided cables crowded the struts, and doubts began to creep through Tally's mind. Was the key really up here? Why would the New Smokies make her risk her life just to pass a test? As the climb grew trickier and the drop more panic-making, Tally found herself wondering how she'd wound up here on this tall and windy spike.

The night before, her only goal had been to become a Crim, pretty and popular, surrounded by a clique of new friends. And she'd managed to get everything she'd wanted—on top of which, Zane had kissed her, a bubbly development she hadn't even imagined before this morning.

Of course, getting what you wanted never turned out the way you'd thought it would. Being a Crim wasn't about being satisfied, and hanging out with Zane apparently involved risking your life and not eating breakfast. Tally had only been voted in last night, and here she was having to prove herself again.

And for what? Did she really want to unlock the rusty shack below? Whatever was in there could only make her head more spinning, and was certain to remind her of

David and the Smoke and everything she'd left behind. It felt as if every time she took a step forward into her new life, something sucked her back toward ugly days.

With her mind tangled by these questions, Tally put her foot wrong.

The sole of one shoe slipped from a thick cable coated in slick plastic, sending her flailing legs away from the tower, yanking her hands from their grip on a strut that was still wet with dew. Tally tumbled downward, the feeling of free fall surging through her body, familiar from all the times she had wiped out on a hoverboard or thrown herself from the top of a building.

Her instincts told her to relax, until she realized the big difference between this fall and all those others: Tally wasn't wearing crash bracelets or a bungee jacket. This time she was really falling; nothing was going to catch her.

Her brand-new pretty reflexes kicked into gear, and her hands flew out to grab a passing braid of cable. Tally's palms slid down the plastic insulation, the friction burning her skin as if the cable had burst into flame. Her legs swung in toward the tower—knees bent, body turning—and Tally absorbed the impact against the metal with her hip, a blow that shook her whole frame but didn't loosen the grip of her burning fingers.

Tally's feet scrabbled to gain purchase, their soles finding a wide strut and mercifully taking most of the weight from her hands. She wrapped her arms around the cable, every muscle tense, barely hearing Zane's shouts above her, and gazed out over the river, amazed at her own vision.

Everything shone, as if diamonds had been scattered across Uglyville. Her mind felt clean, like the air after a morning rain, and Tally understood at last why she had climbed up here. Not to impress Zane or the Smokies, or to pass any test, but because some part of her had wanted this moment, this clarity she hadn't felt since the operation. This was way beyond bubbly.

"Are you okay?" came a distant cry.

She looked back up at Zane. Seeing how far she'd fallen, Tally swallowed, but still managed a smile. "I'm bubbly. Totally. Wait up."

She climbed fast now, ignoring her bruised hip. Her scorched palms complained every time they closed around a handhold, but within a minute she was alongside Zane again. His golden eyes were wider than ever, as if her fall had scared him worse than it had Tally.

She smiled again, realizing that it probably had. "Come on." She left him behind, pulling herself up the last few meters.

Reaching the top, Tally found a black magnet stuck to the bottom of the flagpole, a shiny new key clinging to it. She carefully pulled the key off and slipped it into her pocket while the Valentino flag snapped overhead, the sound as crisp as clothes fresh out of the wall.

"Got it," she yelled, and started down, passing Zane before he'd even moved, the shocked expression still frozen on his face.

It wasn't until she stood on the roof again that Tally realized how sore her muscles were. Her heart was still pounding, and the world remained crystalline. She pulled the key from her pocket, tracing its teeth with one trembling fingertip, her senses registering every detail of the metal's jagged edge.

"Hurry up!" she cried to Zane, who was still only halfway down. He started to climb faster, but Tally snorted and spun on one heel, striding toward the shack.

The padlock popped open when she turned the key, the rusty door groaning with age as its bottom edge skidded across the stone. Tally stepped inside, blind for a moment in the darkness, seeing red traces that pulsed with her heartbeat, full of excitement. If the Smokies had arranged all this to make her bubbly, they'd gotten what they wanted.

The little room smelled very old, the air inside warm and still. As Tally's eyes adjusted, she could see the flaking graffiti that filled every centimeter of wall space, layer upon layer of slogans, scrawled tags, and the names of couples proclaiming their love. Some of the dates included years that made no sense, until Tally realized that they were written in Rusty style, counting all the old centuries before the collapse. The crumbling elevator machinery was decorated with still more graffiti, and the floor littered with ancient contraband: old cans of spray-paint, crushed and empty tubes of notoriously sticky nano-glue, burned-out fireworks smelling like old campfires. Tally saw a yellowed rectangle of paper, squashed and blackened at one end, like a picture of a cigarette from a Rusty history book. She picked it up and sniffed, dropping it when her stomach heaved at the stench.

A cigarette? This place was older than lifters, she reminded herself, maybe even older than the city itself, a strange, forgotten piece of history. She wondered how many generations of uglies and tricky new pretties like the Crims had made it theirs.

The pouch Croy had shown her rested on one of the old rusted gears of the elevator mechanism, waiting.

Tally picked it up. The old leather felt strange in her hands, sending her mind back to the worn textures of the Smoke. She opened it and pulled out a sheet of paper. A small, skittering sound came from the stone floor, and she realized something tiny had fallen from the pouch—two things, in fact. Tally knelt down and squinted, feeling the cool stone with her still burning palms until she found two little white pills.

She stared at them, feeling a memory at the edge of her awareness.

The room darkened, and she looked up. Zane was in the doorway, panting, his eyes flashing in the gloom. "Gee. Thanks for waiting, Tally."

She didn't say anything. He took a step in and knelt beside her.

"You okay?" His hand came to rest on her shoulder. "Didn't hit your head in that fall, did you?"

"No. Just cleared it up. I found this." She handed the sheet of paper to Zane, who smoothed it out and held it up to the light streaming through the door. It was covered with an almost unreadable scrawl.

Tally looked down again at the pills in her hand. Tiny and white, they looked like a pair of purgers. But Tally was pretty sure they would do more than burn calories. She remembered something. . . .

Zane slowly lowered the sheet of paper, his eyes wide. "It's a letter, and it's addressed to you."

"A letter? Who from?"

"You, Tally." His voice echoed softly from the metal walls of the shack. "It's from you."

## NOTE TO SELF

Dear Tally,

You're me.

Or I guess another way to say it is, I'm you—Tally Youngblood. Same person. But if you're reading this letter, then we're also two different people. At least, that's what us New Smokies are guessing has happened by now. You've been changed. That's why I'm writing to you.

I wonder if you remember writing these words. (Actually, I'm telling Shay to write them. She did handwriting in school.) Do they seem like a diary entry from back when you were a littlie, or like someone else's diary altogether?

If you can't remember writing this letter at all, then we're both in big trouble. Especially me. Because not being remembered by myself would mean that the me who wrote this letter has been erased somehow. Ouch. And maybe that means I'm dead, sort of. So please try to remember, at least.

Tally paused and traced the scrawled words with one finger, trying to remember dictating them. Shay liked to demonstrate how they could make letters with a stylus, one of the tricks she'd learned in preparation for their trip to the Smoke. She had left a note for Tally telling how to follow her there. But was this really Shay's handwriting?

More important, were the words true? Tally really couldn't remember. She took a breath and kept on reading. . . .

But, anyway, here's what I'm trying to tell you: They did something to your brain—our brain—and that's why this letter may seem kind of weird to you.

We (that's "we" as in us out in the New

Smoke, not "we" as in you and me) don't know exactly how it works, but we're pretty sure that something happens to everyone who has the operation. When they make you pretty, they also add these lesions (tiny scars, sort of) to your brain. It makes you different, and not in a good way. Look in the mirror, Tally. If you're pretty, you've got them.

Tally heard a sharp intake of breath next to her ear. She turned to find Zane reading over her shoulder. "Looks like you may be right about us pretties," she said.

He nodded slowly. "Yeah. Great." He pointed at the next paragraph. "But how about that?"

She dropped her eyes to the page again.

The good news is, there's a cure. That's why David came and got you, to give you the pills that will fix your brain. (I really hope you remember David.) He's a good guy, even if he had to kidnap you to get you here. Trust him. It might be scary to be out here, away from the city, wherever the New Smokies are hiding you, but the people who gave you the lesions will be looking, and you have to be kept safe until you're cured.

Tally stopped reading. "Kidnapped me?"

"Looks like there's been a change of plan since you wrote this," Zane said.

Tally felt funny for a moment, the image of David now stronger in her head. "If I wrote this. And if it's true. Anyway, Croy came to see me, not . . . David." As she said his name, memories surged through Tally: David's hands roughened from years of work, his jacket made from sewn-together skins, the white scar that went through his eyebrow. A feeling like panic began to well up in her. "What happened to David, Zane? Why didn't he come?"

He shook his head. "I don't know. Were you and he . . . ?"

Tally looked down at the letter again. It blurred before her, and a single teardrop fell onto the paper. Ink bled into the spattered mark, turning the tear black. "I'm pretty sure we were." Her voice was rough, memories tangled inside her. "But something happened."

"Oh?"

"I don't know what." Tally wondered why she couldn't remember. Was it really because of lesions—the scars on her brain that the note had warned about? Or did she simply not want to?

"What's that in your hand, Tally?" Zane asked.

She opened her reddened palm to reveal the tiny white pills resting there. "The cure. Let me finish this." She took a steadying breath.

> One more thing—Maddy (David's mom, who came up with the cure) says I have to add this, something about "informed consent":
>
> I, Tally Youngblood, hereby give my permission for Maddy and David to give me the pills that cure being pretty-minded. I realize this is a test on an unproven drug, and it all might go horribly wrong. Brain-dead wrong.
>
> Um, sorry about that last part. That's the risk we have to take. That's why I gave myself up to become pretty, so we could test the pills and save Shay and Peris, and everyone else in

the world who's had their brain messed with.

So you have to take them. For me. Sorry in advance if you don't want to, and David and Maddy force you to. You'll be better off, I promise.

Good luck.

Love,

Tally

Tally let the paper fall onto her lap. Somehow, the scrawled words had sucked the clarity out of the world, making her head-spinning and fuzzy again. Her heart was still pounding, but not in that beautiful way it had when she'd caught herself falling from the tower. It felt more like panic, as if she were locked inside the little metal shack.

Zane let out a low whistle. "So that's why you came back."

"You believe this, don't you?"

His eyes flashed gold in the darkness. "Of course. It all makes sense now. Why you can't remember David or coming back to the city. Why Shay has so many mixed-up stories about those days. Why the New Smokies are so interested in you."

"Because I'm brain damaged?"

Zane shook his head. "We're all brain damaged, Tally. Just like I thought. But you gave yourself up on purpose, knowing there's a cure." He pointed at the pills in her hand. "Those are the reason why you're here."

She stared down at the pills, which looked small and insignificant in the gloom of the shack. "But the letter said they might not even work. I might wind up brain-dead. . . ."

He took her wrist lightly. "If you don't want to take them, Tally, I will."

She closed her hand. "I can't let you do that."

"But this is what I've been waiting for. A way to escape prettiness, to be bubbly all the time!"

"I wasn't waiting for this," Tally cried. "I didn't want anything but to be a Crim!"

He pointed at the letter. "Yes, you did."

"That wasn't me. She says so herself."

"But you—"

"Maybe I changed my mind!"

"You didn't change your mind. The operation did."

She opened her mouth, but nothing came out.

"Tally, you gave yourself up, knowing you'd have to risk the cure. That's amazingly brave." Zane reached out and touched her face, his eyes shining in the shaft of sunlight that streamed across him. "But if you don't want to, let me take the risk for you."

Tally shook her head, wondering what she was more afraid of: the pills going wrong on her, or watching Zane turn into a vegetable in her place. Or maybe what she really feared was finding out what had happened to David. If only Croy had left her alone, or if she'd never found Valentino 317. If she could just forget the pills and stay dumb and pretty, none of this would ever worry her again. "I just want to forget David."

"Why?" Zane leaned closer. "What did he do to you?"

"Nothing. He didn't do anything. But why did Croy leave these pills for me instead of him coming and taking me away? What if he's—"

The shack shuddered for a moment, silencing her. They both looked up; something big had passed overhead.

"A hovercar . . . ," Tally whispered.

"Probably just flying over. As far as they know, we're in the pleasure garden."

"Unless someone saw us up on the . . ." She fell silent

as a cloud of dust stirred in through the half-opened door, glowing in the shaft of sunlight. "It's landing."

"They know we're here," Zane said, and started tearing up the letter.

"What are you doing?"

"We can't let them find this," he said. "They can't know there's a cure." He stuffed a piece of the letter into his mouth, grimacing at the taste.

She looked at the pills in her hand. "What about these?"

He swallowed the paper with a tortured expression. "I have to take them, now." He bit off another piece of the letter and started chewing.

"They're so small," she said. "We could hide them."

He shook his head, swallowing again. "Getting caught without rings is pretty obvious, Tally. They'll want to know what we were up to. When you get some food in you, you won't be as bubbly—you might chicken out and hand over the pills."

The sound of footsteps approached across the roof outside. Zane yanked the door almost shut, pulling the ends of the chain through to the inside and snapping the padlock closed, plunging them into darkness. "That won't stop them for long. Give me the pills. If they work, I promise I'll make sure you—"

A voice called from outside, and something cold crawled down Tally's spine. The voice had an edge, like razors in her ears. They weren't wardens outside. This was a Special Circumstance.

In the gloom of the shack, the pills stared up at her like two soulless white eyes. Tally was somehow certain that the words in the letter were her own, begging her to take them. Maybe when she did, everything would be clear and bubbly all the time, like Zane said.

Or maybe they wouldn't work, and would leave her a hollow, brain-dead shell.

Or maybe it was David who was dead. Tally wondered if after today part of her would always remember his face, no matter what she did. And unless she took the pills, she would never know the truth.

Tally started to bring them to her mouth, but found she couldn't. She imagined her brain unraveling. Being erased, like that other Tally who had written the letter. She looked into Zane's pleading, beautiful eyes. He had no doubts, at least.

Maybe she didn't have to do this alone. . . .

The door made a sharp screech as someone tried to pull it open, snapping the chain taut. A blow landed on the door, the sound booming like fireworks in the little metal shack. Specials were strong, but could they beat down a metal door?

"Now, Tally," Zane whispered.

"I can't."

"Then give them to me."

She shook her head and leaned closer, whispering to stay unheard under the thundering blows against the door. "I can't do that to you, Zane, and I can't do this alone. Maybe if we each took one . . ."

"What? That's crazy. We don't know how that will—"

"We don't know anything, Zane."

The pounding stopped, and Tally shushed his reply. Specials weren't just strong and fast, they had the sharp hearing of predators.

Suddenly, a bright light sparked through the gap in the door, throwing wildly jittering shadows into the shack, leaving tracers on Tally's vision. The cutting tool hissed as it burned into the chain, and the smell of molten metal reached her nostrils. The Specials would be inside in seconds.

“Together,” she whispered, handing one of the pills to Zane. With a deep breath she placed the other on her tongue. Bitterness exploded through her mouth, like biting into a seed inside a grape. She swallowed the pill, which trailed an acid taste down her throat.

“Please,” she pleaded softly. “Do this with me.”

He sighed and took the pill, grimacing at the taste. He stared at her, shaking his head. “That may have been very stupid, Tally.”

She tried to smile. “At least we were stupid together.” Leaning forward, she grasped the back of his neck and kissed him. David hadn’t come to rescue her. He was either dead or he must not care what happened to her. He was ugly, and Zane was beautiful, and bubbly, and he was here. “We need each other now,” she said.

They were still kissing when the Specials burst in.

# Part II

## THE CURE

and kisses are a better fate
than wisdom
—e. e. cummings, "since feeling is first"

# BREAKTHROUGH

Overnight, the first freeze of winter had come. The trees shone like glass, bare branches alight with icicles. Glittering black fingers stretched across the window, cutting the sky into sharp little pieces.

Tally pressed one hand against the pane, letting the chill leak through the glass and into her palm. The bracing cold made the afternoon light sharper, as brittle as she imagined the icicles outside to be. It focused the part of her mind that still wanted to sink back into pretty dreams.

When she finally pulled her hand away from the window, a fuzzy outline showed its imprint on the glass, then slowly faded.

"Blurry Tally is no more," she said, then grinned, placing her icy palm against Zane's cheek.

"What the . . . ," he muttered, stirring just enough to nudge her hand away.

"Wake up, pretty-head."

His eyes opened a slit. "Make it dark," he told his interface cuff.

The room obeyed, opaquing the window.

Tally frowned. "Another headache?" Zane still sometimes got crippling migraines that could put him out for hours, but they weren't as bad as the first weeks after he'd taken the pill.

"No," he murmured. "Sleepy."

She reached for the manual controls, setting the window back to transparent. "Then it's time to get up. We'll be late for ice skating."

He squinted at her through one eye. "Ice skating is bogus."

"Sleeping's bogus. Get up and be bubbly."

"Bubbly is bogus."

Tally raised one eyebrow, which didn't hurt anymore. She'd been a good pretty and had her forehead all fixed, though she'd memorialized the scar with a flash tattoo: black Celtic swirls just above her eye that spun in time with her heartbeat. For good measure, she'd gotten eye surge exactly like Shay's, backward-running clocks and everything.

"Bubbly is not bogus, lazy-face." Tally placed her hand against the window again to recharge its iciness. Her interface cuff sparkled in the sun like the frozen trees below, and for the millionth time she searched for any seam in its metal surface. But the cuff seemed to have been forged from one piece of steel, perfectly fitted to the oval of her wrist. She pulled at it softly, feeling the slightest give; she was growing skinnier every day. "Coffee, please," she said sweetly to the cuff.

Brewing smells began to percolate into the room, and Zane stirred again. When her hand had grown sufficiently cold, Tally placed it on his bare chest. He flinched but didn't fight back, just squeezed two fistfuls of sheet and took a shuddering breath. His eyes opened, their gold irises shining like the cold winter sun. "Now that was bubbly."

"I thought bubbly was bogus."

He smiled and shrugged drowsily.

Tally smiled back. Zane was extra beautiful when he

first woke up. The edges of sleep softened his intense stare, leaving his severe features almost vulnerable-looking, like a lost and hungry boy. Tally never mentioned this fact, of course, or Zane would probably have gotten surge to fix it.

She made her way to the coffeemaker, stepping over the piles of unrecycled clothes and dirty dishes that occupied every square centimeter of floor. As always, Zane's room was a wreck. His closet lay half-open, too overflowing to shut properly. It was an easy room to hide things in.

Sipping her coffee, Tally told the hole in the wall to make their usual skating ensembles: heavy plastic jackets lined with fake rabbit fur; knee-padded pants for bad falls; black scarves; and, most important, thick gloves that reached halfway to their elbows. While the hole was spitting out clothes, she took Zane his coffee, which finally dragged him to consciousness.

Zane and Tally skipped breakfast—a meal they hadn't eaten for the last month—and layered up in the elevator down to the front door of Pulcher Mansion, speaking fluent pretty along the way.

"Did you see the frost, Zane-la? So icy-making."

"Winter is totally bubbly."

"Totally. Summer is just too . . . I don't know. Warming or something."

"Utterly."

They smiled pleasantly at the door minder and went out into the cold, pausing for a moment on the mansion's front steps. Tally handed Zane her coffee mug and pulled her gloves up inside her sleeves, covering the interface cuff on her left arm with two layers. Then she wrapped that arm with the black scarf to seal the cuff tightly. She took both coffees from Zane, watching steam curl up from the trembling black pools while he did the same with his own gloves.

When he was done, Tally spoke, not too loudly. "I thought we were supposed to act normal today."

"I am acting normal."

"Come on. 'Bubbly is bogus'?"

"What? Too much?"

She shook her head, giggled, and pulled him toward the floating rink.

It had been one month since they'd taken the pills, and Tally and Zane weren't brain-dead yet. The first few hours, though, had been totally bogus. The Specials had searched them and Valentino 317 madly, putting everything they found in little plastic bags. They'd barked a million questions in their grating Special voices, trying to find out why a pair of new pretties would climb the transmission tower. Tally tried to tell them they'd just wanted privacy, but no explanation satisfied the Specials.

Finally, some wardens showed up with the abandoned interface rings, medspray for Tally's palms, and muffins. Tally ate her long-delayed breakfast like a hungry dog until all her bubbliness went away, then smiled prettily and asked to be taken to surge for the previous night's scar. After another really boring hour or so, the Specials let the wardens take her to the hospital with Zane in tow.

That was mostly it, except for the interface cuffs. The doctors slipped Tally's on during her eyebrow surge, and Zane awoke the next morning to find himself wearing one. They worked just like interface rings, except they could send voice-pings from anywhere, like a handphone. That meant the cuffs heard you talking even when you went outside and, unlike rings, they didn't come off. They were manacles with an invisible chain, and no tool Tally and Zane had yet tried could cut them open.

Unexpectedly, the cuffs also became the fashion item of the season. Once the other Crims saw them, it was all Zane could do to keep everyone from requisitioning their own. He got the hole in the wall to make a bunch of nonworking copies and passed them out. Over the next few weeks, word spread that the cuffs were some new marker of criminality, signifying that you had scaled the transmission tower on top of Valentino Mansion; it turned out that hundreds of new pretties had witnessed Tally's and Zane's climb, pinging one another to run to windows and check out the show. Within a few weeks, only the most fashion-missing went around without some kind of metal cuff locked onto their wrists, and minders had to be installed to keep new pretties off the tower.

People were starting to point out Tally and Zane when they were in public, and there were more Crim wannabees every day. It was like everybody wanted to be bubbly.

Tally was nervous about the breakthrough, but she and Zane didn't say much on the way to the skating rink. Although their cuffs couldn't hear anything while wrapped up in the heavy winter gear, silence was a habit that had begun to follow them everywhere. Tally had grown used to communicating in other ways: winks and rolled eyes and silently mouthed words. Living in an unspoken conspiracy filled every gesture with significance, charged every shared touch with unspoken meaning.

Inside the glass elevator that carried them up to the floating sheet of ice, looking down on the great bowl of Nefertiti Stadium, Zane took Tally's hand. His eyes flashed, as they did before a sudden, unexpected trick, like a snowball ambush from the roof of Pulcher Mansion. His playful glance was perfectly timed to settle Tally's nerves a little. It wouldn't do for the other Crims to see her anxious, after all.

Most of them were already there, trading in boots for ice skates, finding bungee jackets in the right size. A few newly voted-in Crims were warming up, looking wobbly ankled on the floating ice, the sound of their skates like a library minder telling you to shush.

Shay glided over to gather Tally in a hug, coming to a halt mostly by bumping into her. "Hey, Skinny-wa."

"Hey, Squint-la," Tally retorted, giggling. Ugly nicknames were back in fashion, but Shay and Tally had switched their old names now that Tally was losing weight. Going food-missing sucked, but sooner or later she hoped to be thin enough to slip the cuff from her wrist.

She saw that Shay had wrapped a black scarf around her forearm in solidarity. Shay also sported a version of Tally's flash tattoo, a nest of snakes coiling around one brow and down her cheek. A lot of the Crims had new facial tattoos with heart-rate triggers—you could see at a glance how bubbly they were. Self-heated coffee mugs sent clouds of steam into the air above the pack of Crims, and everyone's tattoos were spinning.

A chorus of hellos rose up as Tally and Zane were spotted, excitement rising in the pack. Peris glided over with a bungee jacket and Tally's usual skates in hand.

"Thanks, Nose," Tally said, kicking her boots off and sitting down on the ice. Here at the rink, hoverskates weren't allowed; real metal blades glittered in the wintry light like daggers. Tally drew her laces up tight. "Got your flask?" she asked Peris.

He pulled it out. "Double vodka."

"Very thawing." Tally and Zane had stopped drinking alcohol, which turned out to make you more pretty-minded than bubbly, but strong spirits had other uses here on the ice.

She held out her gloved hands, and Peris pulled her up, her momentum sending the two of them into a slippery little waltz. Giggling, they steadied themselves against each other.

"Don't forget your jacket, Skinny," he said.

She took it from him and tied the straps. "That would be bogus, wouldn't it?"

Peris nodded nervously.

"Any word from our friends across the river?" she asked, her voice dropping to just above a whisper.

"Not a ping. They're still totally missing."

Tally frowned. Croy's visit was a month ago now, and the New Smokies hadn't shown themselves since. The silence was ominous, unless this was another of their annoying tests. Either way, she was itching to go looking, once she got this stupid cuff off. "How's Fausto going on tricking that hoverboard?"

Peris only shrugged, looking distractedly at the other Crims, who were invading the rink, laughing and screaming, slashing through the little Zambonies that skittered about polishing the ice.

Tally checked the flash tattoo on Peris's forehead—a third eye that blinked with his heartbeat—and looked into his gorgeous eyes, brown and soft and depthless. Peris seemed bubblier than he had a month ago—all the Crims did—but Tally no longer saw improvement in him from day to day. It was so much harder for the rest of them who hadn't had the pills, who weren't half-cured like Tally and Zane. They could get excited in the short term, but it was hard to keep them focused.

Well, the breakthrough would give them a jolt.

"It's okay, Nose. Let's skate." Tally pushed off against the flat of one blade, building up speed as she swept around the rink's outer edge. She looked down through the mottled window of ice underfoot. The hoverlifters that held the floating rink up in the air were easy to see, spaced in a grid a few meters apart and sending out a sunburst of refrigeration tendrils. Much farther below, the broad oval of the sports stadium was visible, softly out of focus like the world through a pretty-minded haze. The stadium lights were coming on, warming up for the soccer game scheduled in forty-five minutes. As always, there would be fireworks before it started, once the crowd was in their seats. Very pretty-making.

The sky above was an uninterrupted expanse of blue, except for a few hot-air balloons tethered to the tallest party spires. When it was airborne, the skating rink was the highest thing in New Pretty Town. Tally could glimpse the entire city spread out below.

She skated after Zane, catching him as he rounded a turn. "Everybody seem bubbly to you?"

"Mostly nervous." He gracefully reversed, skating backward as easily as breathing. His operation-augmented muscles had been freed from pretty timidity and sloth. He could hold a handstand without trembling, climb up to his window in Pulcher Mansion in seconds, and outrun the monorail that brought crumblies from the burbs into the central hospital. He never broke a sweat and could hold his breath for two solid minutes.

Watching him perform these feats, Tally remembered the Rangers who'd rescued her from a brushfire on her journey to the Smoke. Zane was as physically confident as they had been—fast and strong, but without the twitching inhumanity of Special Circumstances agents. Tally was no slouch herself, but somehow the cure had taken Zane's strength and coordination to a new level. She loved gliding across the ice with him, skating circles around the others, being the graceful center of the Crims' motley vortex of flashing blades.

"Anything from the New Smoke?" he asked, barely audible over the swoosh of skates.

"Peris says nothing."

Zane swore and took a tight turn, spraying ice on a non-Crim struggling slowly along the side of the rink.

Tally caught up to him. "We have to be patient, Zane. We'll get these things off."

"I'm tired of being patient, Tally." He looked down through the ice. The stadium below was teeming, the growing audience awaiting the first game of the intercity playoffs. "How long?"

"Any minute now," she said.

As the words left her mouth the first fireworks exploded below, instantly transforming the rink into a mottled palette of reds and blues. A second later, a tardy boom shuddered up through the ice, followed by a long ahhh of appreciation from the crowd.

"Here we go," Zane said with a grin, his irritation erased.

Tally squeezed his hand and then let him skate away, gliding to a halt in the center of the rink, the farthest point from the supporting hoverstructure around the ice. She raised one hand and waited as the other Crims gathered in a tight pack around her.

"Flasks," she said softly, and heard the whisper spread through the pack.

Flashes of metal caught the sun, and Tally heard the rasp of tops being unscrewed. Her heart was beating fast, her senses sharpened by anticipation. Everyone's tattoos were totally spinning. She saw Zane gathering speed along the outside of the rink.

"Pour," she said softly.

A liquid sound spread through the pack of Crims, double vodka and straight ethyl alcohol gurgling out. Tally thought she heard a creak, the slightest of complaints from the ice as its freezing point was lowered by the spirits.

Even in the old days, Zane had always dreamed of pulling something like this, sometimes pouring champagne on the ice while the Crims skated. But the cure had made him serious; he'd even run a test in the small fridge in his room. He'd filled a tray of ice cubes, each one with a slightly different mix of vodka and water, and stuck it in the freezer. The all-water cube had frozen normally, but those with more alcohol in them got slushier and slushier, leaving the final all-vodka cube completely liquid.

Tally looked down at the layer of spirits slowly spreading across the ice through their skates, melting away the marks of blades and falls. The stadium came into heart-pounding focus, until Tally could see every detail of a rising plume of green and yellow fireworks. When the thunderous boom reached her ears, another ominous creak sounded. The fireworks display was building in intensity, ramping up for the finale.

Tally raised her hand for Zane.

He rounded the next turn, then headed toward them, skating hard. She felt a shimmer of panic in the pack around her, like a herd of gazelles spotting some big cat in the distance. A few Crims took last slugs from their flasks, then squirted boxes of orange juice into them to erase the evidence of what they'd done.

Tally grinned, imagining the pretty befuddlement she would put on for the wardens: We were all just standing there talking and minding our own business, not even skating, and suddenly . . .

"Watch out!" Zane cried, and the pack split in half, opening to create a path for him.

He skated into its center and jumped into the air inhumanly high, eyes and blades flashing, then brought his skates down hard onto the ice, all his weight behind them.

Zane instantly disappeared from view with a noise like breaking glass, and Tally heard the crack spreading with a sound that built like the shriek of a falling tree out in the Smoke. For a strange split second she was pushed up into the air as a large plate of ice teeter-tottered on the fulcrum of a lifter, but then it snapped in half and Tally was falling, her stomach lurching up into her throat. Gloved hands grabbed her coat from every direction in a moment of group panic, then a whoop rose up as the middle of the rink gave way altogether, icy shards and Crims and Zambonies all tumbling down toward the green grass of the soccer field, ten thousand faces staring up at them in shock.

Now this was bubbly.

## BOUNCE

For a moment it was quiet.

All around her, shattered ice fell without a sound, catching the stadium lights as it spun. Wind tore the war cries from the Crims' mouths. The crowd below looked up in stunned silence. Tally spread her arms to slow her fall, clutching the precious seconds with cupped fingers. This part of a bungee jump was always like flying.

Then a burst of light and sound sent Tally spinning, ears pummeled and eyes forced shut by blinding streaks of brilliance. After a few stunned seconds, she shook her head and opened her eyes: Rainbow shards of fire traveled away in every direction, as if Tally were at the center of an exploding galaxy. More booms thundered above her, unleashing a steady rain of incandescence. She realized what had happened. . . .

The grand finale of the fireworks show had detonated just as the pack of falling Crims had broken through the ice. The timing of the breakthrough had been a little too perfect.

One sizzling flare clung to her bungee jacket, burning with the cool insistence of safety fireworks, tickling her face with cast-off sparks. Tally flailed her arms to right herself, but the ground was already rushing up, only seconds away. She was still out of control when the straps of the bungee jacket bit into her, bringing her headfirst plummet to a halt a few meters from the ground.

As the jacket yanked Tally upright and back into the air, she rolled into a ball in case anything big was still falling. The possibility of one of them catching a chunk of ice or a tumbling Zamboni had always been the nervous-making part of this plan. But Tally made the bounce unscathed, and as she reached its apex she heard the ahhh of the crowd's vast confusion. They knew something had gone wrong.

She and Zane had thought about hacking the scoreboard to show a message at this moment, to penetrate the crowd's pretty haze while their heads were spinning. But then the wardens would know the breakthrough had been planned, which would lead to all sorts of bogus complications.

The New Smokies would hear about this trick one way or another, and they, at least, would know what it meant. . . .

The cure had worked. The New Smoke had allies inside the city. The sky was falling.

Tally's hoverbouncing came to a stop about midfield, on grass littered with broken ice, shuddering Zambonies, giggling Crims, and the few innocent skaters who'd fallen through, no doubt suddenly glad that bungee jackets were required in the rink. She looked around for Zane, and saw that his momentum had carried him down the field and into one of the goals. She ran toward that end, checking on Crims along the way. Everyone's tattoos were pulsing madly, spinning with the anti-pretty magic of the breakthrough. But nobody was hurt beyond a few bruises or a little singed hair.

"It worked, Tally!" Fausto said softly as she passed, staring with amazement at a chunk of ice in his hand. She kept running.

Zane was laughing hysterically, tangled up in the net. When he saw Tally, he cried out a long, "Go-o-o-o-o-al!"

She thudded to a halt, relieved, and let herself enjoy the bubbliness of everything, the world transformed around her. It was as if she could take in the whole audience at a glance, every expression crystal clear in the unreal sharpness of the stadium lights. Ten thousand faces stared back at her, awestruck and amazed.

Tally imagined herself making a speech right now, telling them all about the operation, the lesions, the terrible price of being pretty—that lovely meant brainless, and that their easy lives were empty. The bedazzled crowd looked as if they would listen.

She and Zane had wanted to signal the New Smokies, but that hadn't been the only goal of the breakthrough. A trick on this scale would jazz up the Crims for a few days, they knew, but would a truly bubbly experience permanently change pretties who hadn't taken the pills? From the look in Fausto's eyes, Tally thought it might. And now, seeing the faces of the crowd—new and middle pretties and even crumblies all head-spinning together—she wondered if the falling sky had awakened something larger.

The city had definitely noticed. Wardens were streaming onto the field, first-aid kits in hand. Tally had never seen such panicked expressions on middle pretties. Like the crowd, they all looked stunned that anything could have gone so totally wrong here in the city. The hovercameras that had been ready to record the play-off game were panning across the field, taking in the wreckage. By the end of the day, Tally realized, this trick would be broadcast in every city on the globe.

She took a deep breath. It felt like setting off her first firework as a littlie, amazed that one little press of a button could make so much noise, wondering if she was going to get in trouble. As her euphoria wore off, Tally couldn't shake the feeling that, no matter how carefully they had covered up the trick, someone was going to know the breakthrough had been planned.

Suddenly, Tally needed Zane's touch, his silent reassurance, and she ran the rest of the distance to the goal. He was being untangled from the torn net, a pair of wardens treating his face with medspray. Tally pushed them aside and took Zane into her arms.

There were wardens everywhere, so she spoke in pretty. "Bubbly-making, huh!"

"Utterly," he said. Zane didn't have any flash tattoos, but Tally could feel his heart pounding through the heavy winter coat.

"Are you broken anywhere?"

"No. Just ouching." He touched one side of his face gingerly; it bore red lines in the pattern of the net. "Looks like we scored."

She giggled and kissed his wounded cheek as softly as she could, then brought her lips to his ear. "It worked. It really worked. It's like we can do anything."

"We can."

"After this, the New Smokies have to know the cure works. They'll send us more pills, and we can change everything."

He pulled away and nodded, then leaned closer to kiss her ear softly and murmur, "And if they don't notice this, we'll just have to go out looking for them."

## PARTY CRASH

That night was all about champagne. Although they'd sworn off drinking, Tally and Zane felt as if they had to toast the Crims' survival of the Great Collapse of Nefertiti Stadium.

They had all practiced for tonight, every reaction rehearsed, so there was no mention of spirits poured onto the ice, no gloating about a plan that had worked perfectly—just the excited chatter of new pretties recovering from a bubbly and unexpected departure from the norm.

Everyone told and retold the story of their own fall—the shudder of cracking ice, the dazzling interior of the fireworks display, the yank of bungee jackets, and, after it was all over, alarmed calls from crumbly parents who had seen the whole thing replayed again and again on every channel.

Most of the Crims had been interviewed for the feeds, telling their stories with expressions of innocent surprise. The newsfeed story was spreading and mutating: calls for resignations from the city architecture board, a total rescheduling of the soccer play-offs, and the closure of the floating rink forever (a bogus side effect that Tally hadn't anticipated).

But it didn't take long for the feeds to get repetitious—even your own face on a wallscreen was boring after you'd seen it fifty times—so Zane led them outside to build a bonfire in Denzel Park.

The Crims stayed bubbly, their flash tattoos spinning in the firelight as they retold their stories. They all were speaking fluent pretty in case anyone was listening, but Tally heard more than vapid nonsense in their words. It was like the way she and Zane spoke to each other, always aware of the cuffs but loading their pretty-talk with meaning. The silent conspiracy that they had shared was growing beyond the two of them. As Tally stared into the flames, listening to the Crims around her, she began to believe that the bubbly-making excitement of the breakthrough really would stick. Maybe people could think their way out of being pretty-minded, no pills required.

"Better drink that champagne, Skinny," Zane said, his fingers drifting along the back of her neck to interrupt her thoughts. "I hear that alcohol evaporates totally quickly."

"Evaporates? That's terrible." Tally made a serious face, and held her champagne up to the firelight. The news was giving hourly updates on the breakthrough investigation. A bunch of engineers were trying to figure out how twenty centimeters of lifter-supported ice could have buckled under the weight of a few dozen people. Blame had been assigned to shock waves from the fireworks show, heat from the stadium lights, even sympathetic vibrations from skaters moving in tandem like marching soldiers. But none of the experts had guessed that the real reason for the breakthrough had evaporated into thin air.

She raised her glass, clinking it against Zane's. He drained his glass, then took hers, splashing some champagne into his. "Thanks, Skinny," he said.

"For what?"

"For sharing."

She gave him a pretty smile. He meant the pills they'd split, of course, not the champagne. "Anytime. I'm glad there was enough for two."

"Bubbly luck how it worked out."

She nodded. The cure hadn't been perfect, but considering they'd each only had half a dose, the test had been a success. The cure had affected Zane almost instantly, shattering his pretty-mindedness in a few days. Tally's pill had worked more slowly, and she still woke up fuzzy most mornings, needing Zane to remind her to think bubbly thoughts. The good part was, she never got Zane's awful headaches.

"It's better shared, I think," Tally said, clinking his glass again. She remembered the warning in the letter from herself, and shivered despite the fire. Maybe two pills was actually too much, and if Tally had taken both she would have been brain-dead by now.

Zane pulled her closer. "Like I said . . . thanks." He kissed her, his lips warm in the cold night air, eyes flickering with bonfire reflections, and held his mouth to hers for a long time. Between the oxygen-missing kiss and the champagne, Tally felt herself getting pretty-minded, the edges of the firelit party turning fuzzy. Which maybe wasn't always a bad thing. . . .

Zane finally let her go and turned toward the bonfire, nuzzling her ear to whisper, "We have to get these things off."

"Shhh." Even with winter coats and gloves covering their cuffs, Tally felt a little too famous at the moment to make plans out loud. The Crims had already thrown rocks to drive away one hovercamera covering the party for some follow-up story on the rink collapse.

"It's driving me crazy, Tally."

"Don't worry. We'll figure it out." Just stop talking, she pleaded silently.

Zane kicked a fallen branch into the bonfire. As it burst into flame, he let out a pained sound.

"Zane?"

He shook his head, fingers at his temples. Tally swallowed. Another headache. Sometimes they ended after a few seconds, sometimes they lasted for hours.

"No. I'm okay." He sucked in a deep breath.

"You know, you could go to a doctor," she whispered.

"Forget that! They'll know I'm cured."

She pulled him closer to the crackle of the fire and pressed her lips to his ear. "I told you about Maddy and Az, David's parents? They were doctors—surgeons—and for a long time even they didn't know about the brain lesions. They just thought most people were stupid. A regular doctor won't think there's anything wrong with fixing you."

Zane shook his head furiously and turned to whisper in her ear. "It won't stop with a regular doctor, Tally. New pretties don't get sick."

She looked around the fire at the glowing faces. The Crims wound up at the hospital often enough, but only for injuries, not illness. The operation boosted your immune system, strengthened your organs, fixed your teeth forever. An unhealthy new pretty was such a rarity, there would probably be a ton of tests. And if Zane's headaches persisted, the test results would be passed on to experts.

"They're keeping an eye on us already," he whispered. "We can't afford anyone poking around inside my head." He flinched again, pain contorting his features.

"We should go home," she said softly.

"You stay. I can make it to Pulcher okay."

She groaned and pulled him away from the fire. "Come on."

He let her lead him into the darkness, circling around the other Crims. Shay called out to them, but Tally waved her away, saying, "Too much champagne." Shay smiled sympathetically and turned back to the fire.

They trudged home, the bare ground glistening with frost in the moonlight, the cold wind sharp after the lulling heat of the fire. The night was beautiful, but Tally could only wonder about what was happening inside Zane's head. Was it just a minor side effect of the cure? Or a sign of something gone terribly wrong?

"Don't worry, Zane," she said, just above a whisper. "We'll figure this out. Or we'll get out of here and get help from the Smokies. This is Maddy's cure—she'll know what's going on."

He didn't answer, just stumbled up the hill beside her.

When Pulcher Mansion came into view, Zane pulled her to a halt. "Go back to the party. I can make it home okay from here." His voice was too loud.

She looked around, but they were alone—no pretties or hovercams in sight. "I'm worried about you," she whispered.

He lowered his voice. "It's silly to worry, Skinny. It's just a headache. Same thing as always. Probably because I was pretty longer than you." He forced a smile. "It's just taking me longer to get used to having a brain again."

"Come on. Let's get you in bed."

"No, you go back. I don't want them to know about . . . this."

"I won't say anything," Tally whispered. They had told no one about the cure, not until they absolutely trusted that the other Crims were bubbly enough to keep their mouths shut. "I'll just say you drank too much."

"Fine, but go back to the party," he said firmly. "You have to keep them bubbly. Make sure they don't get drunk and start saying stupid things."

Tally looked back at the fire, just visible through the trees below. With enough champagne, someone might start bragging. She looked back at Zane. "You'll be okay?"

He nodded. "Better already."

She took a breath of the cold air. He didn't look any better. "Zane . . ."

"Listen, I'll be fine. And no matter what happens, I'm glad we took the pills."

Tally took a deep breath to steady herself. "What do you mean, 'no matter what happens'?"

"I don't mean tonight. Just whenever. You know."

Tally looked into his gold-flecked eyes, and saw in them the pain he was silently carrying. Whatever was happening to Zane, staying bubbly wasn't worth losing him. She shook her head. "No, I don't know."

He sighed. "I guess that was a stupid way to put it. I'm fine."

"I'm worried about you."

"Just go back to the party."

Tally sighed softly. There was no point in arguing. She held up one arm, indicating the scarf wrapped around her wrist. "Okay. But if you feel worse, ping me."

He smiled bitterly. "At least those things are good for something."

She kissed him softly, then watched him trudge up to the door of the mansion and inside.

On the lonely trip back down to the party, the air seemed to grow colder. Tally almost wished she could be pretty-minded again, just for one night, instead of having to keep watch on the Crims. From the very first kiss, being with Zane had made things complicated.

She sighed. Maybe that was the way it always worked.

Zane would never go to a doctor, Tally knew. If his headaches turned into something worse, could she make him go? Of course, Zane was right: Any doctor who could fix his problem could probably figure out what had caused it, and that was someone who could make Zane pretty-minded again.

If only Croy hadn't disappeared. Tally wondered how long it would take for the New Smokies to get in touch with them now. After the breakthrough, they had to realize the cure had worked. Even if wherever they were hiding didn't have newsfeeds, every ugly in the world would be chattering about the rink collapse, talking about Tally Youngblood looking innocent on their wallscreens.

Of course, she and Zane still had to escape the city. Tally had no idea how to get the cuffs off. As they grew thinner, it seemed like the rings of steel were closer to coming off, but how long was it going to take? Tally didn't much like being in a race between her own starvation and Zane's brain melting.

And when they escaped, she didn't want to go without the other Crims. Peris and Shay, at least. The Crims were so bubbly tonight, they'd probably all jump on hoverboards and head out if she said the word. But how bubbly would they be tomorrow?

Suddenly, Tally felt exhausted. There were too many things to juggle. Too many worries all falling on her alone. All she'd wanted was to become a Crim, to feel safe inside a clique of friends, and now she'd found herself in charge of a rebellion.

"Your friend have too much champagne?"

Tally froze. The words had come out of the darkness, cutting her ears like fingernails scraping metal.

"Hello?"

A figure emerged from the shadows in a hooded winter coat, moving with total silence through the fallen leaves. The woman stood in a shaft of moonlight, ten centimeters taller than Tally, taller even than Zane. She had to be a Special.

Tally forced herself to relax, trying to conquer her nerves and make her face melt into the soft expression of a brand-new pretty. "Shay? Is that you being all scary-making?" she said angrily.

The figure took another step forward into the light of a walkway torch. "No, Tally. It's me." The woman pulled off her hood.

It was Dr. Cable.

## THE DRAGON

"Do I know you?"

Dr. Cable smiled coldly. "I'm sure you remember me, Tally."

Tally took a step back, letting some of her fear show; even the most innocent new pretty would be frightened by the sight of Dr. Cable. Her cruel features, exaggerated by the moonlight, made her look like a beautiful woman half transformed into a werewolf.

Memories flooded into Tally's mind. Being trapped in Dr. Cable's office that awful first time they'd met, learning of the existence of Special Circumstances, and then again when she had agreed to find and betray Shay, the price for becoming pretty. Then, in the Smoke, after Cable had followed Tally with an army of Specials to burn her new home to the ground.

"Yeah," Tally said. "I think I remember. I used to know you, right?"

"Indeed, you did." Cable's sharp teeth glowed in the moonlight. "But what's more important, Tally, is that I know you."

Tally managed a vacant smile. Dr. Cable no doubt remembered their last meeting—Tally and David's rescue of the Smokies—when it had been necessary to crack her on the head.

Dr. Cable gestured at the black scarf that bound Tally's cuff tightly under her glove and winter coat. "Interesting way to wear a scarf."

"What, are you fashion-missing? Everybody does this."

"But I imagine you started the trend. You always were tricky."

Tally beamed prettily. "I guess. I used to play all kinds of tricks back when I was ugly."

"Nothing like today, though."

"Oh, you saw the feeds? Wasn't that totally bogus? The ice just falling out from under us like that!"

"Yes . . . just like that." Dr. Cable's eyes narrowed. "I must admit, at first you had me fooled. That floating rink was a typical architectural folly designed to amuse new pretties. An accident waiting to happen. But then I thought about the timing—the stadium full, a hundred cameras ready."

Tally blinked, shrugged. "I bet it was those fireworks.

You could feel them right through the ice. Who's missing idea was that?"

Dr. Cable nodded slowly. "An almost believable accident. And then I saw your face on the newsfeeds, Tally. All wide-eyed and innocent and telling your bubbly little tale." Cable's upper lip curled into something that was not a smile. "And I realized that you were still playing tricks."

Tally felt something punch into her stomach, something from ugly days: the old feeling of being caught. She tried to turn her fear into a look of surprise. "Me?"

"That's right, Tally: you. Somehow."

Under Dr. Cable's gaze, Tally imagined herself being hauled into the depths of Special Circumstances, the cure reversed, her memories erased again. Or maybe this time they wouldn't bother returning her to New Pretty Town at all. She tried to swallow, but her mouth felt full of cotton. "Yeah, right. Like everything's my fault," she managed.

Dr. Cable stepped closer, and Tally fought to hold her ground, though her whole body screamed run. The woman gazed at her coldly, as if peering at a specimen cut open on a table. "I certainly hope that it was your fault."

Tally frowned. "You hope what?"

"Let's speak frankly, Tally Youngblood. I've had enough of your pretty act. I'm not here to take you away to my dungeon."

"You're not?"

"Do you really think I care if you break things in New Pretty Town?"

"Um . . . kind of?"

Dr. Cable snorted. "Maintenance is not my department. Special Circumstances is only interested in outside threats. The city can take care of itself, Tally. There are so many safety backups, it's hardly worth worrying about. Why do you think skaters on that rink had to wear bungee jackets?"

Tally blinked. It hadn't crossed her mind to wonder about the jackets; everything was always ultra-safe in New Pretty Town, otherwise new pretties would kill themselves left and right. She shrugged. "In case the lifters failed? Like in a power blackout?"

Cable let out a razor-sharp laugh that lasted less than a second. "There hasn't been a blackout in a hundred and fifty years." She shook her head at the thought and continued. "Knock down anything you want, Tally. I don't care about your little tricks . . . except for what they reveal about you."

The woman's gaze focused on her once more, and Tally again had to fight the urge to run. She wondered if this was simply a way to get her to admit what the Crims had done. Probably she'd said too much already. But something about Dr. Cable's cold stare—her razor voice, her predatory movements, her very existence in the world—made it impossible for Tally to act pretty-minded. By now, any real new pretty would have fled screaming or dissolved into a puddle on the spot.

Besides, if Special Circumstances really wanted Tally to confess her tricks, they wouldn't have bothered with a conversation.

"So why are you here?" Tally said in her normal voice, trying hard to keep it steady.

"I've always admired your survival instinct, Tally. You were a good little traitor when you had to be."

"Uh, thanks . . . I guess."

Cable nodded. "And now it turns out you have more of a brain than I gave you credit for. You resist conditioning very well."

"Conditioning. That's what you call it?" Tally swore. "Like it's a hair treatment or something?"

"Amazing." Dr. Cable leaned close again, her eyes focusing on Tally's as if trying to bore through to her brain. "Somewhere in there, you're still a tricky little ugly, aren't you? Most impressive. I could use you, I think."

Tally felt a flush of anger, a fire inside her head. "Um, like, didn't you already use me?"

"So, you do remember. Superb." The woman's cruel-pretty eyes, flat and lusterless and cold, somehow showed pleasure. "I know that was an unpleasant experience, Tally. But it was necessary. We needed to take our children back from the Smoke, and only you could help us. But I do apologize."

"Apologize?" Tally said. "For blackmailing me into betraying my friends, for destroying the Smoke, for killing David's father?" She felt an expression of disgust on her face. "I don't think you'll be using me, Dr. Cable. I've already done you enough favors."

The woman only smiled again. "I agree. So it's time I did you a favor. What I am offering is something quite . . . bubbly."

The word on Cable's thin, cruel lips made Tally laugh dryly. "What would you know about being bubbly?"

"You'd be surprised. We at Special Circumstances know all about sensations, especially the ones you and your so-called Crims are always searching for. I can give it to you, Tally. All day, every day, bubblier than you can imagine. The real thing. Not just an escape from the haze of being pretty—something better."

"What are you talking about?"

"Remember flying on a hoverboard, Tally?" Cable said, her dull eyes igniting with cold fire. "That feeling of being alive? Yes, we can make people pretty inside—empty and lazy and vapid—but we can also make them bubbly, as you call it. More intense than you ever felt as an ugly, more alive than a wolf taking its prey, even bubblier than ancient Rusty soldiers killing one another over some plot of oil-rich desert. Your senses sharper, your body faster than any athlete's in history, your muscles as strong as any human's in the world."

The woman's razor voice fell silent, and Tally could suddenly hear the night around them perfectly—icicles dripping against hard ground, trees creaking in the wind, the bonfire below spitting out random showers of sparks. She could hear the party perfectly: Crims shouting about the exploits of the day, arguing about who had bounced highest or landed hardest. Cable's words had left the world as sharp as broken crystal.

"You should see the world as I see it, Tally."

"You're offering me a . . . job? As a Special?"

"Not a job. A whole new being." Dr. Cable said each word with deliberate care. "You can be one of us."

Tally was breathing hard, her pulse pounding through her entire body, as if the very idea was already changing her. She bared her teeth at Dr. Cable. "You think I'd work for you?"

"Consider your other choice, Tally. Spending your life looking for cheap thrills, managing a few moments at a time truly awake. Never clearing your head completely. But you'd make a fine Special. Traveling to the Smoke on your own was impressive; I always had hopes for you. But now that I see you're still tricky even after the operation"—Dr. Cable shook her head—"I realize that you're a natural. Join us."

A ping went through Tally as she understood something at last. "Tell me something. What were you like as an ugly?"

"Outstanding, Tally." The woman barked her one-second laugh. "You already know the answer, don't you?"

"You were tricky."

Cable nodded. "I was just like you. All of us were. We went to the ruins, tried to run farther, had to be brought back. That's why we let uglies play their little tricks—to see who's cleverest. To see which of you fights your way out of the cage. That's what your rebellion is all about, Tally—graduating to Special Circumstances."

Tally closed her eyes, and knew the woman was telling the truth. She remembered being an ugly, how easy it had always been to fool the dorm minders, how everyone always found ways around the rules. She took a deep breath. "But why?"

"Because someone has to keep things under control, Tally."

"That's not what I meant. What I want to know is, why do you do it to pretties? Why change their brains?"

"Goodness, Tally, isn't that obvious?" Dr. Cable shook her head in disappointment. "What do they teach in school these days?"

"That the Rusties almost destroyed the world," Tally recited.

"There's your answer."

"But we're better than them, we leave the wild alone, we don't strip-mine or burn oil. We don't have wars. . . ." Tally's voice sputtered out as she began to see.

Dr. Cable nodded. "We are under control, Tally, because of the operation. Left alone, human beings are a plague. They multiply relentlessly, consuming every resource, destroying everything they touch. Without the operation, human beings always become Rusties."

"Not in the Smoke."

"Think back, Tally. The Smokies clear-cut the land, they killed animals for food. When we landed, they were burning trees."

"Not that many." Tally heard her voice break.

"What if there had been millions of Smokies? Billions of them, soon enough? Outside of our self-contained cities, humanity is a disease, a cancer on the body of the world. But we . . ." She reached out and stroked Tally's cheek, her fingers strangely hot in the winter air. "Special Circumstances . . . we are the cure."

Tally shook her head, stumbling back from Dr. Cable. "Forget it."

"This is what you've always wanted."

"You're wrong!" Tally shouted. "All I ever wanted was to be pretty. You're the one who keeps getting in my way!"

Her cry left them both in surprised silence, the last words echoing through the park. A hush settled over the party below, everyone probably wondering who was screaming her head off up in the trees.

Dr. Cable recovered first, sighing softly. "Goodness, Tally. Relax. There's no need to shout. If you don't want what I'm offering, I'll leave you to your party. Feel free to age into a smug middle pretty. Soon enough, being bubbly won't matter so much; you'll forget this little conversation."

Tally held the doctor's cruel-pretty stare, almost wanting to tell her about the cure, to spit it back in her face. Tally's mind wasn't going to fade away, not tomorrow, not in fifty years; she wasn't going to forget who she was. And she didn't need Special Circumstances to feel alive.

Her throat still stung from yelling, but Tally said hoarsely, "Never."

"All I ask is that you think about it. Take your time deciding—it's all the same to me. Just remember the way it felt falling through that ice. You can have that feeling every second." Dr. Cable waved a hand casually. "And if it makes a difference, I may even find space for your friend Zane.

I've had my eye on him for some time. He was once of help to me."

A chill went through Tally, and she shook her head. "No."

Dr. Cable nodded. "Yes. Zane was very forthcoming about David and the Smoke, that time he didn't run away."

She turned and disappeared into the trees.

## BREAKUP

Tally stumbled back to the party.

The bonfire had grown bigger, its heat pushing back the revelers into a wide circle. Someone had requisitioned industrial-size logs of peat, big enough to burn through the Crims' collective carbon allowance for a month. The fire was topped off with fallen branches gathered from the park, and the hiss of still-green wood reminded Tally of cook-fires in the Smoke, when the water inside fresh-cut trees would boil, steam spitting out as if giving voice to the angry spirits of the forest.

She looked up at the column of smoke rising, ominously dark against the sky. That's how the Smoke had gotten its name. As Dr. Cable had said, the Smokies burned trees ripped alive from the ground. Human beings had been pulling that particular trick for thousands of years; a few centuries before, they'd almost put enough carbon in the air to screw up the climate for good. Only when someone had released an oil-transforming bacteria into the air had Rusty civilization been brought to a halt, and the planet saved.

And now, at their bubbliest, the Crims were instinctively headed in the same direction. Suddenly, the warm, cheery fire just made Tally feel worse.

She listened to the voices around her—bragging about how far they'd hoverbounced on the soccer field, debating who'd done the best interview for the feeds. Her unhappy conversation with Dr. Cable had left Tally's senses sharpened; she could separate every sound, tease apart every strand of conversation. Suddenly the Crims all sounded foolish, repeating the stories of their petty victories to one another again and again. Just like pretties.

"Skinny?"

She turned from the fire to find Shay next to her.

"Is Zane okay?" Shay peered closer, and her eyes widened. "Tally-wa, you look . . ."

Tally didn't need her to finish, she could see it in Shay's eyes: She looked terrible. Tally smiled tiredly at this news. That was part of the cure, of course. She might still be gorgeous—her bone structure perfect, her skin flawless—but Tally's face revealed the turmoil inside. Now that she could think unpretty thoughts, she would no longer be beautiful every minute of the day. Anger, fear, and anxiety were not pretty-making.

"Zane's all right. It's just me."

Shay leaned her weight against Tally, putting an arm around her. "Why so sad, Skinny? Tell me."

"It's just"—she glanced around at the boasting Crims—"it's everything, kind of."

Shay lowered her voice. "I thought today went perfectly."

"Sure. Perfect."

"Until Zane went and drank too much, of course. That's all it was, right?"

Tally made a noncommittal sound. She didn't want to lie to Shay. Eventually, she would tell her all about the cure, which would mean explaining Zane's headaches.

Shay sighed, squeezing Tally harder. There was a moment of silence, and then she asked, "Skinny, what happened to you guys up there?"

"Up where?"

"You know—when you climbed the transmission tower. It changed you, somehow."

Tally played with the scarf around her wrist, wishing she could tell her friend everything. But it was too risky to share news of the cure until they were safely outside the city. "I don't know what to say, Squint. It was really bubbly-making up there. You can see the whole island, and you can fall at any moment. Die, even. That makes a difference."

"I know," Shay whispered.

"You know what?"

"How it feels. I climbed the tower. Fausto and I figured out how to hack the minders, and last night I decided to go for it. To make myself bubbly for the breakthrough."

"Really?" Tally stared at her. Shay's face glowed with pride in the firelight, her implanted eye-jewels glittering. All the Crims were changing, but if Shay was hacking minders and scaling the Valentino tower, she was way ahead of the rest of them. "That's great. And you climbed up at night?"

"Only way to get away with it, since you and Zane got so totally busted. Fausto said I should wear a bungee jacket, but I wanted to do it like you did. I could have fallen—died, like you said. I even cut myself on a cable." With a smile, she showed a red mark that stretched across her palm, but then paused a moment, unpretty lines appearing on her forehead. "But it was kind of disappointing."

"How?"

"It didn't change me as much as I thought it would."

Tally shrugged. "Well, everyone's different. . . ."

"I suppose so," Shay said softly. "But it made me

wonder . . . It wasn't just you guys climbing the tower, was it? There was something else that happened that day, Skinny. You'd never even hung out alone with Zane before, but since then you two have your own secret club, smiling at your own jokes and whispering all the time. You never go anywhere without each other."

"Squint . . . ," Tally said, and sighed. "Sorry if we've been all coupley. But, you know, it's my first crush as a pretty."

Shay stared at the fire. "That's what I thought, at first. But it's gone way past that, Tally. You're so different from the rest of us—both of you." Her voice rose above a whisper. "Zane gets those weird headaches that he tries to hide, and that was you screaming a minute ago, wasn't it?"

Tally swallowed.

"What changed you guys that day?"

Tally pointed at her wrist. "Shhh."

"Don't shush me! Tell me."

Tally looked around them nervously. The fire consumed more fallen branches, hissing loudly, and most of the Crims were singing drinking songs. No one had heard Shay's outburst, but Tally could feel the hard metal of the cuff around her wrist, always listening. "I can't tell you, Squint."

"Yes, you can." Shay's face seemed to change in the firelight, the pretty softness burning away as her anger grew. "You see, Tally, I remembered some things when I was up in that tower, staring down at the ground and wondering if I was going to die. And then I remembered a few more while I was falling through the ice and bouncing on the soccer field. A lot of things came back from ugly days. Isn't that great?"

Tally turned away from the harsh expression on Shay's face. "Yeah, sure it is."

"Glad you agree. So here's what I remembered: It's

because of you that I'm here in the city, Tally. All those stories I used to tell? They were bogus. What really happened is that you followed me out to the Smoke to betray me, right?"

Tally felt it again, the same gut-punch as when she'd seen Dr. Cable in the trees: caught. From the moment she'd felt the pills working on her, Tally had known somewhere inside her that this moment would come, that Shay would eventually remember what had really happened back when they were uglies. But Tally hadn't expected it so soon. "Yeah, I followed you to bring you back here. It's my fault, what happened to the Smoke. The Specials tracked me there."

"Right, you betrayed us. After you stole David from me, of course." Shay laughed bitterly. "I hate to bring the whole David thing up, but who knows if I'll remember it tomorrow, you know? So I thought I'd mention it while I'm bubbly."

Tally turned to her. "You'll remember it."

Shay only shrugged. "Maybe. But tricks like today's don't come around that often. So you might be off the hook again by tomorrow."

Tally took a deep breath, inhaling the smell of wood smoke, burning peat, pine needles, and spilled champagne. The firelight revealed everything as bright as day, even the whorls of her fingerprints. She didn't know what to say.

"Look at me," Shay said. Her flash tattoo was spinning hard, its halo of snakes blurring together like the spokes of a bicycle wheel. "Tell me what happened to you that day. Keep me bubbly. You owe me."

Tally swallowed. She and Zane had promised each other not to tell anyone—not yet. But neither of them had realized how far Shay had come—bubbly enough to climb the tower on her own, to finally remember what had really happened back in ugly days. Probably she could keep a secret, and telling her about the cure would give her hope, at least. It was the only way Tally could begin to make up for what she'd done.

And Shay was right: Tally owed her.

"Okay. Something else happened that day."

Shay nodded slowly. "I thought so. What was it?"

Tally pointed at Shay's scarf, and together they pulled it off and wrapped it tightly around Tally's wrist, another layer over the cuff. After another breath, she said in the softest whisper she could manage, "We found a cure."

Shay's eyes narrowed. "It's about starving yourself, isn't it?"

"No. Well, that helps. Hunger, coffee, playing tricks—all that stuff Zane's been doing for months. But the real cure is . . . simpler than that."

"What is it? I'll do it."

"You can't."

"The hell with you, Tally!" Shay's eyes flashed. "If you can do it, I can!"

Tally shook her head. "It's a pill."

"A pill? Like vitamins?"

"No, a special pill. Croy brought it to me, the night of the Valentino bash. Try to remember, Shay. Before you and I came back to the city, Maddy had figured out how to reverse the operation. You helped me write a letter, remember?"

Shay's face went blank for a moment, then she frowned. "That's when I was pretty."

"Right. After we rescued you, when we were hiding out in the ruins."

"Funny, those days are harder to remember than back when I was ugly." Shay shook her head.

"Well, Maddy figured out a cure. But it was untested, dangerous. She wouldn't give it to you because you refused.

You wanted to stay pretty. So I had to give myself up to test it. That's why I'm here."

"And Croy brought it to you a month ago?"

Tally nodded, taking Shay's hand. "And it works. You've seen how it changed me and Zane. It makes us bubbly all the time. So once we get out of here, you can—" Shay's expression brought Tally to a halt. "What's the matter?"

"You and Zane both took some?"

"Yeah," Tally said. "There were two pills, and we split them. I was afraid to do it on my own."

Shay turned to the fire, pulling her hand away. "I can't believe you, Tally."

"What?"

Shay whirled to face her. "Why him? Why didn't you ask me?"

"But I—"

"You're supposed to be my friend, Tally. I've done everything for you. I was the one who first told you about the Smoke. I was the one who introduced you to David. And when you came to New Pretty Town, I helped you become one of the Crims. Did it even occur to you to share the cure with me? It's your fault I'm like this, after all!"

Tally shook her head. "There wasn't time . . . I didn't even—"

"No, of course you didn't," Shay spat. "You barely even knew Zane, but he was the leader of the Crims, so hooking up with him was the next trick on your list. Just like David out in the Smoke. That's why you split the cure with him."

"It wasn't like that!" Tally cried.

"You are like that, Tally. You have always been like that! No cure is going to make you any different—you were busy betraying people a long time ago. You didn't need any operation to make you selfish and shallow and full of yourself. You already were."

Tally tried to answer, but something horrible rose up in her throat, choking off her words. Then she noticed the quiet around them, and realized that Shay had been yelling. The other Crims looked on in puzzlement, only the hiss of the fire filling the silence. Pretties didn't fight. They hardly ever argued, and they certainly never shouted at one another in the middle of a party. That sort of obnoxious behavior was strictly for uglies.

She looked down at her wrist, wondering if Shay's raised voice had gotten through the layers of cloth and plastic. If so, it would all end tonight.

Shay pulled away and whispered fiercely, "I may be my pretty self again tomorrow, Tally. But I'll remember this, I swear. No matter what sweet things I say to you, trust me, I am not your friend." She turned and walked into the trees, thrashing through frozen branches.

Tally looked around at the other Crims, the champagne glasses in their hands glittering sharply in the moonlight, reflecting the wasteful fire. She felt alone and exposed with all of them staring at her. But after a few more horrible moments of silence, they turned away and started telling breakthrough stories again.

Tally's head spun. The change in Shay had been so shocking, so complete, and she hadn't even taken a pill. A few minutes of real anger had transformed her from a placid pretty to a wild beast. . . . It didn't make sense.

Suddenly, Tally remembered Dr. Cable's last words, about Zane helping Special Circumstances. After his friends had run away, he must have been taken to see her, confessing everything he knew about the Smoke and the mysterious David who took uglies there. Maybe that was what had kept him bubbly all these months—his shame about not running away, his guilt over having betrayed his friends to Dr. Cable.

Of course, Tally had her own guilty secrets. So she'd stayed bubbly too, never quite fitting in, never quite sure of what she wanted, no matter how much champagne she drank. Old and ugly emotions were always waiting, hidden inside, ready to change her.

And Shay had been transformed as well—not by guilt, but by buried anger. Concealed behind her pretty smiles were suppressed memories of the betrayals that had cost her David, the Smoke, and finally her freedom. All it had taken was climbing up the tower and falling through the ice—enough stimulation to break the logjam in her memories—to bring that anger to the surface. And now she hated Tally.

Maybe Shay wouldn't need the pills at all—maybe old memories from ugly days were enough. Perhaps, thanks to every terrible thing that Tally Youngblood had ever done to her, Shay would find her own way to a cure.

# RAIN

Tally woke up with an ugly mind.

It was what she used to call bubbly—the gray morning light somehow bright and glittery, sharp enough to cut flesh. The rain beat against Zane's window in malicious, half-frozen drops, tapping like impatient fingernails.

But Tally didn't mind the rain. It blurred the city's spires and gardens, reducing the view to gray and green blotches, the lights of other mansions casting halos on the wet glass.

The downpour had started late the night of the party, finally extinguishing the Crims' bonfire, as if Dr. Cable had called the heavens down to drown their celebration. For the two days since, Tally and Zane had been trapped inside, unable to speak freely within the smart walls of Pulcher Mansion. She hadn't even had a chance to tell him about Shay's outburst of old memories, or about meeting Dr. Cable in the woods. Not that she was looking forward to revealing what she'd confessed to Shay, or bringing up what Cable had told her about Zane's past.

This morning had brought another mountain of pings, but Tally couldn't face any more requests to join the Crims. The stadium collapse and the last two days of feed coverage had made them the hottest clique in New Pretty Town, but a bunch of new members was exactly what the Crims didn't need. What they needed was to stay bubbly. Tally worried, though, that a third day stuck inside by the rain would bore everyone back into being pretty-heads.

Zane was already awake, sipping coffee and staring out the window, absently spinning his cuff with one finger. He glanced at her as she stirred, but didn't make a sound. The silence between them since they'd been cuffed had felt conspiratorial, their secret whispers intimate, but Tally wondered if talking so little was gradually shutting them off from each other. Shay had been right about one thing: Tally had hardly known Zane before that day they'd climbed the tower. What Dr. Cable had told her made Tally realize that she still didn't know him very well.

But once the cuffs were off and they were outside the city, their memories freed from the blur of pretty-headedness, there would be nothing to stop them from telling each other everything.

"Bogus weather, huh?" she said.

"Just a few degrees colder and it'd be snowing."

Tally brightened. "Yeah, snow would be totally pretty-making." She fished a dirty T-shirt from the floor, wadded it up, and threw it at his head. "Snowball fight!"

He let it bounce off him, smiling softly. Zane's headache from the night of the party had passed, but it had left him in a serious mood. Without having said a word, they both knew they would have to escape the city soon.

It all came down to the cuffs.

Tally gave hers an experimental pull. It slipped from her wrist onto her hand, catching only centimeters from coming off. She'd hardly eaten anything the day before, determined to fade away to nothing if that's what it took to get the thing off, but Tally wondered if she would ever be skinny enough. The cuff's circumference looked just smaller than the width of the bones in her hand, a measurement that no amount of starvation was going to alter.

She stared at the red marks left by the metal. The big bone that was the joint of her left thumb was most of the problem. Tally envisioned pulling the thumb back hard enough to snap the bone, leaving room for the cuff to slip off, and couldn't imagine anything more painful.

A ping came from the door, and Tally sighed. Someone had gotten sick of being ignored and had come around in person.

"We're not here, are we?" Zane said.

Tally shrugged. Not if it was Shay outside, or some wannabe trying to get into the Crims. Come to think of it, there was no one she was in the mood to see.

The ping came again.

"Who is it, anyway?" Tally asked the room, but the room didn't know. Which meant whoever it was wasn't wearing their interface ring.

"That's . . . interesting," Zane said. They looked at each other for a moment, and Tally felt the moment when curiosity got the better of them.

"Okay, open up," she told the room.

The door slid away to reveal Fausto, looking like a kitten pulled out of a river. His hair was plastered to his head, his clothing soaked, but his eyes were bright. Under his arms he carried two hoverboards, their knobbly surfaces dripping water on the floor.

He walked into the room without a word and dropped the boards. They came to a hovery stop at knee height, while Fausto unloaded four crash bracelets and two belly sensors from his pockets. He took one of the boards and turned it over, gesturing at the access panel on its bottom. Tally rolled out of bed to take a closer look. The nuts securing the panel were stripped, and two red wires snaked out, their ends twisted together and sealed with black tape.

Fausto mimed pulling the wires apart, then opened his hands in a gesture that meant, Where is it? He grinned.

Tally nodded slowly. Fausto was still bubbly from the breakthrough, his flash tattoo spinning. He, at least, hadn't wasted the last rainy days and nights. These boards were tricked up, ugly-style. When the wires were disconnected, their governors and trackers would crash, freeing the boards from the city interface.

Once they'd gotten rid of the cuffs, Zane and Tally could fly anywhere they wanted.

"Awesome," she said aloud, not caring if the walls heard it.

They didn't wait for sunshine.

Flying through the rain was like standing under a freezing shower. The hole in the wall had coughed up goggles and grippy shoes, so it was possible to stay on board, but just barely. The high winds plastered Tally's soaking winter coat against her skin, pulling her hood back from her head and threatening to spill her on every turn.

Her reflexes from ugly days hadn't disappeared, though. If anything, the operation had improved her balance, and the almost freezing rain kept Tally from slipping into a pretty haze, even with her coat's heating turned to maximum. With a pounding heart and chattering teeth, her mind stayed crystal clear.

She and Zane shot down to the river at treetop level, following the winding path of Denzel Park. The branches danced in the wind under them, like flailing hands trying to reach up and drag them down. As Tally leaned into turns, cutting the wind with her hands, the last traces of her morning pretty-mindedness disappeared. The weight of the sensor clipped to her belly ring—which told the board where her center of gravity was—brought back memories of expeditions to the Rusty Ruins with Shay, reminding her how easy it had been to sneak out of the city back in ugly days.

Only the inescapable presence of the interface cuff spoiled her mood. The crash bracelets were big enough to fit over the metal ring, their soft, smart plastics conforming to its shape. Still, Tally imagined the manacle cutting into her flesh.

They reached the river and turned onto it, skimming under bridges, her board slapping the churning whitecaps stirred up by the wind. Laughing maniacally, Zane pulled in front of Tally and dipped his board's tail into the water, sending up a wall of spray.

She crouched low on the board, ducking the worst of the water, and tipped it forward to shoot into the lead. Banking across Zane's path, she slapped the river with her board, raising up a wall of water in front of him. She heard him whoop as he zoomed straight through it.

Soaking and panting hard, Tally wondered if this is what it would be like to be a Special—her senses sharp, every moment intense, her body a perfectly tuned machine. She remembered Maddy and Az saying that Specials didn't have the lesions—they were cured.

Of course, there was a price for being Special—the small matter of a new face: wolflike teeth and cold, dull eyes that terrified everyone you met. And the horror-movie look was nothing compared with having to work for Special Circumstances—tracking down runaway uglies and crushing anyone the city felt threatened by.

And what if the Special operation changed your mind in some other way: making you obedient instead of empty-headed? With all that speed and strength, running away from the city would be easy, but what if the Special operation put something like the cuff inside you, something that would always tell them where you were?

A faceful of water reminded Tally to keep her mind on the game, and she shot high into the air, soaring over a foot-bridge. Below, Zane was looking back uncertainly, trying to figure out where she'd disappeared to.

Tally dropped down just ahead of him, hitting the river with a sound like a face being slapped, throwing up an explosion of water. But she knew instantly she'd hit too fast. At this speed, the water was as hard as concrete, and her feet slipped at the impact—Tally felt herself sliding off. . . .

She was falling for a moment, then the crash bracelets kicked in, gripping her wrists cruelly and spinning her to a safe halt.

She wound up waist-deep in the freezing water, hanging from the bracelets, crying out as she discovered a whole new level of being soaked. She was glad to see that her attack had also dumped Zane.

"Really bubbly move, Skinny," he shouted, pulling himself back onto his hoverboard. Too out of breath to answer, she crawled onto hers and lay on her stomach, laughing. The two of them wordlessly coasted over to the ground to recover their breath.

On the muddy riverbank, they huddled close for warmth. Her heart still pounded, the expanse of rain-struck water stretched before them like a field of glittering flowers.

"So beautiful," Tally said, trying to imagine what it would be like in the wild with Zane, feeling this way every day, free from the mind-numbing restrictions of the city.

Her wrist was throbbing, and she pulled her crash bracelet off to take a look. In the wipeout, the metal cuff underneath had cut into her skin. Tally gave it a tug, but even with her soaking skin, it stopped at its usual spot.

"Still stuck," she said.

Zane took her hand and said softly, "Don't push it, Tally." He covered the cuff with her coat and whispered, "You'll only make your wrist swell up."

She swore, pulling on her hood. The rain beat on the plastic, impatient fingers drumming on her head. "I thought maybe with the water . . ."

"Nah. Cold makes metal contract, so they're probably tighter out here."

Tally looked at Zane, raising an eyebrow. "So," she whispered, "do they get bigger when they get hot?"

He was silent for a moment. Then, so softly that she could barely hear him above the rain, he whispered, "If they got really hot? I guess they'd get a little bigger."

"How much?"

He shrugged, the gesture almost invisible under his

winter coat, but he was interested now. "How much heat can you stand?"

"You're not talking about a candle, are you?"

Zane shook his head. "Something much hotter than that. Something we could control, so it wouldn't roast our hands off. We'd still get burned, though."

She looked at the bulge in her sleeve and sighed. "Beats breaking your own thumb, I guess."

"Doing what?"

"Just something I was . . ." Her voice trailed off.

Zane's gaze followed hers across the river. On the opposite bank, two figures on hoverboards stood watching them, faceless in their hooded raincoats.

Tally fought to keep her voice down. "Smokies?"

Zane shook his head. "Those are dorm jackets."

"What would city uglies be doing out in this rain?"

He stood up. "Maybe we should ask."

## CUTTERS

On the Uglyville side of the river, the four of them sheltered together under a tarp covering a paper recycler, hidden from view and out of the rain. The two uglies weren't wearing rings, Tally was glad to see; the four of them wouldn't be recorded by the city interface as having hung out together.

"Is that really you, Tally?" the girl whispered.

"Uh, yeah. Recognize me from the feeds?"

"No! It's me, Sussy. And this is Dex," she said. "Don't you remember us?"

"Remind me."

The girl just stared. She was wearing a crude leather strap around her neck, which looked like the sort of thing a Smokey might own—handmade and discolored by age. Where had she gotten it?

"We helped you with that 'New Smoke Lives' thing, remember?" the boy offered. "Back when you were . . . ugly."

An image came slowly into Tally's mind: huge burning letters lit as a diversion while she and David had broken into Special Circumstances. These were two of the uglies who had organized that trick, and then helped them hide out in the Rusty Ruins, bringing news and supplies from the city, playing more tricks to keep the wardens and Specials busy.

"You really forgot us," Dex said. "So it's true. They do something to your brains."

"Yeah, it's true," Zane said. "But a little softer, please." The rain was as loud as a jet engine on the plastic tarp, making it hard to hear. The two uglies needed reminding to keep their voices down.

Dex's stare dropped to Tally's wrist, covered by a crash bracelet and bound in a scarf, as if he didn't believe the cuff was really under there, listening. "Sorry."

When his eyes crept back up to stare at her face, Dex couldn't hide his amazement at her transformation. Sussy was silent—awestruck and hanging on every word. Under their gaze, Tally felt self-conscious and weirdly powerful. It was obvious the two would do anything she or Zane asked. Back when her brain had been prettified, she'd felt entitled to this sort of awe. But now, with her head clear, it was kind of embarrassing.

But talking to the two uglies was less awkward than it might have been. Tally's unpretty thoughts over the last month had made it easier to look at their imperfect faces. They didn't horrify her as much as her first glance at Croy had. The tiny gap between Sussy's two front teeth seemed more charming than revolting, and even Dex's zits didn't make her skin crawl.

"But the damage wasn't permanent," Zane was saying. "We're starting to get smarter. Which, by the way, is not something you can spread around to everyone, okay?"

The two nodded dumbly, and Tally wondered if hinting about the cure to random uglies was worth the risk. Of course, enlisting Sussy and Dex might be the quickest way to get a message to the New Smoke.

"What's the news from the ruins?" she asked.

Sussy leaned closer, remembering to whisper. "That's why we came down here. As far as we could tell, the New Smokies had all disappeared. Until last night."

"What happened last night?" Tally asked.

"Well, since they went missing, we've been going to the ruins every few nights," Dex said. "To check out the old spots, light sparklers. But we haven't seen anything all month."

Tally and Zane shared a glance. A month ago was about the same time Croy had left the pills for Tally to find. The timing probably wasn't a coincidence.

"But last night we found some stuff in an old hideout," Sussy said. "Burned-out lightsticks and some old magazines."

"Old magazines?" Tally asked.

"Yeah," Sussy said. "From the Rusty era. Those ones that showed how ugly everyone used to be."

"I don't think the New Smokies would have left those lying around," Tally said. "Those are precious. I knew someone who died to save them. So they must be back."

"But they're lying low," Dex said. "Playing it safe."

"Why?" Zane said softly. "And for how long?"

"How would we know?" Dex said. "That's why we came down here today. We were going to sneak over in the rain and find you, Tally. We thought you guys might have a clue."

"After you were all over the news the other day, we figured something was up," Sussy added. "Like, that stadium thing was a trick, right?"

"Glad you noticed," Tally said. "The New Smokies were supposed to notice too. Apparently, they did."

"We figured you knew something about it," Sussy said. "Especially after we spotted some of your pretty friends out here in Uglyville."

Tally frowned. "Pretties? Out here?"

"Yeah, in Cleopatra Park. I recognized a couple of them from the feeds. I think they were Crims. That's your clique, right?"

"Yeah, but . . ."

Sussy frowned. "You didn't know?"

Tally shook her head. After the last couple of days, she had gotten a few pings from other Crims—mostly complaints about the rain. But no one had said anything about going to Uglyville.

"What were they up to?" Zane asked.

Dex and Sussy looked at each other, unhappy expressions on their faces.

"Um, we're not sure," Sussy said. "They wouldn't talk to us, just chased us off."

Tally let out a slow breath through her teeth. Pretties were allowed on this side of the river—they could go anywhere they wanted in the city—but they never came to Uglyville. Which meant that Cleopatra Park would be a great place for a pretty to find some privacy, especially in the driving rain. But privacy for what?

"Didn't you tell everyone to lie low for a while?" Zane asked her.

"Yeah, I did." Tally wondered which of the Crims was behind this. And what "this" was.

"Take us there," she said.

Sussy and Dex led them up toward the park, flying slowly in the steady rain. Figuring that someone was monitoring the cuffs' positions, Tally had asked them to take an indirect route. The journey wound through half-familiar sights of her childhood: ugly dorms and schools, sodden parks, and empty soccer fields.

Despite the downpour, there were a few uglies out. One bunch was taking turns skidding down a hill, screaming as they ran to throw themselves onto a mudslide. A few played tag in a dorm courtyard, slipping and falling and winding up just as muddy as the first group. They were all having too much fun to notice the four hoverboarders gliding silently past.

Tally wondered if she'd had that much fun as an ugly. All she could recall from those days was dying to turn pretty, to get across the river and leave all this behind. Floating above the earth, her perfect face hidden by a hood, she felt like some risen spirit, enviously watching the living and trying to remember what it was like to be one of them.

Cleopatra Park, high in the greenbelt on the outer edge of Uglyville, was empty. The walking paths had been transformed into small creeks carrying the rain down toward the swollen river. The wildlife seemed to be in hiding except for a few miserable-looking birds that clung to the branches of the great pines that drooped low under their loads of water.

Sussy and Dex brought them to a clearing marked with slalom flags, and Tally felt a flush of recognition. "This is one of Shay's favorite spots. She taught me to hoverboard here."

"Shay?" Zane said. "But she'd tell us if she was up to some kind of trick, wouldn't she?"

"Um, maybe not," Tally said softly. No pings had come from Shay since the fight. "I've been meaning to tell you, Zane: She's kind of pissed off at me right now."

"Wow," Sussy said. "I thought pretties all liked each other."

"Usually, they do." Tally sighed. "Welcome to the new world."

Zane narrowed his eyes. "I think Tally and I need to talk." He glanced at the two uglies.

It took them a moment to realize what he meant, but then Sussy said, "Oh, sure. We'll be going. But what if . . . ?"

"If the New Smokies show up again, send me a ping," Tally said.

"Doesn't the city read your mail?"

"Probably. Don't say anything except that you saw us on the feeds and you want to join the Crims when you turn sixteen. Leave the real message hidden under that recycler, and I'll send someone to pick it up. Got that?"

"Got it," Sussy said with a gap-toothed smile. Tally figured the two would be headed out to the ruins every night now, rain or not, looking for the New Smokies, happy to have a mission.

She gave them a pretty smile. "Thanks for everything."

Tally and Zane sat in silence for a minute after the uglies had left, watching the clearing from a thick stand of trees. The plastic slalom flags drooped miserably in the rain, the wind barely lifting them. Rainwater gathered in spots, the shallow pools reflecting the gray sky like rippling mirrors. Tally remembered flying between the flags on her hoverboard in ugly days, learning to bank and turn. Back when she and Shay were really friends . . .

It was impossible to guess why Shay would be visiting this spot. Maybe it was nothing but a few Crims practicing their hoverboarding, figuring it was a great way to stay bubbly. No big deal.

As they sat, Tally realized she was out of excuses for not telling Zane everything. It was time to admit what she'd done to the Smoke and how she'd told Shay about the cure, and past time to bring up what Dr. Cable had revealed about Zane. But Tally wasn't looking forward to the conversation, and being soaking wet and cold wasn't helping. Her coat's heating was already turned up to maximum. The bubbliness from hoverboarding had worn off, replaced by Tally's anger at herself for having waited this long. The always-listening cuffs made it too easy to avoid mentioning uncomfortable subjects.

"So what happened between you and Shay?" Zane said. His voice stayed soft, but carried an edge of frustration.

"Her memories are starting to come back." Tally stared into a mud puddle before her, watching drops that had made their way down through the soaked pine trees distort its surface. "On the night of the breakthrough, she got really mad at me. She blames me for the Specials finding the Smoke. Which, I guess, is pretty much what happened. I betrayed them."

He nodded. "I figured that. All the stories you two told—back before the cure—they had you rescuing her from the Smoke. That sounds like pretty-talk for betrayal."

Tally looked up at him. "So you knew?"

"That you'd gone undercover for Special Circumstances? I'd guessed it."

"Oh." Tally didn't know whether to feel relieved or ashamed. Of course, Zane had cooperated with Dr. Cable himself, so maybe he understood. "I didn't want to do it, Zane. I mean, at first I went out there to bring Shay back, so they'd make me pretty, but then I changed my mind. I wanted to stay in the Smoke. I tried to destroy the tracker they'd given me, but I wound up setting it off. Even when I tried to do the right thing, I betrayed everyone."

Zane faced her, his eyes intense under his hood. "Tally, we're all manipulated by the people who run this city. Shay should know that."

"I wish that was all," Tally said. "I also stole David from her. Back when we were in the Smoke."

"Oh, him again." Zane shook his head. "Well, I guess she's pretty pissed off at you right now. At least that'll keep her bubbly."

"Yeah, really bubbly." Tally swallowed. "And there's one more thing that's got her mad."

He waited silently, rain dripping from his hood.

"I told her about the cure."

"You what?" Zane's whisper cut through the rain like a hiss of steam.

"I had to." Tally spread her hands imploringly. "She had it halfway figured out already, Zane, and was thinking she could cure herself. She climbed the Valentino tower like we did, thinking that was what had changed us. But of course it didn't work, not like the pills. She kept asking me what happened to us. She said I owed her, after everything I did to her back in ugly days."

Zane swore under his breath. "So you told her about the pills? Great. That's one more thing that can go wrong."

"But she's totally bubbly, Zane. I don't think she'll give us away," Tally said, then shrugged. "If anything, finding out about the pills made her furious enough to stay bubbly for life."

"Furious? Because you're cured and she's not?"

"No." Tally sighed. "Because you are."

"What?"

"I owed her, and you got the other pill."

"But there wasn't time to—"

"I know that, Zane. But she doesn't. To her, it looks like . . ." She shook her head, feeling hot tears in her eyes. The rest of her was so cold, her fingers were slowly going numb. She began to tremble.

"It's okay, Tally." Zane reached out and took her hand, squeezing hard through the thick glove.

"You should have heard her, Zane. She really hates me."

"Listen, I'm sorry about that. But I'm glad it was me."

She looked up, her vision blurring with tears. "Yeah. Thanks for all the headaches, you mean."

"Better than staying a pretty-brain," he said. "But that's not what I meant. That day was about more than just finding those pills. I'm glad about . . . you and me."

She looked up and found him smiling. His fingers, still interlaced with hers, also trembled in the cold. Tally managed to smile back. "Me too."

"Don't let Shay make you feel bad about us, Tally."

"Of course not." She shook her head, realizing how much she meant it. Whatever Shay thought, Zane had been the right person to share the cure with. He had kept her bubbly, pushing her to pass the Smokies' tests, pressing her to dare the unproven pills. Tally had found more than a cure for pretty-headedness that day—she'd found someone to move forward with, past everything that had gone wrong last summer.

It had been littlie days when Peris had promised to stay her best friend forever—but the day he'd turned sixteen, Peris had left her behind in Uglyville. Then Tally had lost Shay's friendship, betraying her to Special Circumstances and stealing David from her. Now even David was gone, missing somewhere in the wild and half-erased from her memories. He hadn't even bothered to bring her the pills—he'd left that job to Croy. Tally could guess what that meant.

But Zane . . .

Tally stared into his golden, perfect eyes. He was here with her right now, in the flesh, and she'd been stupid to let what was between them get tangled up in her messy past. "I should have told you about Shay earlier. But the smart walls . . ."

"It's okay. But you can trust me. Always."

She pressed his hand in both of hers. "I know."

He reached up to touch her face. "We didn't really know each other very well that day, did we?"

"We took a chance, I guess. Weird how that happened."

He laughed. "I think that's the way it always happens. Usually without mysterious pills or Special Circumstances pounding on the door. But it's always taking a risk, when you . . . kiss someone new."

Tally nodded, and leaned forward. Their lips met, the kiss slow and intense in the chill of the rain. She could feel him trembling, and the muddy ground beneath them was cold, but their two hoods joined to block out the world, making a space that became warm from their mingling breath.

Tally whispered, "I'm so glad it was you with me that day."

"Me too."

"I—Ah!" She pulled away, wiping at her face. A trickle of water had crawled inside Tally's hood and was running down her cheek like a cold, malevolent tear.

He laughed and stood up, pulling her to her feet. "Come on, we can't stay here forever. Let's go back to Pulcher and get breakfast, and some dry clothes."

"I wasn't uncomfortable."

He smiled, but indicated his wrist and lowered his voice. "If we sit in one place too long, someone might get curious about what the big deal is out here in Uglyville."

"Whatever it is," she whispered.

But Zane was right. They should go home. They hadn't eaten anything all day except for a few calorie-purgers and some coffee. Their winter coats were heated, but between the physical effort of hoverboarding and the shock of getting dumped into the freezing river, Tally was starting to feel exhaustion and cold down in her bones. Hunger, the cold, and the kiss were all dizzy-making.

Zane snapped his fingers, and his board rose into the air.

"Wait a second," she said softly. "There's one more thing I should tell you about the night of the breakthrough."

"Okay."

"After I took you home . . ." The thought of Dr. Cable's feral face made her shiver, but Tally took a calming breath. She'd been stupid not to drag Zane outside sooner, getting him away from Pulcher Mansion's smart walls to tell him about her encounter with the doctor. She didn't want any secrets between them.

"What's wrong, Tally?"

"She was waiting for me . . . ," she said. "Dr. Cable."

The name made Zane's face go blank for a moment, then he nodded. "I remember her."

"You do?"

"She's kind of hard to forget," Zane said. He paused, staring out into the clearing. Tally wondered if he was going to say more.

Finally, she said, "She made me a weird sort of offer. She wanted to know if I—"

"Shhh!" he hissed.

"What—," she began, but Zane silenced her with a gloved hand. He turned and crouched in the mud, pulling her down beside him. Through the trees, a group of figures were marching into the clearing. They moved slowly, huddled in almost identical winter gear, their left wrists wrapped in black scarves. But Tally recognized one of them instantly, copper eyes bright and flash tattoo spinning in the cold.

It was Shay.

## RITUAL

Tally counted ten of them, slogging with quiet determination across the muddy ground. They reached the middle of the clearing and arranged themselves in a wide circle around one of the slalom flags. Shay moved to stand in the center, turning slowly, peering at the others from under her hood. The others settled into place about an arm's length apart, facing Shay and waiting silently.

After a long moment motionless, she dropped her winter coat to the ground, pulling off her gloves and spreading her arms. She wore only trousers, a sleeveless white T-shirt, and the fake metal cuff on her left wrist. Tipping her head back, she let the rain pound against her face.

Tally shivered and gathered her own coat tighter around her. Was Shay trying to freeze herself to death?

The other figures did nothing for a moment. Then, slowly and with awkward glances at one another, they followed her example, pulling off coats and gloves and sweaters. As their hoods came down, Tally recognized two more Crims. Ho was there—one of Shay's old friends who had run away to the Smoke only to come back on his own. Tally also recognized Tachs, who'd joined the clique a few weeks before she had.

But the other seven pretties weren't Crims at all. They placed their coats on the ground gingerly, hugging themselves against the bitter cold. When Ho and Tachs spread their arms, the others followed reluctantly. Rain ran down their faces and plastered the white shirts to their skin.

"What are they doing?" Zane whispered.

Tally only shook her head. She noticed that Shay had gotten new surge, some sort of raised tattoo hash marks on her arms. They extended from elbow to wrist, and Ho and Tachs seemed to have copied the design.

Shay began to speak, facing upward, addressing the flag overhead like a crazy person talking to nobody in particular. Her voice didn't carry across the clearing except for a word here and there. Tally couldn't make sense of it—the cadence sounded like a chant, almost like the prayers that Rusties and pre-Rusties had once offered up to their invisible superheroes in the sky.

After a few minutes, Shay fell silent, and again the group stood without saying a word, all shivering in the cold except the apparently insane Shay. Tally realized that the non-Crims all had flash tattoos on their faces, fresh-looking surge that glistened in the rain. She guessed that since the stadium disaster, swirly face tattoos must be the rage, but it was an awfully big coincidence that all seven of the unknown pretties had them.

"Those pings from wannabees," she whispered. "Shay's been recruiting."

"But why?" Zane hissed. "We all agreed that newbies were the last thing we need right now."

"Maybe she needs them."

"For what?"

A shiver went through Tally. "For this."

Zane swore. "We'll just veto them."

Tally shook her head. "I don't think she cares about vetoes. I'm not sure if she's still a—"

Shay's voice cut through the rain again. She reached into her back pocket and produced an object that glittered coldly in the gray light. It unfolded into a long knife.

Tally's eyes widened, but none of the pretties in the circle looked surprised; their expressions revealed a mix of queasy fear and excitement.

Holding the knife aloft, Shay spoke more words in the same slow, deliberate cadence, and Tally heard one repeated enough to make it out.

It sounded like "Cutters."

"Let's get out of here," she said so softly that Zane must not have heard. She wanted to climb on her hoverboard and flee, but Tally found she couldn't move, or look away, or close her eyes.

Shay took the knife with her left hand and placed its edge against her right forearm, the wet metal gleaming. She raised both arms, turning slowly, fixing each of the others with her burning gaze. Then she looked up into the rain.

The movement was so slight that Tally hardly saw it from their hiding place, but she knew what had happened from the reactions of the others. Their bodies shuddered, eyes widening with horrified fascination—like Tally, they couldn't look away.

Then she saw the blood begin to trickle from the wound. It ran thinly in the rain, spreading down Shay's upraised arm and onto her shoulder, reaching her shirt, spreading a color that was more pink than red.

She turned around once to give them all a good look, her slow, deliberate movements as disturbing as the blood running down her arm. The others were shivering visibly now, shooting furtive glances at one another.

Shay finally lowered her arm, swaying a little on her feet, and held out the knife. Ho stepped forward to take it from her, and she took his place in the circle.

"What is this?" Zane whispered.

Tally shook her head and closed her eyes. The rain became suddenly deafening around her, but she heard her own words through the torrent. "This is Shay's new cure."

The others followed one by one.

Tally kept on expecting them to run, thinking that if only one of them would make a break for it, the rest would scatter into the forest like scared rabbits. But something—the bleak setting, the spirit-sapping rain, or maybe the crazed expression on Shay's face—bound them to their spots. They all watched, and then, one by one, they cut themselves. And as each did so, their faces transformed to become more like Shay's: ecstatic and insane.

With every cut, Tally felt something hollowing out inside her. She couldn't forget that there was more to this ritual than madness. She remembered the night of the costume party. Her fear and panic had made her bubbly enough to pursue Croy, but had left her still pretty-minded. It wasn't until after Peris's knee had struck her as he hoverbounced—opening up her eyebrow—that Tally's head had really become clear.

Shay had admired that scar; she'd been the one to suggest getting a tattoo to commemorate it. Apparently she'd also understood how that injury had changed Tally, leading her to Zane, to the top of the transmission tower, and finally to the cure.

And now Shay was sharing her knowledge.

"This is our fault," Tally whispered.

"What?"

Tally opened her gloved hands toward the tableaux before them. She and Zane had given Shay what she needed to spread this cure: citywide fame, hundreds of pretties all dying to become Crims—bleeding to become Crims.

Or whatever they were becoming. "Cutters," Shay had said.

"She's not one of us anymore."

"Why are we just sitting here?" Zane hissed. His fists were clenched, his face reddening in the shadow of his hood.

"Zane, calm down." Tally took his hand.

"We should make her . . ." His voice trailed off with a choked-sounding cough, his eyes wide.

"Zane?" she whispered.

He was struggling for breath, hands clutching at empty air.

"Zane!" Tally cried aloud. She grabbed his other hand, staring into his bulging eyes. He wasn't breathing.

Tally glanced into the clearing, desperate for help from someone, anyone—even the Cutters. A few of the distant figures had heard her cry, but they only stared wide-eyed at her, blood flowing and flash tattoos spinning, too zoned out to be of any help.

She reached for her cuff, tearing off the black scarf to send a distress ping. But Zane's hand reached out to grab her. He shook his head painfully. "No."

"Zane, you need help!"

"I'm okay. . . ." The words tore from his throat.

She paused a moment, imagining him dying here in her arms. But if she called the wardens, they might both wind up under the surgeon's knife, pretty-minded for good—leaving Shay's cure as the only one in town. "All right," she said. "But I'm taking you to the hospital."

"No!"

"Not inside. Just as close as we can get. We'll wait there and see what happens."

Tally rolled Zane onto her hoverboard and snapped her fingers, watching as it rose into the air. She lay on top of him, feeling the board settle uneasily under their combined weight. The lifters held, and she pushed forward carefully.

As the board began to move, she glanced back at the clearing. All ten of them were staring at Tally and Zane now. Shay was walking toward them, her glare as cold as the rain.

Suddenly, Tally was overwhelmed with fear, the same terror she felt at the sight of Specials. She pushed off hard with her feet, leaning forward and climbing into the trees, leaving the place behind.

The ride down to the river was terrifying. Zane's limbs sprawled out in all directions, his shifting weight threatening to tip the board over with every turn. Tally wrapped her arms around him, fingernails scraping across the board's knobbly underside. She steered with her flailing legs, her turns as wide as a stumbling drunk's. The cold rain spat into her face, and Tally remembered the goggles in her coat pocket, but there was no way of getting at them without stopping.

And there wasn't time to stop.

They hurtled among the trees, the board picking up speed as they descended toward the river. Pine branches, heavy and glistening with captured raindrops, reared up out of the rain to slash her face. When they finally burst out of Cleopatra Park, Tally cut across a belt of muddy sports fields at top speed, angling toward the far end of the central island.

At this distance, the hospital was invisible in the driving rain, but Tally spotted the running lights of a hovercar headed in that direction. It was moving fast and high, probably an ambulance taking someone in. Squinting against the barrage of freezing rain, she managed to keep her eyes on it, following its course. As the hovercar pulled out of sight, they reached the river, and the overweighted board began to lose lift over the open water.

Tally realized too late what was happening: The buried metal grid that magnetic lifters used to push against was lower here—in the ground under ten meters of water. As they neared the middle of the river, the board descended closer and closer to the cold and choppy surface.

Halfway across, the board struck water with a slap, Zane's hands bouncing off the river as if it was solid. But the hoverboard rebounded into the air, and as the far shore grew closer, the lifters gained purchase and carried them higher.

"Tally . . . ," a croaking voice came from beneath her.

"It'll be okay, Zane. I've got you."

"Yeah. Feels very under control."

Tally dared a glance down at him. His eyes were open, his face no longer red. She realized that his chest rose and fell beneath her, his breathing normal. "Just relax, Zane. I'll stop when we're close to the hospital."

"Don't take me there."

"I'm just taking you closer. In case."

"In case what?" he said raggedly.

"In case you stop breathing again! Now shut up!"

He fell obediently silent, his eyes closing.

As the river's rain-spattered surface shot by underneath them, the lights of the hospital rose up, its dark bulk reassuringly close. Tally spotted the flashing yellow lights of the emergency bay, but pulled off the river before they reached it, climbing the bank slowly. She brought the board to rest in the shelter of a rack of empty ambulances, the hovercars stacked three high in their giant metal frame, apparently awaiting some major disaster.

When the board settled, Zane rolled off onto the wet ground with a groan.

She kneeled next to him. "Talk to me."

"I'm fine," he said. "Except my back."

"Your back? What . . ."

"I think it has to do with riding a hoverboard on it." He snorted. "And under you."

She took his face in her hands, staring into his pupils. He looked exhausted and bedraggled, but he smiled and winked at her tiredly.

"Zane . . ." She felt herself starting to cry again, tears running hot among the cold raindrops. "What's happening to you?"

"Like I said: I think we need some breakfast."

Sobs wracked her body. "But . . ."

"I know." He put his hands on her shoulders. "We have to get out of here."

"But what about the New Smo—"

His hand shot up to cover her mouth, muffling her next words. She pulled away in surprise. Zane pushed himself up on one elbow, staring at her cuff, which was uncovered in the rain. She'd taken her glove off to make a call when his attack had started.

"Oh . . . I'm sorry."

He shook his head, pulling her closer and whispering, "It's okay."

Tally closed her eyes, trying to remember what they had said on the mad trip here. "We argued about taking you to the hospital," she whispered.

He nodded and stood shakily, saying aloud, "Well, since we're here." He turned and punched his fist against the metal of the ambulance rack. It rebounded with a dull ring.

"Zane!"

He doubled over with pain, then shook his head, waving his wounded hand in the air for a moment. He regarded the blood on the knuckles. "As I said, since we came all this way, I might as well get this looked at. But next time ask me, okay?"

She stared at him, finally understanding. For a moment, she'd thought Shay's insanity was contagious. But a wounded hand was a plausible reason for their wild ride here, and would square with most of what the cuff had heard. Tally could also tell the wardens that they hadn't eaten in a couple of days. Maybe a vitamin- and blood-sugar drip in Zane's arm would help his headache.

He still looked like crap, muddy and soaking wet, but he walked without any stagger. In fact, Zane seemed pretty bubbly after cracking his hand. Maybe Shay wasn't as insane as she looked—at least she knew what worked.

"Come on," he said.

"Want a ride?" Tally asked, pointing. The second hoverboard was coasting toward them across the grass, having followed the signal in Zane's crash bracelets.

"I think I'll walk," he said, trudging toward the flashing lights of the emergency bay. Tally saw then that his hands shook, and how pale he was. And she resolved that the next time he had an attack, she was calling the wardens.

Even the cure wasn't worth dying for.

## HOSPITAL

It turned out that Zane's punch had broken three bones in his hand, which were going to take half an hour to fix.

Tally shared the waiting room with two brand-new pretties waiting for a friend with a broken leg—something about running down wet stairs outside Lillian Russell Mansion. She ignored the details of the story, scarfing down cookies and coffee with lots of milk and sugar, luxuriating in the hospital's warmth and total absence of pounding rain. The rare sensation of calories entering her body softened the world a little, but Tally was glad for a few moments of pretty haze. Her memories of what Shay and company were up to in Cleopatra Park were all too clear.

"So what happened to you?" one of the pretties finally asked, the emphasis on the last word indicating her soaked and muddy clothes, exhausted expression, and generally shaming appearance.

Tally shoved a chocolate-chip cookie into her mouth and shrugged. "Hoverboarding."

The other pretty elbowed her friend, widening her eyes and angling one nervous thumb at Tally.

"What?" he said.

"Shhh!"

"What?"

The second pretty sighed. "Sorry," she said to Tally. "My friend is brand new. And totally brain-missing." She explained to him in a whisper, "That's Tally Youngblood."

The first one opened his mouth wide, then shut it.

Tally just smiled and stuffed another cookie into her face. Of course you'd run into Tally Youngblood in the emergency bay, they were thinking. Where else? They were probably wondering what piece of major architecture had crumbled under her this time.

Though her celebrity kept the two mercifully quiet, their furtive glances were unsettling. These two pretties weren't the type to become Cutters, Tally was fairly certain. But she couldn't escape the realization that her criminal notoriety was feeding Shay's little project, creating pretties hungry to explore a certain kind of bubbliness. Even full of coffee, milk, and cookies, Tally's stomach began to feel sour as she wondered if trips to the emergency bay were going to be the rage this winter.

"Tally?" An orderly stood by the waiting room door, beckoning her in. Finally. Tally was ready to get out of this place.

"Take care, kids," she said to the pretties, and followed the orderly down the hall.

When the door closed behind her, Tally realized that she hadn't been taken to the outpatient center. The orderly had brought her to a small room dominated by a huge, cluttered desk. A wallscreen showed a grassy field on a sunny day—the sort of visuals they showed in littlie school right before nap time.

"Been out in the rain?" the orderly said brightly, pulling

off his powder blue paper robe. He was wearing a suit underneath—semiformal, her brain informed her—and Tally realized that he wasn't an orderly at all. He had the beaming smile favored by politicians, nursery teachers, and headshrinks.

She sat in the chair across from him, her damp clothes squelching. "You totally guessed it."

He smiled. "Well, accidents happen. You were wise to bring your friend in. And lucky me, being here when you did. The thing is, I've been trying to get in touch with you, Tally."

"You have?"

"Indeed." He smiled again. There was a species of middle pretty who smiled at everything: happy smile, disappointed smile, you're-in-trouble smile. His was welcoming and enthusiastic, trustworthy and calm, and it set Tally's teeth on edge. He was the sort of middle pretty Dr. Cable had promised Tally she would become: smug and self-assured, his handsome face marked with just the right lines of laughter, age, and wisdom.

"You haven't been opening your mail the last couple of days, have you?" he said.

She shook her head. "Too many bogus pings. From being on the feeds, you know? Totally famous-making."

The words earned Tally a proud smile. "I suppose it's all been very exciting for you and your friends."

She shrugged, going for false modesty. "It was bubbly at first, but now it's getting bogus. So, who are you again?"

"Dr. Remmy Anders. I'm a trauma counselor here on the hospital staff."

"Trauma? Is this about the stadium thing? Because I'm totally—"

"I'm sure you're fine, Tally. It's a friend of yours I've been wanting to ask you about. Frankly, we're a little worried."

"About who?"

"Shay."

Behind her pretty expression, a serious ping went through Tally. She tried to keep her voice steady. "Why Shay?"

Slowly, as if controlled by a remote, Dr. Anders's concerned smile bent into a frown. "There was a disturbance the other night at your little bonfire party. An argument between you and Shay. Quite troubling."

Tally blinked, stalling as she recalled Shay screaming at her by the fire. Even under all those layers, the cuff must have heard how upset Shay had been—way beyond the usual soft-spoken tiff between new pretties. Tally tried to recall exactly what Shay had shouted, but the combination of champagne and horrible guilt wasn't very memory-improving. She shrugged. "Yeah. She was pretty drunk. Me too."

"It didn't sound very happy-making."

"Dr. Remmy, are you, like, spying on us? That's bogus."

The counselor shook his head and went back to the concerned smile. "We have had a particular interest in all of you who suffered that unfortunate accident. It can sometimes be difficult to recover from frightening and unexpected events. That's why I've been assigned as your post-stress counselor."

Tally pretended not to notice that he'd totally dodged the spying question—she already knew the answer, anyway. Special Circumstances might not care if the Crims knocked down New Pretty Town, but the wardens were always on the job. Given that the city was designed to keep people pretty-minded, it made sense that they would assign a counselor to anyone who'd had any serious bubbly-making experience. Dr. Anders was here to make sure that the breakthrough hadn't given the Crims any new and exciting ideas.

She summoned up a pretty smile. "In case we go crazy?"

Dr. Anders laughed. "Oh, we don't think you'll go crazy. I'm just here to make sure there aren't any long-term effects. Friendships can be negatively impacted by stress, you know."

She decided to throw Remmy a bone, and let her eyes widen. "So that's why she was being such a pain that night?"

He brightened. "Yes, it's all about stress, Tally. But remember, she probably didn't mean it."

"Well, I didn't go all crazy on her."

Reassuring smile. "Everyone reacts differently to trauma, Tally. Not everyone's as tough as you. Instead of getting angry, why don't we think of this as an opportunity to show Shay your support. You're old friends, aren't you?"

"Yeah. Since we were uglies. Same birthday."

"That's wonderful. Old friends are best at times like these. What was the fight about?"

Tally shrugged. "I don't know. Nothing, really."

"Can you remember at all?"

Tally wondered if this room was rigged to polygraph her, and if so, how big a lie she could get away with. She closed her eyes, concentrating on the calories moving through her half-starved body, letting a pretty haze settle over herself.

"Tally?" he prompted.

She decided to give Dr. Anders a little bit of the truth. "It was just . . . old stuff."

He nodded, folding his hands in satisfaction. Tally wondered if she'd said too much. "From ugly days?" he asked.

She shook her head, not trusting her voice.

"How have you and Shay been getting along since that night?"

"Just fine."

He smiled happily, but Tally caught him glancing away into the middle distance—probably at an eyescreen that was invisible to her. Was he checking the city interface? It would know that she and Shay hadn't pinged each other since the party, and three whole days without any mail between them was pretty unusual. Or was Dr. Anders looking to see if her voice was wavering?

He gave his invisible data, or whatever it was, a small nod. "Has she seemed in better spirits to you since then?"

"She's okay, I guess." Just a little self-mutilation, crazy chanting, and maybe wanting to start her own very disturbing clique. "I haven't seen her since this bogus rain started coming down, actually. But me and her are best friends forever."

The last words came out wrong, Tally's voice sounding rough. She coughed a little, which was marked by a deepening of Dr. Anders's concerned smile. "I'm glad to hear that, Tally. And you're feeling all right as well, aren't you?"

"Bubbly," she said. "A little hungry, though."

"Yes, yes. You and Zane really must eat more. You're looking a bit thin, and I'm told his blood sugar was terribly low when he came in."

"I'll make sure he has some of those chocolate-chip cookies in the waiting room. They're awesome."

"A wonderful idea. You're a good friend, Tally." He stood, offering his hand. "Well, I see that Zane's all patched up, so I won't keep you. Thanks for your time, and make sure you let me know if you or any of your friends ever need to talk."

"Oh, I will," she said, giving the doctor her prettiest smile. "This has really been great."

*

Outside, the cold rain embraced Tally like an old and unavoidable friend, the discomfort almost a relief after Dr. Anders's radiant smiles. She told Zane about him on the way home. Although her cuff was bound up again, she spoke softly enough for the wind to tear her words away as they climbed into the gray sky.

He sighed when she was done. "Sounds like they're as worried about her as we are."

"Yeah. They must have heard our fight the other night. She was screaming at me in a very unpretty way."

"Perfect." His teeth were bared against the cold. It didn't look like the painkillers they'd given him for his hand were helping Zane's headache much. His feet shuffled on the board, finding their balance clumsily.

"I didn't say anything much. Just that she was drunk and acting up." Tally allowed herself a thin smile of self-congratulation. This one time, at least, she hadn't betrayed Shay. She hoped.

"Of course you didn't, Tally. Shay might need help, but not from some middle-pretty headshrink. What we have to do is get her out into the wild and give her the real cure. As soon as possible."

"Yeah. The pills are a lot better than cutting yourself." If they don't wind up giving you brain damage, she didn't add. Tally had decided not to tell Zane about her resolve to take him to the hospital the next time he had an attack; hopefully it wouldn't come to that. "So how were your doctors?"

"The usual. They spent the first hour lecturing me about eating more. When they finally got around to knitting my bones up, I was only unconscious about ten minutes. But other than being skinny, they didn't seem to notice anything weird about me."

"Good."

"Of course, that doesn't mean I'm fine. They didn't look at my head, after all, just my hand."

Tally took a deep breath. "Your headaches are getting worse, aren't they?"

"I think it was more hunger and cold than anything else."

She shook her head. "I haven't eaten anything today either, Zane, and you didn't see me—"

"Forget about my head, Tally! I'm not any worse or any better. It's Shay's arms I'm worried about." He angled his board closer and lowered his voice. "They're going to be keeping an eye on her, too, now. If your Dr. Remmy gets a good look at what she's been doing to herself, all hell will break loose."

"Yeah. I can't argue with that." Tally visualized the row of scars along Shay's arms. From a distance, she'd thought they were tattoos, but from close up, anyone would know what they were. If Dr. Anders saw them, Tally doubted very much that he would have a smile appropriate to the occasion. Alarms would go off all over the city, and the wardens' interest in everyone who'd been involved in the stadium disaster would go way off the scale.

Tally reached out and brought them to a stop, lowering her voice to just above a whisper. "We don't have much time, then. He could decide to talk to Shay any day now."

Zane took a deep breath. "You'll have to talk to Shay first. Tell her to lay off the cutting."

"Oh. Fun. What if she doesn't want to?"

"Tell her we're about to leave. Tell her we'll get her the real cure."

"Leave? How?"

"We just go—tonight, if we can. I'll pack up everything we need, you get the other Crims ready."

"What about these?" She was too exhausted to raise her swaddled wrist, but he took her meaning.

"We'll get them off. Tonight. There's a trick I've been saving."

"What trick, Zane?"

"I can't tell you yet. It'll work, though—it's just a little risky."

Tally frowned. She and Zane had tried every tool they could think of, and nothing had so much as scratched the cuffs. "What is it?"

"I'll show you tonight," he said, his jaw tight.

Tally swallowed. "Must be more than a little risky."

Zane stared at her, his face pale and half-starved, his eyes dull through the goggles. "Give the girl a hand." He chuckled. "Might need one."

Tally had to turn her eyes away from his smile.

## CRUSHER

The shop shed wasn't far from the hospital, on the downstream end of New Pretty Town where the two arms of the river rejoined each other. This late at night, the lathes, imaging tables, and injection molds sat unused, the place almost empty. The only light came from the other end of the shed, where a middle pretty was blowing molten glass into shape.

"It's freezing in here," Tally said. She could see the words coiling from her mouth in the soft red glow of work lights. The rain had finally stopped while they were getting the Crims ready to run, but the air was still damp and chill.

Even inside the shed, Tally, Fausto, and Zane were huddled in their winter coats.

"They've usually got smelting furnaces going," Zane said. "And some of these machines put out a ton of heat." He pointed at the two sides of the shed that were open to the night. "But the ventilation means no smart walls, see?"

"I see." Tally pulled her coat tighter around her, reaching into one pocket to turn up its heater.

Fausto pointed out a machine that looked like a huge press. "Hey, I remember playing with one of those back in ugly school, for industrial design class," Fausto said. "We made these lunch trays with runners on the bottom, for sliding on the snow."

"That's why I brought you along," Zane said, leading Tally and Fausto across the concrete floor.

The bottom part of the machine was a metal table, which seemed to be etched with a million tiny dots. Parallel with the table was suspended an identical expanse of metal.

"What? You want to use a crusher?" Fausto raised his eyebrows. Zane still hadn't told them what he was up to, but Tally didn't like the look of the massive machine.

Or its name, for that matter.

Zane put down the champagne bucket he'd brought, sloshing ice water onto the floor. He pulled a memory card from one pocket and shoved it into the crusher's reader slot. The machine booted up, lights winking around the edge and the floor rumbling powerfully under Tally's feet.

A ripple seemed to pass through the table, a wave traveling across the surface as if the metal had suddenly become liquid and alive.

When the movement subsided, Tally took a closer look at the crusher's surface. The tiny etched-looking dots were in fact the tips of thin rods, which could be raised up and down to make shapes. She ran her fingers across the table, but the rods were so thin and perfectly aligned, it felt like smooth metal. "What's it for?"

"Stamping out stuff," Zane said. He pushed a button, and the table sprang to life again, a tiny, symmetrical collection of mountains rising up in its center. Tally noticed that identically shaped cavities had appeared in the upper surface of the crusher.

"Hey, that's my lunch tray," Fausto said.

"Of course. You thought I forgot? Those things were awesome for sledding," Zane said happily. He pulled a sheet of metal from under the machine and carefully aligned its edges to the table's.

"Yeah. I always wondered why they never mass-produced them," Fausto said.

"Too bubbly-making," Zane said. "But I bet some ugly reinvents them every few years. Heads up. I'm going to shoot it."

The other two each took a healthy step back.

Zane grasped two handles at the edge of the table, squeezing both at the same moment. The machine made a rumbling noise for a fraction of a second, then leaped suddenly into motion, the top half slamming down onto the lower with an earsplitting clang. The sound echoed through the shed, and Tally's ears were still ringing as the crusher's jaws slowly parted to reveal the sheet of metal.

"Sweet, isn't it?" Zane said. He picked up the sheet, whose contours had been reshaped by the impact. It looked like a lunch tray now, with little sections to divide a meal into salad, main, and dessert. Turning it over in his hands, Zane ran a finger down the grooves that marked the back side of the tray. "On good, powdery snow you could go a thousand klicks an hour on these babies."

Fausto's face had turned pale. "It won't work, Zane."

"Why not?"

"Too many safeties. Even if you could get one of us to—"

"Are you kidding, Zane?" Tally cried. "You are not sticking your hand in there. That thing'll take it off!"

Zane just smiled. "No, it won't. Like Fausto said: too many safeties." He pulled the memory card out of the crusher's reader slot and stuck another in. The table rippled again, leaving a set of sharp ridges at its edge, like a row of teeth. He placed his left wrist alongside the metal jaws. "It's hard to tell with the glove on, but see where it'll snip the cuff?"

"But what if it misses, Zane?" Tally said. She had to fight to keep her voice down. Their cuffs were bound as usual, but she didn't want the middle pretty at the other end of the shed to hear them.

"It doesn't miss. You can stamp out parts for a stopwatch with these things."

"It won't work at all," Fausto proclaimed. He stuck his own hand under the crusher. "Shoot it."

"I know, I know," Zane said, grasping the handles and squeezing.

"What?" Tally cried in horror, but the machine didn't move. A row of yellow lights flashed around its edge, and a tinny industrial voice said, "Clear, please."

"It detects humans," Fausto said. "Body heat."

Tally swallowed, her heart pounding in her chest as Fausto took his hand out from under the crusher. "Don't do that!"

"And even if you trick it, what's the point?" Fausto continued. "It'll only crush the cuff, which will squish your hand."

"Not at fifty meters per second. Look here." Zane leaned over the table, running one finger along the formation of teeth he had programmed. "That edge will cut it, or at least smack it hard enough to kill whatever's inside. Our cuffs will just be hunks of dead metal after this thing hits them."

Fausto leaned in to look closer, and Tally turned away from the sight of them with their heads between the metal jaws. Dead metal. She stared at the glassblower at the other end of the shed. Unaware of their insane conversation, the woman was calmly holding a chunk of glass inside a small, radiant furnace, turning it slowly over the flame.

Tally walked toward the woman until she was out of earshot of Zane and Fausto, then unwrapped her cuff. "Ping Shay."

"Not available. Message?"

Tally scowled, but said, "Yes. Listen, Shay, I know this is my eighteenth message today, but you've got to answer. I'm sorry we were spying on you, but . . ." Tally didn't know what to add, assuming that the wardens—maybe even Specials—might be listening. She could hardly explain that they were escaping tonight. "But we're worried about you. Get back to me as soon as you can. We need to talk . . . face-to-face."

Tally signed off and rewrapped the scarf around her wrist. Shay, Ho, and Tachs—the Cutters—had pulled a big disappearing act, refusing to answer any pings. Probably Shay was sulking about having her secret ceremony spied on. But hopefully one of the Crims would find them and tell them about tonight's escape.

Tally and Zane had spent the afternoon getting everyone ready. The Crims were packed up and positioned around the island, ready to start moving once the signal came from the shop shed that Tally and Zane were free.

The woman blowing glass had finished heating it up.

She pulled the glowing mass from the furnace and began to blow into it through a long tube, making the molten material bubble up into sinuous shapes. Tally reluctantly turned away from the sight and returned to the crusher.

"But what about the safeties?" Fausto was arguing.

"I can get rid of my body heat."

"How?"

Zane kicked the champagne bucket. "Thirty seconds in ice water and my hand will be as cold as a chunk of metal."

"Yeah, but your hand is not a chunk of metal," Tally cried. "And neither is mine. That's the problem."

"Look, Tally, I'm not asking you to go first."

She shook her head. "I'm not going at all, Zane. Neither are you."

"She's right." Fausto was staring at the metal teeth rising up from the table, comparing them with their twins jutting down from the top half. "High marks for good design, but sticking your hand in there is crazy. If you've miscalculated by one centimeter, the crusher will hit bone. They told us about that in shop class. The shock wave will travel all the way up your arm, shattering everything along the way."

"Hey, if it misses, they'll put me back together. And it won't miss. I even made a different cast for your hand, Tally," Zane said, waving another memory card. "Since your cuff's smaller."

"If this goes wrong, they'll never fix you," she said quietly. "Not even the city hospital can rebuild a flattened hand."

"Not flattened," Fausto said. "Your bones will be liquifacted, Zane. That means the shock will melt them."

"Listen, Tally," Zane said, reaching down to fish the bottle out of the champagne bucket. "I didn't want to do this either. But I had an attack this morning, remember?" He popped the cork.

"You had a what?" Fausto said.

Tally shook her head. "We have to find some other way."

"There's no time," Zane said, taking a swig from the bottle. "So, Fausto, will you help?"

"Help?" Tally asked.

Fausto nodded slowly. "It takes two hands to shoot the crusher—another safety feature, so you can't leave one in there by accident. He needs one of us to pull the triggers." Fausto crossed his arms. "Forget it."

"And I'm not helping you either!" Tally said.

"Tally." Zane sighed. "If we don't leave the city tonight, I might as well stick my head in there. These headaches have been coming every three days or so, and now they're getting worse. We have to leave."

Fausto frowned. "What are you talking about?"

Zane turned to him. "Something's wrong with me, Fausto. That's why we have to go tonight. We think the New Smokies can help me."

"Why would you need them? What's wrong with you?"

"What's wrong with me is, I'm cured."

"Come again?"

Zane took a deep breath. "You see, we took these pills. . . ."

Tally groaned and turned away, realizing that another line was being crossed. First Shay, and now Fausto. Tally wondered how long it would be before all the Crims knew about the cure. Which would only make it more urgent for her and Zane to escape the city, no matter what they had to risk.

Tally watched the glassblower with growing unhappiness. She could sense Fausto's disbelief fading as Zane explained what had happened to the two of them over the last month: the pills, the growing bubbliness of the cure, and Zane's crippling headaches.

"So Shay was right about you guys!" he said. "That's why you're so different now. . . ."

Shay had been the only one to call Tally on it, but all the Crims must have seen the changes and wondered what had happened. They all wanted the strange new bubbliness that Tally and Zane had. Now that Fausto knew the cure existed, that it was as simple as swallowing a pill, maybe risking a couple of hands in the crusher wouldn't seem so crazy to him.

Tally sighed. Maybe it wasn't crazy. That very morning she had delayed taking Zane to the hospital, waiting outside in the rain for what might have been precious minutes—risking his life, not just a hand.

She swallowed. What was the word Fausto had used? Liquifacted?

The glass object was growing in the woman's grasp, bubbling into overlapping spheres that looked supremely delicate, impossible to repair if shattered. The woman held the glowing shape carefully; some things couldn't be put back together if you broke them.

Tally thought about David's father, Az. When Dr. Cable had tried to erase Az's memories, the process had killed him. The mind was even more fragile than the human hand—and none of them had a clue what was going on inside Zane's head.

She looked down at her own left glove, flexing the fingers slowly. Was she brave enough to put it in the crusher's metal jaws? Maybe.

"Are you sure we can find the New Smokies out there?" Fausto was saying to Zane. "I thought no one had seen them for a while."

"The uglies we met this morning said there were signs they'd come back."

"And they can cure you?"

Tally heard it then in Fausto's voice—he was justifying it to himself aloud, slowly but surely, and would eventually agree to shoot the crusher. It even made perfect sense, in a horrible way. There was a cure for Zane's condition somewhere out in the wild, and if they didn't get him to it, he was as good as dead, anyway.

What was risking a hand?

Tally turned and said, "I'll do it. I'll pull the triggers."

They looked at her in shocked silence for a moment, then Zane smiled. "Good. I'd rather it was you."

She swallowed. "Why?"

"Because I trust you. Don't want to be shaking."

Tally took a deep breath, fighting to keep tears from her eyes. "Thanks, I guess."

There was a moment of uncomfortable silence.

"Are you sure, Tally?" Fausto finally said. "I could do it."

"No. It should be me."

"Well, no sense waiting around." Zane dropped his winter coat to the floor. He unwrapped his scarf from his wrist and pulled off the glove that had covered his cuff. His bare left hand looked small and fragile next to the crusher's dark mass. Zane made a fist and thrust it into the ice bucket, wincing as the freezing water began to leech his body heat away. "Get ready, Tally."

She glanced at their backpacks on the floor, felt to make sure she was wearing her belly sensor, checked the hoverboards at the edge of the shed one more time; the wires under the boards were yanked apart, disconnected from the city grid. They were ready to go.

Tally looked at her cuff. Once Zane's was shattered, the tracking signal would be interrupted. They'd have to do hers right away and get moving. They would have a long run just to reach the edge of the city.

Two dozen Crims waited all over the island, ready to scatter into the wild and draw pursuit in every direction. Each carried a Roman candle with a special mix of colors—purple and green—to spread the signal once Zane and Tally were free.

Free.

Tally looked down at the crusher's controls and swallowed. The two handles were cast in cheery bright yellow plastic and shaped like thumbgame joysticks, each with a fat trigger. When she took hold of them, the power of the idling machine shuddered in her hands, like the rumble of a suborbital plane passing overhead.

She tried to imagine herself pulling the triggers, and couldn't. Tally was out of arguments, though, and the time for discussion was past.

After thirty long seconds in the ice water, Zane pulled his hand out.

"Close your eyes in case the metal shatters. The cold will make it brittle," Zane said in a normal voice. It didn't matter what the cuff heard now, Tally realized. By the time anyone figured out what they were talking about, they'd be flying at top speed toward the Rusty Ruins.

Zane placed his wrist on the edge of the table, closing his eyes tightly. "Okay. Do it."

Tally took a deep breath, her hands trembling on the controls. She closed her eyes and thought, Okay, do it now. . . .

But her fingers didn't obey.

Her mind started to spin, thinking of everything that could go wrong. She imagined flying Zane to the hospital again, his left arm a mass of jelly. She imagined Specials bursting in at that moment and stopping them, having figured out what they were up to. She wondered if Zane had made all the right measurements, and if he'd remembered that the cuff would have shrunk a bit from the ice water.

Tally paused at that thought, thinking maybe she should ask him. She opened her eyes. The wet cuff glimmered like a piece of gold in the crusher's yellow work lights.

"Tally . . . do it!"

Cold would make the metal contract, but heat . . . Tally glanced at the glassblower on the other side of the shed, blissfully unaware of the violent, horrible thing that was about to happen.

"Tally!" Fausto said softly.

Heat would make the cuff expand. . . .

The woman held the red-hot glass in her hands, turning it over to inspect it from every side. How was she holding molten glass?

"Tally," Fausto said. "If you want, I'll do—"

"Hang on," she said, taking her hands from the crusher's controls.

"What?" Zane cried.

"Stay here." She pulled the memory card from the crusher's slot, ignoring the sounds of protest behind her, and ran past hulking lathes and furnaces to the other side of the shed. At her approach, the woman looked up placidly, smiling with middle-pretty calm.

"Hello, dear."

"Hi. That's beautiful," Tally said.

The pleasant smile grew warmer. "Thank you."

Tally could see the woman's hands now, how they shimmered silver in the glowing red light. "You're wearing gloves, aren't you."

The woman laughed. "Of course! It's rather hot in that furnace, you know."

"But you can't feel it?"

"Not through these gloves. I think the material was

invented for shuttles coming back through the atmosphere. It can reflect a couple of thousand degrees."

Tally nodded. "And they're really thin, aren't they? From across the room, I couldn't even tell you had them on."

"That's right." The woman nodded happily. "You can feel the texture of the glass right through them."

"Wow." Tally smiled prettily. The gloves would fit on under the cuffs, she could see now. "Where can I get a pair?"

The woman nodded at a cupboard. Tally opened it and found dozens of gloves crammed inside, their reflective material glittering like fresh snow. She pulled two out. "They're all the same size?"

"Yeah. They stretch to fit, all the way up past the elbows," the woman said. "Just make sure you throw them away after one use. They don't work very well the second time."

"No problem." Tally turned away with the gloves in a tight grip, relief flooding through her as she realized she wouldn't have to pull the triggers, wouldn't have to watch the crusher snap down on Zane's hand. A new and better plan unfolded in her mind like clockwork—she knew exactly where to find a powerful furnace, one they could take right to the edge of the city.

"Wait a second, Tally," the woman said, a troubled note entering her voice.

Tally froze, realizing that the woman had recognized her. Of course, everyone who watched the feeds knew Tally Youngblood's face now. She wracked her brain for an innocent reason for needing the gloves, but everything she thought of sounded totally bogus. "Um, yeah?"

"You've got two left gloves there." The woman laughed. "Not very useful, whatever trick you're planning."

Tally smiled, letting a slow chuckle escape her lips.

That's what you think. But she turned back to the cupboard and fished out two right gloves. It wouldn't hurt to protect both hands. "Thanks for all your help," she said.

"No problem." The woman smiled beautifully, turning away, staring again into the curves of her piece of glass. "Just be careful."

"Don't worry," Tally said. "I always am."

## HIJACKING

"Are you kidding? How do we requisition one in the middle of the night?" Fausto asked.

"We can't. We'll have to hijack it." Tally put a backpack over her shoulder, and snapped for her board to follow. "In fact, we should get a few. The more of us who go out that way, the better."

"Hijack?" Zane said, checking the rewrapped scarf around his forearm. "You mean steal them?"

"No, we'll ask nicely." She grinned. "Don't forget, Zane, we're the Crims. We're famous. Follow me."

Outside the shop shed, she jumped on board and headed up toward the center of the island, where the tops of the party spires were always surrounded by parasails, hot-air balloons, and fireworks. The other two scrambled to follow. "You pass the word to the rest of the Crims," she shouted to Fausto. "Tell them about the change in plans."

He glanced at Zane for approval, then nodded, relieved that the crusher concept had been replaced by something less violent. "How many of us do you want to go up with?"

"Nine or ten," she said. "Anyone who's not afraid of

heights—the rest can go by hoverboard, as planned. We'll be ready in twenty minutes. Meet us in the center of town."

"I'll be there," Fausto said, and angled away into the night sky.

Tally turned to Zane. "You okay?"

He nodded, slowly flexing the fingers of his gloved hand. "I'll be fine. It's just taking me a second to switch gears."

She brought her board closer to Zane's, taking his bare hand. "It was brave, what you wanted to do."

He shook his head. "I guess it was stupid."

"Yeah, maybe. But if we hadn't gone to the shop, I wouldn't have thought of this."

He smiled. "I'm pretty glad you did, to tell you the truth." His hand flexed nervously again. Then he pointed ahead of them. "There's a couple."

She followed his gaze to the center of the island, where a pair of hot-air balloons floated like big bald heads above a party spire, the tethers that kept them in place catching the trembling light of safety fireworks.

"Perfect," she said.

"One problem," Zane said. "How do we get that high on hoverboards?"

She thought for a moment. "Very carefully."

They climbed higher than she ever had, rising slowly alongside the party spire, close enough to reach out and touch its concrete wall. The metal inside the building provided barely enough push for the boards' lifters, and Tally felt a nervous-making tremble under her feet, like standing at the end of the highest diving board as a littlie. After a slow minute, they reached the spot where one of the balloons was tethered to the tower. Tally touched the tether with her bare hand, feeling its rain-slick links. "No problem. It's metal."

"Yeah, but is it enough metal?" Zane asked.

Tally shrugged.

He rolled his eyes. "And you thought my plan was risky. Okay, I'll take the stupid-looking one." He slid around the tower's girth to where the other balloon bobbed in the breeze. Tally grinned, seeing that it was shaped like a giant pig's head, with protruding ears and two big eyes painted on the pink nylon of its envelope.

At least her own balloon was a normal color: silvery and reflective, with a blue stripe around its equator. From up in the gondola she heard the unmistakable sound of a champagne cork popping, then laughter. It wasn't far away, but getting up was going to be tricky.

Her eyes followed the length of the tether, which drooped down before curving up to where it was attached to the gondola's bottom. The sinuous line reminded her of the roller coaster out in the Rusty Ruins. Of course, the roller coaster had a lot more metal in it, almost as if it had been designed for hoverboarding. This slender length of chain would provide slim pickings for her board's magnetic lifters.

And, unlike the roller coaster, the tether was in constant motion; the balloon was drifting slowly downward as the air in its envelope cooled, but Tally knew it would suddenly jump up and pull the tether taut if the burner was ignited. Worse, the Hot-airs might get bored of hovering around and decide to go for a night ride, releasing the tether and leaving nothing between Tally and the ground.

Zane was right: This wasn't the easiest way to get hold of a balloon, but there was no time to requisition one properly, or wait for the Hot-airs in the gondola to get bored and decide to land. If they were going to make it to the Rusty Ruins before dawn, the escape had to start soon. Maybe someone would find Shay while this new plan was unfolding.

Tally crept farther up the spire wall, rising until the tether ring was just under the center of her board. She nudged herself away from the party spire, drifting out over open space, balancing her hoverboard across the tether like a tightrope walker on a plank of wood.

She moved slowly forward, the lifters straining and trembling, their invisible magnetic fingers pushing down the chain. Once or twice, the board actually scraped the links, sending a shudder through Tally. She saw the balloon dip a little as her weight disrupted the delicate balance between hot air and gravity.

Tally descended until she reached the halfway point, then began to climb toward the balloon. Her board trembled harder as it left the party spire behind, until she was certain the lifters were about to fail, dumping her into a fifty-meter fall. From this height, crash bracelets were much worse than a bungee jacket—being jerked to a halt by her wrists would probably dislocate a shoulder.

Of course, that was nothing compared to what the crusher might have done.

But the lifters didn't fail; the board continued to rise, climbing up toward the gondola of the balloon. She heard a few shouts from the party spire's balcony behind her, and knew she and Zane had been spotted. What sort of bubbly new game was this?

A face appeared over the edge of the gondola, looking down with a surprised expression.

"Hey, look! Someone's coming!"

"What? How?"

The other three pretties in the balloon crowded onto

the near side to peer down at her, their shifting weight making the tether wobble. Tally swore as her board swayed perilously under her feet.

"Stay still up there!" she shouted. "And don't pull the burn chain!" Her barked commands were met by surprised silence, but at least they stopped moving around.

A minute later, Tally's shuddering board had pulled almost to within reach of the gondola. She bent her knees and jumped, in free fall for a sickening moment before her hands grasped the wicker rail. Hands reached down to help pull her up, and soon Tally was inside, facing four wide-eyed Hot-airs. Relieved of her weight, her board followed her up, and she pulled it in.

"Whoa! How'd you do that?"

"I didn't know hoverboards could come this high!"

"Hey, you're Tally Youngblood!"

"Who else?" She grinned and leaned over the side. The ground was coming closer, her weight and the board's tugging the balloon earthward. "Now, I hope you don't mind landing this thing. Me and my friends need to go for a little ride."

By the time the balloon was settling on the lawn in front of Garbo Mansion, a pack of Crims on hoverboards had arrived, Fausto at their head. Tally saw the pink-eared shape of Zane's balloon coming to rest nearby, bouncing slowly to a halt.

"Don't get out yet!" she told the hijacked Hot-airs. "We don't want this thing to shoot up into the air empty." They waited while Peris and Fausto cruised over and climbed into the gondola.

"How many will it hold, Tally?" Fausto said.

The gondola was made of wicker. She ran her hand

across the woven cane, which was still the perfect substance if you wanted something strong, light, and flexible. "Let's take four in each."

"So what are you guys doing?" one of the Hot-airs got up enough nerve to ask.

"Wait and see," Tally said. "And when they interview you for the feeds, feel free to tell them all about it."

The four of them stared at her with widened eyes, realizing that they were going to be famous.

"But keep quiet for the next hour or so. Otherwise, our little trick won't work, and it won't be as bubbly a story."

They nodded obediently.

"How do you release the tether?" Tally asked, realizing that for all her plans to do so, she'd never been up in a balloon.

"Pull this cord to cut loose," one of the Hot-airs answered. "And push this button when you want a hovercar to come get you."

Tally smiled. That was one feature they wouldn't be needing.

Seeing her expression, one of the Hot-airs said, "Hey, you guys are going somewhere really far, aren't you?"

Tally paused for a moment, knowing that what she said would wind up on the feeds, and then be repeated down through generations of uglies and new pretties. It was worth the risk to tell the truth, she decided. These four wouldn't want to short-circuit their brush with criminal fame, so they wouldn't be talking to the authorities until it was way too late.

"We're going to the New Smoke," she said in a slow, clear voice. They stared at her with disbelief.

Chew on that, Dr. Cable! she thought happily.

The gondola shook, and Tally turned to find that Zane had jumped in. "Mind if I join you? There's four in my balloon," he said. "And we've got another bunch taking over one more."

"The rest are set to go out on our signal," Fausto said.

Tally nodded. As long as she and Zane escaped by balloon, it didn't matter how the others went. She looked up at the burner hanging over their heads, purring like an idling jet engine, waiting to heat the air in the envelope again. Tally just hoped it was powerful enough to expand the cuffs wider than their wrists, or at least destroy the transmitters in them.

She pulled the fire-resistant gloves from her pocket and handed a pair to Zane.

"Much better plan, Tally," he said, looking at the idling burner. "A furnace that can fly. We'll be at the edge of the city by the time we're free."

She smiled at him, then said to the Hot-airs, "Okay, guys. You can get out now. Thanks for all your help, and remember not to mention this to anyone for at least an hour."

They nodded and jumped out of the gondola one by one, retreating a few meters to give it room as it gained buoyancy, bobbing impatiently in the breeze.

"Ready?" she called to the pig-faced balloon. The Crims inside gave the thumbs-up. A third balloon was coming down not far away; they would be headed up soon. The more rogue balloons, the better. If they all left their interface rings in the gondolas when they jumped, the wardens would have a busy night.

"We're all set," Zane said softly. "Let's go."

Tally's eyes swept the horizon—taking in Garbo Mansion, the party spires, the lights of New Pretty Town—the world she had looked forward to her whole ugly life. She wondered if she would ever see the city again.

Of course, Tally had to return, if Shay still hadn't gotten

the word. Her cutting was really just a struggle to be cured. There was no way Tally could leave her behind for good, whether Shay hated her or not.

"Okay, let's go," she said, then whispered, "Sorry, Shay. I'll come back for you."

She reached up and pulled the ascent chain. The burner burst into a full-throated roar, blistering heat washing over them, the envelope beginning to swell overhead. The balloon began to rise.

"Whoa!" Peris cried. "We are out of here!"

Fausto let out a whoop and pulled the release cord, the gondola bucking as the tether's weight fell away.

Tally locked eyes with Zane. They were rising fast now, passing the top of the party spire, a dozen pretties on its balcony drunkenly hailing them.

"I'm really leaving," Zane said softly. "Finally."

She grinned. There would be no backing out for Zane this time. She wouldn't let him.

The balloon quickly left the party spire below, rising higher than any building in New Pretty Town. Tally could see the silver band of river all around them, the darkness of Uglyville, and the dull lights of the burbs in every direction. Soon they would be high enough to glimpse the sea.

She released the ascent chain, silencing the burner. They didn't want to get too high. The balloons weren't fast enough to escape the wardens' hovercars; they would need their boards for that. Soon, they would have to jump, free-falling until their hoverboards could pick up the city's magnetic grid and catch them.

Not as simple as falling with a bungee jacket, but not too dangerous, she hoped. Looking down, Tally shook her head and sighed. Sometimes it felt like her life was a series of falls from ever-greater heights.

Tally could see that the wind was carrying them quickly now, pushing the balloon away from the sea, though, strangely, the air felt motionless around them. Of course, Tally realized, the balloon was moving along with the air currents, as if she were perfectly still, and the world sliding along beneath her.

The Rusty Ruins were slipping away behind them, but there were lots of rivers around the city, their beds filled with mineral deposits that could support a hoverboard. The Crims had planned on heading out in lots of directions—everyone knew how to get back to the ruins no matter where the wind took them.

Tally dropped her winter coat, crash bracelets, and gloves to the gondola's floor. Warmth still radiated from the glowing burner, so she didn't feel too cold. She pulled on her heat-resistant gloves, sliding the left one underneath the interface cuff, pulling it up past her elbow and almost to her armpit. Across from her, Zane was also getting ready.

Now to bring their cuffs within reach of the flame.

She looked up. The burner was held to the gondola by a frame with eight arms, stretching over them like a giant metal spider. She put one foot on the railing and held tightly to the burner frame, pulling herself up. From this precarious perch, Tally glanced down at the city passing below, hoping the balloon wasn't going to start rocking in some sudden wind.

She took a deep breath. "Fausto, the signal."

He nodded and lit his Roman candle, which began to hiss and to spit out green and purple flares. Tally watched the signal repeated by nearby Crims, and then spread across the island in a series of colored plumes. They were committed now.

"Okay, Zane," she said. "Let's get these things off."

# BURNER

The four nozzles of the burner were barely a meter from her face, still glowing, radiating heat into the cold night air. Tally reached out and tapped one gingerly. The woman in the shop had been telling the truth. Tally could feel the burner's ridges through the heat-resistant fabric, her fingertips sensing a few stray bumps where it had been welded together. But she had no sense of temperature at all; the burner wasn't hot, or cold . . . nothing. The feeling was uncanny, as if her hand were immersed in body-temperature water.

She looked across at Zane, who had pulled himself up on the other side of the burner. "These things really work, Zane. I can't feel a thing."

He looked at his own gloved left hand, unconvinced. "Two thousand degrees, you said?"

"That's right." As long as you believed every statistic tossed off by a middle-pretty artist blowing glass in the middle of the night. "I'll go first," she offered.

"No way. We'll do it together."

"Don't be dramatic." Tally looked down at Fausto, whose face was as pale as when Zane's hand had been in the crusher. "Give the burner cord a little tug, as short as you can, on my signal."

"Hang on!" Peris said. "What are you guys doing?"

Tally realized that no one had brought Peris up to speed on the plan. He stared at her with a look of total confusion. Well, there wasn't time for explanations now. "Don't worry, we have gloves on," she said, and placed her left hand on the burner.

"Gloves?" Peris said.

"Yeah . . . special gloves. Hit it, Fausto!" Tally cried.

A wave of heat struck, the pure blue flame of the burner blindingly bright. Tally slammed her eyes shut, the inferno like a desert wind on the skin of her face. She ducked her head below the burner frame, and heard the cry of horrified surprise that escaped from Peris's lips.

A half-second later, the burner stopped.

Tally opened her eyes, yellow afterimages of the flame crowding her vision. But she saw her fingers flexing in front of her, still whole.

"My hand didn't feel a thing!" she shouted. She blinked away the dancing yellow spots, and saw that the metal of her cuff was glowing a bit. It didn't look any bigger, though.

"What are you doing?" Peris shouted. Fausto shushed him.

"All right," Zane said, thrusting his hand out over the burner. "Let's do it fast. They must know we're up to something by now."

Tally nodded—the cuff had to have felt the scorching burst of flame. Like the locket Dr. Cable had given Tally before her trip to the Smoke, it probably was designed to send some kind of signal if damaged. She took a deep breath of the cold night air, placing her hand over the burner again and ducking her head. "Okay, Fausto. Burn it until I say stop!"

Another wash of blistering heat poured over Tally. Peris stared up at her, his terrified expression turned demonic by the intense fire, and she had to look away from him. Above them, the envelope began to swell, and the balloon was tugged upward by its load of superheated air. The gondola swayed, testing Tally's grip on the burner frame.

Her left shoulder, covered only by her T-shirt, was taking the worst of the inferno. Past the glove's protection, her skin itched like a bad sunburn. Sweat trickled down her back in the relentless heat.

Weirdly, the parts of Tally that felt the furnace the least were her gloved hands, even her left, sitting in the inferno's very center. She imagined the cuff hidden within that blaze, turning red, then white . . . gradually expanding.

After what seemed like a solid minute, she yelled, "Okay, hold it!"

The burner stopped, and the air was instantly cool around her, the night suddenly black. Tally stood up from her crouch, feet still on the gondola's railing, and blinked, amazed at how still and silent it was with the raging flame extinguished.

She pulled her hand from the burner, expecting it to be a blackened stump, no matter what her nerve endings told her. But all five fingers wiggled in front of her. The cuff glowed blazing white, mesmerizing blue flickers traveling around its edge. The smell of molten metal struck her nose.

"Quick, Tally!" Zane yelled, jumping down into the gondola. He started tugging at his cuff. "Before they cool off."

She leaped down from the rail and started pulling—glad that she had brought two gloves for each of them. The cuff slid down her arm, but came to a halt as it always did, catching at the usual spot. She squinted at the glowing band, trying to see if it had grown. It seemed bigger, but maybe the heat-resistant glove was thicker than she'd thought, making up the difference.

Tally squeezed the fingers of her left hand together and tugged again; the cuff crept another centimeter along. Heat still radiated from the ring of metal, but it was gradually turning a dull red, its light fading. . . . As it cooled, would it shrink around her hand now, crushing her wrist?

She gritted her teeth and pulled once more, as hard as

she could . . . and the cuff slipped off, dropping onto the floor of the gondola like a glowing coal.

"Yes!" Finally, she was free.

Tally looked up at the others. Zane was still struggling; Fausto and Peris were scrambling to avoid her glowing cuff as it rolled, steaming and hissing, across the gondola floor. "I did it," she said softly. "It's off."

"Well, mine's not," Zane grunted. His cuff was wedged around the thick of his wrist, its glow faded to a dull red. He swore and stepped back up onto the gondola's railing. "Hit it again."

Fausto nodded, and gave another long blast on the burner.

Tally turned away from the heat, looking down at the city, trying to clear the spots from her eyes. They were past the greenbelt now, over the burbs. She could see the factory belt coming up, dotted with industrial orange work lights, and past that the absolute blackness that marked the edge of the city.

They had to jump soon. In a few more minutes they would pass beyond the metal grid that underlay the city. Without the grid, their hoverboards wouldn't fly or even stop a fall, and they'd be forced to crash-land the balloon instead of bailing out.

She looked up at the swollen envelope, wondering how long it would take the still rising balloon to settle back to earth. Maybe if they could rip the envelope open somehow to get themselves down faster . . . but how hard would a torn balloon crash-land? And without working hoverboards, the four of them would have to hike until they reached a river, giving the wardens plenty of time to find the crumpled balloon and track them down.

"Come on, Zane!" Tally said. "We've got to hurry!"

"I'm hurrying! Okay?"

"What's that smell?" Fausto said.

"What?" Tally pulled back into the gondola, sniffing at the still, hot air.

Something was burning.

## THE CITY'S EDGE

"It's us!" Fausto shouted. He jumped back, releasing the burner chain, staring down at the gondola floor.

Tally smelled it then: burning cane, like the smell of brush thrown onto a campfire. Somewhere under their feet, her red-hot cuff had ignited the wicker gondola.

She glanced up at Zane still perched on the railing—he ignored the others' panicked cries, tugging fiercely at his glowing cuff. Peris and Fausto were hopping around, trying to find the source of the smell.

"Relax!" she said. "We can always jump!"

"I can't! Not yet," Zane shouted, still struggling with the cuff. Peris looked as if he was about to leap out of the balloon without bothering to take his hoverboard.

Her vision was finally clearing from burner's glare, and Tally looked down at her feet. A bottle lay there, left behind by the Hot-airs. She reached for it with her gloved hands; it was full.

"Hold on, you guys," she said, and with a practiced motion twisted off the foil and placed both thumbs beneath the cork. She popped it, watching the cork soar into the dark void. "Everything's under control."

Froth bubbled out, and Tally put one thumb over the

bottle's mouth. Shaking the bottle, she sprayed champagne across the floor of the gondola. An angry sizzle came from the smoldering flames.

"Got it!" Zane cried at that moment. His cuff fell off and rolled under her feet, and Tally calmly emptied the rest of the bottle onto it. The smell of molten metal rose up around her, tinged with an oddly sweet smell: boiled champagne.

Zane was staring with amazement at his freed left hand. He pulled off the heat-resistant gloves and tossed them overboard. "It worked!" he said, and swept Tally into a hug.

She laughed, letting the bottle drop to the floor and pulling off her own gloves. "Time for that later. Let's get out of here."

"Okay." He balanced his board on the gondola's railing, looking down. "Damn, that's a long fall."

Fausto tugged at a dangling cord. "I'll vent some hot air—maybe we can get a little lower."

"No time," Tally cried. "We're almost at the end of town. If we get separated, meet at the tallest building in the ruins. And remember: Don't let go of your board on the way down!"

They all scrambled to put on their backpacks, bumping into one another in the small space, Zane and Tally struggling back into their winter coats and crash bracelets. Fausto pulled off his interface ring and threw it to the gondola floor, grabbed his board, and jumped out with a whoop. The balloon pitched upward as his weight left it behind.

When Zane was ready, he turned and kissed her. "We did it, Tally. We're free!"

She looked into his eyes, dizzy with the thought that they were finally here, at the edge of the city, at the beginning of freedom. "Yeah. We made it."

"See you down there." He looked over his shoulder at the distant earth, then turned back to her. "I love you."

"I'll see you down . . . ," she began, but the words sputtered out. It took a moment to replay in her mind what Zane had said. Finally she managed, "Oh. Me too."

He laughed, then let out a wordless cry as he tumbled over the rail, the gondola bucking again under its two remaining passengers.

Tally blinked, dazzled for a moment by Zane's unexpected words. But she shook her head to clear it. This was no time to get pretty-headed; she had to jump now.

She pulled the straps of her backpack tight, wrestling her hoverboard up onto the rail. "Hurry up!" she shouted at Peris.

He was just standing there, staring over the side.

"What are you waiting for?" she cried.

He shook his head. "I can't."

"You can do it. Your board will stop your fall—all you have to do is hang on!" she shouted. "Just jump! Gravity does the rest!"

"It's not the fall, Tally," Peris said. He turned to face her. "I don't want to leave."

"What?"

"I don't want to leave the city."

"But this is what we've been waiting for!"

"Not me." He shrugged. "I liked being a Crim, and being bubbly. But I never thought we'd get this far. I mean, like, leaving home forever?"

"Peris . . ."

"I know you've been out there before, you and Shay. And Zane and Fausto always talked about escaping. But I'm not like you guys."

"But you and me, we're . . ." Tally's voice caught. She

was about to say "best friends forever," but the old words wouldn't come anymore. Peris had never been to the Smoke, had never tangled with Special Circumstances, had never even been in trouble. Everything had always gone smoothly for him. Their lives had been so different for so long.

"You're sure you want to stay?"

He nodded slowly. "I'm sure. But I can still help. I'll keep them busy for you. I'll stay airborne as long as I can, then push the pickup button. They'll have to come out and get me."

Tally started to argue, but she couldn't help remembering sneaking across the river right after Peris's operation, visiting him in Garbo Mansion. He had adjusted so quickly, loving New Pretty Town right from the beginning. Maybe the whole Crim thing had just been a joke to him. . . .

But she couldn't leave him here in the city alone. "Peris, think. Without us around, you won't be bubbly anymore. You'll go back to being a pretty-head."

He smiled sadly. "I don't mind, Tally. I don't need to be bubbly."

"You don't? But don't you feel how much . . . better it is?"

He shrugged. "It's exciting. But you can't keep fighting the way things are forever. At some point, you have to . . ."

"Give up?"

Peris nodded, the smile still on his face, as if giving up wasn't really that bad, as if fighting was only worthwhile as long as it was amusing.

"Okay. Stay, then." She turned away, not trusting herself to say anything more. But when Tally looked down, all she saw was darkness. "Oh, crap," she said softly.

The city had run out. It was too late to jump.

*

Side by side, they stared into the darkness, the wind carrying them farther and farther away.

Peris finally broke the silence. "We'll come down eventually, right?"

"Not soon enough." She sighed. "The wardens probably already know that our cuffs are fried. They'll come looking for us soon. We're sitting ducks up here."

"Oh. I really didn't mean to screw things up for you."

"It's not your fault. I waited too long." Tally swallowed, wondering if Zane would ever find out what happened. Would he think she'd fallen to her death? Or would he guess that she'd chickened out, like Peris?

Whatever he thought, Tally saw their future fading out, disappearing like the distant lights of the city behind them. Who knew what Special Circumstances would do to her brain when they caught her again?

She looked at Peris. "I really thought you wanted to come."

"Listen, Tally. I just got caught up in everything. Being a Crim was exciting and you were my friends, my clique. What was I supposed to do? Argue against running away? Arguing's bogus."

She shook her head. "I thought you were bubbly, Peris."

"I am, Tally. But tonight is about as bubbly as I want to get. I like breaking the rules, but living out there?" He waved his hand at the wild below them, a cold, unfriendly sea of darkness.

"Why didn't you tell me before now?"

"I don't know. I guess it wasn't until we got up here that I realized you guys were so serious about . . . never coming back."

Tally closed her eyes, remembering what having a pretty mind was like—everything vague and fuzzy, the world nothing but a source of entertainment, the future nothing but a blur. A few tricks weren't enough to make everyone bubbly, she supposed; you had to want your mind to change. Maybe some people had always been pretty-heads, even back before the operation had been invented.

Maybe some people were happier being that way.

"But now you can stay with me," he said, putting his arm around her. "It'll be like it was supposed to be. You and me pretty—best friends forever."

Tally shook her head, a sickening feeling sweeping over her. "I am not staying, Peris. Even if they take me back tonight, I'll find a way to escape."

"Why are you so unhappy there?"

She sighed, looking out over the darkness. Zane and Fausto would already be headed toward the ruins, thinking she wasn't far behind. How had she let this opportunity slip away? The city always seemed to claim her in the end. Was she really like Peris, somewhere deep inside?

"Why am I unhappy?" Tally repeated softly. "Because the city makes you the way they want you to be, Peris. And I want to be myself. That's why."

He squeezed her shoulder and gave her a sad look. "But people are better now than they used to be. Maybe they have good reasons for changing us, Tally."

"Their reasons don't mean anything unless I have a choice, Peris. And they don't give anyone a choice." Tally shook his hand from her shoulder, staring back at the distant city. A set of winking lights was rising into the air, a fleet of hovercars gathering. She remembered that the Specials' cars were held aloft by spinning blades, like the Rusties' ancient helicopters, so they could fly beyond the grid. They must be headed this way, pursuing the final signals of the cuffs.

She had to get out of this balloon now.

Before he'd jumped, Fausto had tied off the descent cord, and hot air was spilling from the envelope every moment. But the balloon, superheated as they'd burned off the cuffs, was losing altitude so slowly . . . the ground hardly looked any closer.

Then Tally saw the river.

It stretched out below them, catching moonlight like a silver snake, winding out of the ore-rich mountains to make its way toward the sea. On its bed would be centuries' worth of metal deposits, enough to make her hoverboard fly. Maybe enough to catch her fall.

Maybe she could get her future back.

She pulled her board back up onto the rail. "I'm going."

"But, Tally. You can't—"

"The river."

Peris looked down, his eyes wide. "It looks so small. What if you miss?"

"I won't." She gritted her teeth. "You've seen those formation bungee jumpers, haven't you? They've only got their arms and legs to guide themselves down. I've got a whole hoverboard. It'll be like having wings!"

"You're crazy!"

"I'm leaving." She kissed Peris quickly, then threw one leg over the rail.

"Tally!" He grabbed her hand. "You could die! I don't want to lose you. . . ."

She shook him off violently, and Peris took a fearful step back. Pretties didn't like conflict. Pretties didn't take risks. Pretties didn't say no.

Tally was no longer pretty. "You already have," she said.

And, clutching her hoverboard, she threw herself into the void.

# Part III

## OUTSIDE

The beauty of the world . . . has two edges, one of laughter, one of anguish, cutting the heart asunder.
—Virginia Woolf, *A Room of One's Own*

# DESCENT

Tally dropped into silence, spinning out of control.

After the stillness in the balloon, the rush of passing air built around her with unexpected strength, almost tearing the hoverboard from Tally's hands. She held it tightly to her chest, but the wind's fingers continued to search for purchase, hungry to pry away her only hope of survival. She clasped her hands around the board's underbelly, kicking her legs, trying to control the spinning. Gradually, the dark horizon steadied.

But Tally was upside down, looking up at the stars and hanging from the board. She could see the dark orb of the balloon above. Then its flame ignited, giving the envelope a silvery glow against the darkness, like a huge, dull moon in the sky. She guessed that Peris was headed upward to throw off the pursuit. At least he was trying to help.

His change of heart stung her, but she didn't have time to worry about it, not while plummeting toward the earth.

Tally struggled to turn herself over, but the hoverboard was wider than she was—it caught the air like a sail, threatening to pull itself from her grasp. It was like trying to carry a large kite in a strong wind, except that if she lost control of this particular kite, she'd be splattered all over the ground in about sixty seconds.

Tally tried to relax, letting herself hang there. Something was tugging at her wrist, she realized. Up here in the void, the board's lifters might be useless for flying, but they would still interact with the metal in her crash bracelets.

She adjusted her left bracelet to maximize the connection. Her grip on the board made surer, she straightened out her right arm into the rushing air. It was like riding in her parents' groundcar as a littlie, her hand stuck out a window. Flattening her palm increased the resistance, and Tally found herself slowly beginning to turn over.

A few seconds later, the hoverboard was beneath her.

Tally swallowed at the sight of the earth spread out below, vast and dark and hungry. The rushing cold seemed to cut straight through her coat.

She'd been falling for what felt like forever, but the ground didn't look any closer. There was nothing to give it scale except the winding river, still no bigger than a piece of ribbon. Tally angled her outstretched palm experimentally, and watched the curve of moonlit water turn clockwise beneath her. She pulled her arm in, and the river steadied.

Tally grinned. At least she had some control over her wild descent.

As she fell, the silvery band of river grew in size, first slowly, then faster, the dark horizon of earth expanding like some huge predator advancing toward her, blotting out the starlit sky. Clinging to the hoverboard with both hands, Tally discovered that her outstretched legs could guide her descent, keeping the river directly below her.

And then in the last ten seconds, she began to realize how large the river was, its surface wide and troubled. She saw things moving in it.

It grew, faster and faster. . . .

When the board's lifters kicked in, it was like a door

slamming in her face, flattening her nose and breaking open her lower lip, the taste of blood instantly in her mouth. Her wrists were twisted cruelly by the crash bracelets, and her momentum squashed her against the braking hoverboard, forcing the breath from her lungs like a giant vice. She struggled to pull in a breath.

The hoverboard was slowing rapidly, but the river's surface still grew, stretching farther in all directions like a huge mirror full of starlight, until . . .

Slap!

The board struck the water like the flat of a giant hand, catching Tally's body with another battering jolt, an explosion of light and sound filling her head. And then she was underwater, ears filled with a dull roar. She let go of the board and clawed for the surface, her lungs emptied by the impact. Forcing her eyes open, Tally saw only the faintest glimmer of light filtering down through the murky river. Her arms struggled weakly, and the light grew slowly closer. Finally, she broke into the air, gasping and coughing.

The river raged around her, the swift current kicking up whitecaps in every direction. She dog-paddled hard, the weight of her pack trying to pull her back under. Her lungs sucked in air, and she coughed violently, tasting blood in her mouth.

Turning from side to side, Tally realized that she hit her mark too well—she was in the dead center of the river, fifty meters from either shore. She swore and kept paddling, waiting for a tug on her crash bracelets.

Where was her hoverboard? It should have found her by now.

It had taken so long for the lifters to kick in—Tally had expected to pull up in midair, not hit the river at speed. But after a few moments' thought, she realized what had happened. The river was deeper than she'd anticipated; the minerals on its floor were a long way below her kicking feet. She remembered how hoverboards sometimes got wobbly over the middle of the city river—too far from the mineral deposits for the lifters to work at full strength.

It was lucky the board had slowed her fall at all.

Tally looked around. Too dense to float, the hoverboard had probably sunk to the bottom, the raging current carrying her away from it. She turned up her crash bracelets' calling range to a whole kilometer, and waited for the board's nose to push itself above the surface.

Shapes bobbed along in the water all around her, knobby and irregular, like a flotilla of alligators in the fast-moving current. What were they?

Something nudged her. . . .

She spun around, but it was just an old tree trunk—not an alligator, and not her hoverboard. Tally grabbed on to it gratefully, though, already exhausted from paddling. In every direction were more trees, as well as branches, clots of reeds, masses of rotting leaves. The river was carrying all sorts of cargo on its surface.

The rain, Tally thought. Three days of downpour must have flooded the hills, washing all manner of stray matter down into the river, swelling its size and accelerating its current. The trunk she clung to was old and rotted black, but a few strands of green wood showed from a break. Had the flooding ripped it from the ground alive?

Tally's fingers traced where the tree had broken, and she saw that something unnaturally straight had struck it.

Like the edge of a hoverboard.

A few meters away, another log floated, cut with the same sharp edge. Tally's crash-landing had snapped the old, rotten tree in half. Her face was bleeding from the impact; she could still taste blood. So what damage had been done to the hoverboard?

Tally twisted the call controls of her crash bracelets higher, setting them to burn their batteries down. Every second, the current was carrying her farther from where she'd landed.

No hoverboard rose up above the surface, no tugging came at her wrists. As the minutes passed, Tally began to admit to herself that the board was dead, a piece of junk at the bottom of the river.

She switched her bracelets off and, still clinging to the log, began to kick her way toward shore.

The riverbank was slippery with mud, the ground saturated by the rains and the swollen river. Tally waded to shore in a small inlet, struggling through branches and reeds in the hip-deep water. It seemed the flood had collected everything that floated and dumped it in this one spot.

Including Tally Youngblood.

She stumbled up the bank, desperate to reach dry ground, every instinct impelling her to keep moving away from the rushing water. Her exhausted body felt full of lead, and Tally slid back down the slope, becoming covered with mud. Finally, she gave up and huddled on the muddy ground, shaking in the freezing cold. Tally couldn't remember feeling so tired since becoming a new pretty, as if the river had sucked away her body's vitality.

She took the firestarter from her backpack and, with trembling fingers, gathered a pile of washed-up twigs. But the wood was so wet from three days of rain that the firestarter's tiny flame only made the twigs hiss dully.

At least her coat was still working. She turned its heater

up to full, not worrying about the batteries, and gathered herself into a ball.

Tally waited for sleep to come, but her body wouldn't stop trembling, like a fever coming on back in ugly days. But new pretties almost never got sick, unless she'd run herself too far down this last month—eating almost nothing, staying out in the cold, running on adrenaline and coffee, with hardly an hour in the last twenty-four when she hadn't been soaking wet.

Or was she finally getting the same reaction from the cure as Zane? Was the pill beginning to damage her brain, now that she was beyond any hope of medical care?

Tally's head pounded, fevered thoughts swirling through her. She had no hoverboard, no way of getting to the Rusty Ruins except on foot. No one knew where she was. The world had been emptied of everything but the wild, the freezing cold, and Tally Youngblood. Even the absence of the cuff on her wrist felt strange, like the gap left behind by a missing tooth.

Worst was the absence of Zane's body next to her. She'd stayed with him every night for the last month, and they'd spent most of every day together. Even in their enforced silence, she had grown used to his constant presence, his familiar touch, their wordless conversations. Suddenly he was gone, and Tally felt as if she'd lost some part of herself in the fall.

She had imagined this moment a thousand times, finally reaching the wild, free from the city at last. But never once had she imagined being here without Zane.

And yet here she was, utterly alone.

Tally lay awake a long time, replaying in her mind those last frantic minutes in the balloon. If she'd only jumped sooner, or had thought to look down before the city grid ran out. After what Zane had said, she shouldn't have hesitated, knowing that this escape was their only chance for freedom together.

Once again, things were screwed up, and it was all her fault.

Finally Tally's exhaustion overpowered her worries, and she drifted into troubled sleep.

## ALONE

So, there was this beautiful princess.

She was locked in a high tower, one whose smart walls had clever holes in them that could give her anything: food, a clique of fantastic friends, wonderful clothes. And, best of all, there was this mirror on the wall, so that the princess could look at her beautiful self all day long.

The only problem with the tower was that there was no way out. The builders had forgotten to put in an elevator, or even a set of stairs. She was stuck up there.

One day, the princess realized that she was bored. The view from the tower—gentle hills, fields of white flowers, and a deep, dark forest—fascinated her. She started spending more time looking out the window than at her own reflection, as is often the case with troublesome girls.

And it was pretty clear that no prince was showing up, or at least that he was really late.

So the only thing was to jump.

The hole in the wall gave her a lovely parasol to catch her when she fell, and a wonderful new dress to wear in the fields and forest, and a brass key to make sure she could get back into the tower if she needed to. But the princess, laughing pridefully, tossed the key into the fireplace, convinced she would never need to return to the tower. Without another glance in the mirror, she strolled out onto the balcony and stepped off into midair.

The thing was, it was a long way down, a lot farther than the princess had expected, and the parasol turned out to be total crap. As she fell, the princess realized she should have asked for a bungee jacket or a parachute or something better than a parasol, you know?

She struck the ground hard, and lay there in a crumpled heap, smarting and confused, wondering how things had worked out this way. There was no prince around to pick her up, her new dress was ruined, and thanks to her pride, she had no way back into the tower.

And the worst thing was, there were no mirrors out there in the wild, so the princess was left wondering whether she in fact was still beautiful . . . or if the fall had changed the story completely.

When Tally awoke from this bogus dream, the sun was halfway across the sky.

She struggled to her feet, having to pry herself from the sucking embrace of the mud. At some point during the night, her winter coat had run out of charge. Without batteries, it was a cold thing clinging to her skin, still damp from her soaking in the river, and it smelled funny. Tally unstuck the coat from herself and laid it across the broad surface of a rock, hoping that the sun would dry it out.

For the first time in days the sky was cloudless. But in clearing, the air had turned crisp and cold—the warmer weather that had arrived with the rain had departed with it as well. The trees glittered with frost, and the mud under her feet sparkled, its thin layer of rime crackling underfoot.

Her fever had passed, but Tally felt dizzy standing, so she knelt beside her backpack to look through its contents—the sum of everything she possessed. Fausto had managed to gather up some of the usual Smokey survival gear: a knife, water filter, position-finder, firestarter, and some safety sparklers, along with a few dozen packets of soap. Remembering how valuable dehydrated food had been in the Smoke, Tally had packed three months' worth, which was all wrapped up in waterproof plastic, fortunately. When Tally saw the two rolls of toilet paper she'd brought, however, she let out a groan. They were soaked through, reduced to bloated, squishy blobs of white. She placed them on the rocks next to her jacket, but doubted that it was even worth drying them out.

She sighed. Even back in her Smokey days, she'd never gotten used to the leaf thing.

Tally found her pitiful pile of twigs, and remembered trying to light a fire the night before, too delirious to realize how stupid that would have been. The Special Circumstances hovercars that had come after the balloon would have easily spotted a fire in the darkness.

There was no evidence of pursuit in the sky this morning, but Tally decided to put some distance between herself and the river. Without a working heater in her jacket, she would need to build a fire that night.

But first things first, which meant food.

She trudged down to the river to fill the purifier, dried mud crumbling from her skin and clothing with every step. Tally had never been so dirty in her life, but she wasn't up to bathing in the freezing water, not without a fire to warm her up afterward. Last night's fever might have passed, thanks to her new-pretty immune system kicking in, but she didn't want to take any risks with her health out here.

Of course, Tally realized, it wasn't her own health she should be worrying about. Zane was somewhere out here too, maybe just as alone as she was. He and Fausto had jumped almost at the same moment, but they might have landed kilometers apart. If Zane had one of his attacks on the way to the ruins, with no one to help him . . . .

Tally shook the thought from her head. All she could do right now for Zane or anyone else was get to the ruins herself. And that meant making food, not worrying about things she couldn't control.

The purifier took two fillings before it had strained enough pure water from the silty inlet to make a meal. She chose a packet of PadThai and set the purifier to boil; the smell of reconstituting noodles and spices soon rose from the gurgling water.

By the time the meal pinged that it was ready, Tally was ravenous.

As she reached the end of the PadThai, she realized there was no longer any point in going hungry, and immediately boiled up a packet of CurryNoods. Starvation might have been useful for getting off the cuffs and staying bubbly, but her cuff was gone, and Tally now had the whole of the wild, dangerous and cold, to keep her bubbly. Not much chance of sinking into a pretty haze out here.

After breakfast, the position-finder offered up its bad news. Tally had to check her calculations twice before she believed the distance she'd traveled the night before. The winds from off the ocean had pushed the balloon a long way east, in the opposite direction from the Rusty Ruins, and then the river's current had carried her another long distance southward. She was more than a week's journey by foot to the ruins, if she went in a straight line. And straight lines wouldn't come into it: She had to go the long way around the city, staying in the forest to hide herself from searchers in the air.

Tally wondered how long the Specials would bother to keep looking for her. Luckily, they didn't know that her hoverboard had disappeared into the river, so they would assume she was flying, not trudging along on foot. As far as they knew, Tally would have to stay near the river or some other natural vein of mineral deposits.

The sooner she got away from the riverbank, the better.

Tally packed up her pitiful camp unhappily. Her backpack held more than enough food for the journey, and the hills would be full of ready water after the long rains, but she felt defeated already. From what Sussy and Dex had said, the New Smokies hadn't set up a permanent camp in the ruins. They might leave any day now, and she was a week away.

Her only hope was that Zane and Fausto would stay behind, waiting for her to show up. Unless they thought that she had been captured, or killed by the fall, or had simply chickened out.

No, she told herself, Zane wouldn't think that last one of her. He might be worried, but Tally knew that he would wait for her, however long it took.

She sighed as she tied the still-damp coat around her waist and hoisted her backpack onto her shoulders. There was no point wondering about where the others were; her only choice was to hike toward the ruins and trust that someone would be waiting when she arrived.

Tally had nowhere else to go.

The way through the forest was rugged, every step a battle. Back in the Smoke, Tally had mostly traveled by hoverboard. When she had been forced to hike cross-country, it had been on paths hacked through the trees. But this was nature in the raw, hostile and unrelenting. The dense undergrowth tugged at her feet, trying to trip her, throwing up thick bushes and ankle-twisting roots and impenetrable walls of thorn.

Among the trees, the downpour still echoed. Pine needles sparkled with frost, which the day's heat was slowly changing to water, generating a constant rain of chill, sparkling mist. It was like a magnificent ice palace, with spears of sunlight shooting between the trees, visible in the mist like lasers through smoke. But every time Tally dared disturb a branch, it unloaded its freight of freezing water onto her head.

She remembered traveling to the Smoke through the ancient forest that had been devastated by the Rusties' biologically engineered weeds. At least walking through that flattened landscape had been easier than this dense growth. Sometimes, you could almost see why the Rusties had tried so hard to destroy nature.

Nature could be a pain.

As she walked, the struggle between the forest and Tally began to feel more and more personal. The grasping brambles seemed almost conscious of her, corralling Tally the way they wanted her to go, no matter what her direction-finder said. The dense undergrowth would split open welcomingly, offering easy paths that wound pointlessly off her course. Hiking in a straight line was impossible. This was nature, not some Rusty superhighway cutting through mountains and across deserts without any regard for the terrain.

But as the afternoon progressed, Tally slowly became convinced that she was following an actual path, like the nature trails that the pre-Rusties had used a millennium before.

She remembered what David had told her out in the Smoke, that most of the pre-Rusty trails had originally been made by animals. Even deer, wolves, and wild dogs didn't want to fight their way through virgin growth. Just like people, animals stuck to the same paths for generation after generation, forging tracks through the forest.

Of course, Tally had always imagined that animal trails were something that only David could see. Having grown up in the wild, he was practically a pre-Rusty himself. But as the shadows lengthened around her, Tally found her path becoming easier and straighter, as if she had stumbled onto some uncanny fissure in the wild.

A gnawing feeling started in her stomach. The random sounds of dripping trees began to play with her mind, and Tally's nerves began to twitch, as if she was being watched.

It was probably just her perfect new-pretty eyesight helping her spot the subtle marks of animal passage. She must have picked up more skills than she knew out in the Smoke. This was an animal path. Certainly, no people could live out here. Not this close to the city, where they would have been detected by the Specials decades ago. Even out in the Smoke, no one knew of any other communities living outside the cities. Humanity had decided two centuries ago to leave nature alone.

Alone, Tally kept reminding herself. No one else was out here. Though, oddly, she couldn't decide whether being the only person in the forest made it feel less creepy, or more.

Finally, as the sky was fading to pink, Tally decided to come to a halt. She found an open clearing where the sun had beaten down all day, maybe drying out enough wood for a fire. The brutal hike had raised a sweat—Tally's shirt clung to her, and she'd never once worn her coat—but once the sun set, she knew the air would turn freezing cold again.

Finding dry twigs was easy, and Tally weighed a few small logs in her hand to find the lightest, which would contain the least water. All her Smokey knowledge seemed to have come back, with no scraps of pretty-mindedness remaining after the escape. Now that she was out of the city, the cure had settled over Tally's mind for good.

But she hesitated before putting the firestarter to the pile, paranoia staying her hand. The forest still made its sounds—dripping water, bird cries, the skitterings of small animals among the wet leaves—and it was easy to imagine something watching her from the darkened spaces between the trees.

Tally sighed. Maybe she still was a pretty-head, making up irrational stories about the empty forest. The longer she stayed alone out here, the more Tally understood why the Rusties and their predecessors had believed in invisible beings, praying to placate spirits as they trashed the natural world around them.

Well, Tally didn't believe in spirits. The only things she had to worry about were Specials, and they would be looking along the river, kilometers behind her. Darkness had fallen as she built the fire, and it was already halfway to freezing. She couldn't risk another fever out here in the wild, alone.

The firestarter flicked to life in her hand, and Tally held it to the twigs until a blaze erupted. She nursed the fire along with larger and larger branches until it was strong enough to ignite the lightest of her logs, then banked it with the others to dry them out.

Soon, the blaze was hot enough to push her back on her heels, and Tally felt warmth stealing into her bones for what seemed like the first time in days.

She smiled as she stared into the flames. Nature was tough, it could be dangerous, but unlike Dr. Cable or Shay or Peris—unlike people in general—it made sense. The problems it threw at you could be solved rationally. Get cold, build a fire. Need to get somewhere, walk there. Tally knew she could make it to the ruins, with or without a hoverboard under her. And from there she would eventually find Zane and the New Smoke, and everything would be all right.

Tonight, Tally realized happily, she was going to sleep well. Even without Zane beside her, she had made it through her first day of freedom in the wild, still bubbly and still in one piece.

She lay down, watching the fire's embers pulsing beside her, warm as old friends. After a while, her eyelids began to flicker, then to fall.

Tally was deep in pleasant dreams when the shrieking woke her.

## HUNT

At first, she thought the forest was on fire.

There were flames moving through the trees, casting jittering shadows across the clearing, darting through the air like wild, burning insects. Shrieks rose up from every side, inhuman calls strung with meaningless words.

Tally staggered to her feet and stumbled straight into the remains of her fire. Kicked embers flared to life in all directions. She felt hot needles through the soles of her boots, and almost fell to her hands and knees among the glowing coals. Another shriek came from close by—a high-pitched cry of anger. A human form ran toward her, a torch raised in one hand. The torch hissed and sparked with every step, as if the flame were a living thing impelling its carrier onward.

The figure was swinging something across its path—a long, polished stick, gleaming in the firelight. Tally leaped back just in time, and the weapon whistled through empty air. She rolled backward on the ground, feeling the sting of the scattered embers in the middle of her back. Jumping to her feet, she spun away, dashing toward the trees. Another figure blocked her path, also brandishing a club.

His face was obscured by a beard, but even in the jittering torchlight Tally could see that he was an ugly—fat and with a bloated nose, the pale skin of his forehead pocked with disease. He had ugly reflexes, too: The swing of the club was slow and predictable. Tally rolled under the flailing weapon, lashing out with her feet to take his knees out from under him.

By the time she heard the thump of his body hitting the earth, Tally was up and running again, slashing through branches, angling toward the darkest part of the forest.

Another chorus of shrieks rose up behind her, the pursuers' torches casting flickering shadows onto the trees ahead. Tally crashed through the undergrowth almost blind, half-falling as she ran, wet branches whipping her face. A vine grasped her ankle, jerking Tally off-balance and throwing her to the ground. She stretched out both hands to catch herself, and felt one wrist bend too far backward with a wrenching burst of pain.

She cradled the injured hand for a moment, glancing back at the ugly hunters. They weren't as fast as Tally, but they ducked and weaved through the forest skillfully, knowing the way through the trees even in darkness. The hovering lights of their torches flowed into place around where Tally lay, the racket from their reedy cries surrounding her once more.

But what were they? They looked small in stature, and they yelled back and forth in some language she didn't recognize. Like pre-Rusty ghosts risen from the grave . . .

Whatever they were, there wasn't time to ponder the question. Tally rose to her feet and made another dash for the darkness, aiming for the gap between two torches.

The two hunters closed on her as she approached: bearded men, their ugly faces marked with scars and sores. Tally crashed between them, close enough to feel the heat of the torches. A wildly swung club caught her shoulder with a glancing blow, but Tally managed to keep her feet, and found herself stumbling down a hill into blackness.

The two cried out as they followed her, and more shrieks came from up ahead. How many of them were there? They seemed to be rising up from the ground itself.

Suddenly, her feet splashed into cold water, and Tally found herself slipping, falling into a shallow creek. Behind, her two closest pursuers tumbled down the slope, their torches spitting out sparks as they bumped trees and branches. It was a wonder the whole forest wasn't aflame.

Tally got to her feet and dashed down the streambed, thankful for the route it cut through the undergrowth. She stumbled on the slick, rocky bottom, but found herself outpacing the burning eyes that darted along either bank. If she could only reach some sort of open ground, Tally knew that she could outrun the smaller, slower uglies.

The sound of splashing feet came from behind her, and then a grunt and a stream of curses in their unknown tongue. One of them had fallen. Maybe she was going to make it.

Of course, her food and water purifier were in her backpack in the clearing, back among the shrieking, club-wielding uglies. Lost.

She forced the thought from her mind and kept running. Her wrist still throbbed from the fall, and she wondered if it was broken.

A loud roar rose up before Tally, the stream boiling around her ankles, the ground rumbling. Then suddenly the earth seemed to disappear from under her feet as she ran. . . .

Flailing through the air, Tally realized too late that the roar was behind her now—she'd run straight off the top of a waterfall. Her flight through emptiness lasted only a moment, then she hit water, a deep, churning pool that wrapped its chill around her, sound suddenly reduced to a low rumble in her ears. She felt herself hurtling downward into darkness and silence, slowly turning head over heels.

One shoulder brushed the bottom, and Tally pushed herself upward. She came up gasping, clawing at the water until her fingers found a rocky edge. Clinging to it, she pulled herself up into the shallows, on hands and knees, coughing and trembling.

Caught.

Torches hovered all around her, reflected in the churning water like swarms of fireflies. Tally raised her eyes and found at least a dozen pursuers glowering down from the stream's steep banks, their pale and ugly faces made even more hideous by the torchlight.

A man was standing in the stream in front of her—his fat belly and big nose marking him as the hunter she'd knocked over at the clearing. His bare knee was bleeding where she'd kicked it. He bellowed a wordless cry, raising his crude club high into the air.

Tally stared up at him in disbelief. Was he really going to hit her? Did these people murder total strangers for no reason at all?

But no blow came. As he stared down at her, fear gradually filled the man's expression. He thrust his torch toward her, and Tally shrank back, covering her face. The man sank to one knee before her, taking a closer look. She dropped her hands.

His milky eyes squinted in the torchlight, staring in confusion.

Did he recognize her?

Warily, Tally watched the thoughts racing across his exaggerated features: growing fear and doubt, and then a sudden realization that something terrible had happened . . .

The torch fell from his hand and into the stream, where it was extinguished with a strangled hiss and a puff of foul smoke. The man bellowed once more, this time as if in pain, the same word repeated again and again. He pitched forward, lowering his face almost into the water.

The others followed, dropping to their hands and knees, their torches falling to sputter against the ground. They all set up the same wailing cry, almost drowning out the roar of the waterfall.

Tally rose to her knees, coughing a little and wondering what the hell was going on.

Looking around, she noticed for the first time that all the hunters were men. Their clothes were irregular, far cruder than the Smokies' handmade clothing. They all had unhealthy marks on their faces and arms, and long beards that were matted and tangled. Their hair looked as if they'd never combed it in their lives. They were paler than pretty average, with the sort of freckly, pinkish skin of those occasional littlies born extra sensitive to the sun.

None of them stared back at her. Their faces were buried in their hands or pressed to the ground.

Finally, one of them crawled forward. He was thin and horribly wrinkled, his hair and beard white, and Tally remembered from her time in the Smoke that this was what old uglies looked like. Without the operation, their bodies grew decrepit, like ancient ruins abandoned by their builders. He trembled as he moved, either from fear or ill health, and stared closely at her for what seemed an endless time.

At last he spoke, his wavering voice barely audible above the waterfall. "I know little the gods' tongue."

Tally blinked. "You what?"

"We saw fire and thought outsider. Not a god."

All the others had gone silent, waiting fearfully, ignoring their torches guttering on the ground. Tally saw a bush crackle to life, but the man crouching next to it seemed too paralyzed by fear to move.

So she terrified them all of a sudden? Were these people crazy?

"Never gods use fire before. Please understand." His eyes begged her for forgiveness.

She stood unsteadily. "Um, that's okay. No problem."

The old ugly rose from his crouch so suddenly that Tally stepped backward, almost toppling back into the churning pool. He yelled a single word, and the hunters repeated it. The cry seemed to release them from their spell; they stood up, stamping out the small fires that had sprung up around their dropped torches.

Suddenly, Tally felt outnumbered again. "But, hey," she added, "just no more with the . . . clubs, okay?"

The old man listened, bowed, and yelled out more words in the unknown language. The hunters sprang into action: Some propped their clubs against trees and split them with a kick; others pounded them against the ground until they shattered, or threw the weapons off into the darkness.

The old man turned back to Tally, his hands spread open, clearly waiting for approval. His club lay split in two at her feet. The others raised their free hands, empty and open.

"Yeah," she said. "Much better."

The old man smiled.

And then she saw it, the familiar glimmer in his ancient, milky eyes. The same look Sussy and Dex had given her when they'd first seen her pretty face. The same awe and eagerness to please, the same instinctive fascination—the sure result of a century of cosmetic engineering and a million years of evolution.

Tally looked around at the others, and found all of them shrinking from her gaze. They could barely meet her huge, copper-flecked eyes, almost couldn't stand to face her beauty.

God, he'd said. The old Rusty word for their invisible superheroes in the sky.

This was their world out here—this raw, cruel wilderness with its disease and violence and animal struggle for survival. Like these people, this world was ugly. To be pretty was to be from somewhere beyond.

Out here, Tally was a god.

## YOUNG BLOOD

The hunters' camp took about an hour to reach. With torches extinguished, the party followed pitch-black trails and waded down freezing streams, never uttering a word.

Tally's guides displayed a strange combination of crudity and skill. They were small and slow, a few even disfigured, shuffling along carrying all their weight on one leg. They smelled as if they never bathed, and wore shoes so poor, their feet were scarred. But they knew the forest, moving gracefully through the tangled undergrowth, guiding Tally unerringly through the darkness. The hunters didn't use direction-finders, or even pause to check the stars.

The suspicions that Tally had nursed the day before were proven right. These hills were laced with human-made paths. The trails she'd only half-glimpsed in daylight now seemed to open up magically in the darkness, the old man who led her taking turns and switchbacks without hesitation. The group moved in a single line, making no more noise than a snake among leaves.

The hunters had enemies, it seemed. After their cacophonous attack on Tally, she wouldn't have imagined them capable of stealth or cunning. But now they sent signals up and down the line with clicking sounds and birdlike chirps instead of words. They seemed perplexed whenever Tally tripped over an invisible root or vine, and nervous when she let out a string of curses as a result. They didn't like being unarmed, she realized. Perhaps they regretted breaking their weapons at the first sign of her displeasure.

Tough luck, Tally thought. No matter how friendly the hunters had become, she was glad they'd discarded the clubs, just in case they changed their minds. After all, if she hadn't fallen into the water, washing the day's mud and muck from her pretty face, Tally doubted she would be alive now.

Whoever the hunters' enemies were, the grudge was serious.

Tally smelled the village before they reached it. It made her nose wrinkle unhappily.

It wasn't just the scent of wood smoke, or the less welcome tang of animal slaughter, which she knew from watching rabbits and chickens killed for food back in the Smoke. The smell at the outskirts of the hunters' camp was much worse, reminding Tally of the outdoor latrines the Smokies had used. That was one aspect of camping she'd never quite gotten used to. Mercifully, the smell faded as the village came into sight.

The camp wasn't big—a dozen huts made of mud and reeds, a few sleeping goats tied to each, the furrows of vegetable plots casting ruffled shadows in the starlight. One big storehouse sat in the middle of everything, but there were no other large buildings that Tally could see.

The village's borders were marked by watch fires and armed guards. Having reached home, the hunters felt safe enough to raise their voices again, shouting the news that they'd brought back a . . . visitor.

People began to flow out of the huts, the hubbub growing as the village gradually awoke. Tally found herself at the center of a gathering crowd of curious faces. A circle formed around her, but the adult villagers never pressed too close, as if held back by the force field of her beauty. They kept their eyes averted.

The littlies, on the other hand, showed more courage. Some actually dared to touch her, darting out to lay a hand on her silvery jacket before retreating back into the crowd. It was strange seeing kids out here in the wild. Unlike their elders, the littlies looked almost normal to Tally. They were too young for their skin to show the ravages of bad nutrition and disease, and, of course, even in the city no one got the operation until they were sixteen. She was used to seeing asymmetrical faces and squinty eyes on littlies, and they were cute, anyway.

Tally knelt and reached out a hand, letting the bravest of them nervously stroke her palm.

She also saw women for the first time. Given that almost every man wore a beard, it was easy to tell the sexes apart. The women hung back in the crowd, tending to the smallest littlies and hardly daring a glance at Tally. A few were building a fire on a blackened pit in the middle of town. No men bothered to help them, she noticed.

Tally dimly remembered learning in school about the pre-Rusty custom of assigning different tasks to men and women. And it was usually women who got the crappy jobs, she recalled. Even some Rusties had doggedly clung to that little trick. The thought gave Tally a queasy feeling in her stomach, and she hoped similar rules didn't apply to gods.

She wondered exactly where the god idea had come from. Tally had her firestarter and other equipment in her backpack, recovered before she and the hunters had started on their way here. But none of them had seen those miracles yet. All it had taken was one glance. From what she knew of mythology, being divine meant more than having a pretty face.

Of course, she wasn't the first pretty they'd seen. At least some of them knew Tally's language. They might know something about high technology as well.

Someone shouted from the outskirts of the throng, and the crowd parted before her, growing silent. A man came into the circle, oddly shirtless in the cold. He walked with an air of unmistakable authority, striding right through Tally's divine force field and to within arm's length. He was almost her height, a giant among these people. He looked strong as well, wiry and hard, though Tally guessed that his reflexes were no match for hers. In the firelight, his eyes sparkled with curiosity rather than fear.

She had no idea what his age might be. His face had some of the lines of a middle pretty, but his skin looked better than most of the others'. Was he younger than most of them? Or simply healthier?

Tally also noticed that he wore a knife, the first metal

tool she'd seen. Its handle shone with the matte black of plastic. She raised an eyebrow: The knife had to be city-made.

"Welcome," he said.

So he also spoke the gods' tongue. "Thanks. Um, I mean . . . thank you."

"We did not know you were coming. Not for many days."

Did gods usually call ahead before visiting? "Oh, sorry," she mumbled, but her response only seemed to confuse him. Maybe gods weren't supposed to apologize.

"We were confused," he said. "We saw your fire, and thought you were an outsider."

"Yeah, I got that. No harm done."

He tried to smile, but then frowned and shook his head. "We still do not understand."

You and me both.

The man's accent sounded slightly unusual, like someone from another city on the continent, but not from another civilization altogether. On the other hand, he seemed to lack words for the questions he wanted to ask, as if he wasn't accustomed to making small talk with gods. Possibly he was searching for: What the hell are you doing here?

Whatever concept of the divine these people had, Tally evidently wasn't fitting into it very well. And she had a feeling that if they decided she wasn't really a god, that would only leave one other category: outsider.

And outsiders got their heads caved in.

"Forgive us," he said. "We don't know your name. I am Andrew Simpson Smith."

A strange name for a strange situation, she thought. "I'm Tally Youngblood."

"Young Blood," he said, beginning to look a little happier. "So, you are a young god?"

"Uh, yeah, I guess. I'm only sixteen."

Andrew Simpson Smith closed his eyes, evidently relieved. Tally wondered if he wasn't very old himself. His earlier swagger seemed to abandon him during his moments of confusion, and he hardly had any beard yet. If you didn't notice the lines and a few pockmarks, his face could almost be an ugly of about David's age, maybe eighteen or so.

"Are you the . . . leader here?" she asked.

"No. He is headman." He pointed at the fat hunter with the bloated nose and bleeding knee, the one Tally had knocked down during the chase. The one who'd been totally about to cave her head in with his club. Great.

"I am the holy man," Andrew continued. "I learned the gods' tongue from my father."

"You speak it really well."

His face broke into a crooked-toothed smile. "I . . . thank you." He laughed, then a look that was almost sly crossed his face. "You fell, didn't you?"

Tally held her injured wrist. "Yeah, during the chase."

"From the sky!" He looked around with a stagey bafflement, spreading his empty hands. "You have no hovercar. So you must have fallen!"

Hovercar? That was interesting. Tally shrugged. "Actually, I guess you've got me there. I did fall from the sky."

"Ahh!" He sighed with relief, as if the world was beginning to make sense again. He called out a few words to the crowd, who murmured sounds of understanding.

Tally found herself beginning to relax. They all seemed much happier now that her presence on earth had a perfectly rational explanation. Falling from the sky, they could deal with. And hopefully young gods were held to different standards of conduct.

Behind Andrew Simpson Smith, the fire exploded to

life with a crackle. Tally smelled food, and heard the unmistakable squawk of a chicken being captured for slaughter. Apparently, divine visitation was a good enough excuse for a midnight feast.

The holy man spread one arm toward the fire, and the crowd parted again to open a path toward it. "Will you tell the story of falling? I will change your words to ours."

Tally sighed. She was exhausted, bewildered, and injured—her wrist still throbbed. She wanted nothing more than to curl up and sleep. But the fire looked warm and cheery after her soaking under the waterfall, and Andrew's expression was hard to resist.

She couldn't disappoint the whole village. There were no wallscreens here, no newsfeeds or satellite bands, and touring soccer teams were no doubt few and far between. Just like back at the Smoke, that made stories a valuable commodity, and it probably wasn't very often that a stranger dropped in from the sky.

"Okay," she said. "One story, but then I'm passing out."

The whole village gathered around the fire.

The smells of roasting chicken came from long spits held over the flames, and earthen pots were shoved in among the coals, something white and yeasty-smelling gently rising in them. The men sat in the front row, eating noisily, wiping their greasy hands on their beards until they glowed in the firelight. Women tended to the food while littlies ran amok underfoot, the older ones feeding the fire with branches scavenged from the darkness. But when the signal went up that Tally was going to speak, everyone settled down.

Perhaps it was sharing a meal with her, or possibly young gods weren't so intimidating, but many of the villagers now dared to catch her eye, some even gazing unapologetically at her pretty face as they waited for the story.

Andrew Simpson Smith sat beside her, proudly ready to translate.

Tally cleared her throat, wondering how to explain her journey here in a way that would make sense to these people. They knew about hovercars and pretties, apparently. But did they know about Specials? What about the operation? The Crims? The Smoke?

The difference between bubbly and bogus?

Tally doubted her story would make any sense to them at all.

She cleared her throat again, looking down at the ground to escape their expectant gazes. She felt tired, almost pretty-headed from the night's interrupted sleep. The whole trip from the city to this fireside seemed almost like a dream.

A dream. She smiled at that thought, and gradually the words for her story began to find their way to her lips.

"Once upon a time, there was a beautiful young goddess," Tally said, then waited as her words were translated into the tongue of the villagers. The strange syllables that came from Andrew's mouth made this firelit setting even more dreamlike, until the story was flowing from her without effort.

"She lived in a high tower in the sky. It was a very comfortable tower, but there was no way down and out into the world. And one day the young goddess decided that she had better things to do than look at herself in the mirror. . . ."

# REVENGE

Tally awoke to unfamiliar smells and sounds: sweat and morning breath, a soft chorus of snores and snuffling, the heavy, humid warmth of a small and crowded space.

She stirred in the darkness, and a ripple of movements spread out from her, intertwined bodies shifting to accommodate one another. Beneath the fur blankets, soft, comforting warmth suffused her senses. It felt almost like a pretty dream, except for the overwhelming smell of unwashed humans and the fact that Tally really had to pee.

She opened her eyes. Light filtered through the chimney, which was just a hole in the roof that let smoke out. Judging by the angle of the sun, it was midmorning; everyone was sleeping late. That was no surprise—the feast had lasted until dawn. Everyone told more stories after Tally's was over, competing to see whose tale could keep the sleepy god awake, with Andrew Simpson Smith tirelessly translating the whole time.

When at last they'd let her go to bed, Tally discovered that "bed" was in fact a foreign concept here. She had wound up sharing this hut with twenty other people. Apparently, in this village, staying warm on winter nights meant sleeping in piles, fur blankets strewn across everyone. It had been weird, but not weird enough to keep Tally awake another minute.

This morning, unconscious bodies lay all around her, more or less clothed, tangled up with one another and with the animal skins. But the casual contact hardly seemed sexual. It was just a way of keeping warm, like kittens in a pile.

Tally tried to sit up, and found an arm wrapped around her. It was Andrew Simpson Smith, snoring softly with his mouth half-open. She pushed his weight away from her, and he turned over without waking, draping his arm over the old man asleep on the other side of him.

As she moved through the semidarkness, Tally began to find the crowded hut dizzying. She had known that these people hadn't invented hoverboards or wallscreens or flush toilets, probably not even metal tools, but it had never occurred to Tally that there was ever anyone anywhere who hadn't invented privacy.

She made her way across the unconscious forms, stumbling over arms and legs and who-knew-what-else to reach the door. Stooping, she gratefully crawled out into the bright sun and fresh air.

The freezing cold goose-pimpled her bare arms and face, every breath carrying ice into her lungs. Tally realized that her coat was back in the hut, but she only wrapped her arms around herself, deciding she would rather shiver than run the gauntlet of all those sleeping bodies again. Out here in the cold, she felt her wrist throbbing from the fall the night before, and the sore muscles from the long day's hike. Maybe the human warmth of the hut hadn't been so bad, but first things first.

To find the latrine, Tally only had to follow her nose. It was nothing but a ditch, and the overwhelming smell made her glad for the first time that she had run away in winter. How did people live here in summer?

Tally had faced outdoor toilets before, of course. But the Smokies treated their waste, using a few simple, self-propagating nanos borrowed from city recycling plants. The nanos broke down sewage and routed it straight back into the soil, which helped produce the best tomatoes Tally had ever eaten. More important, they kept the latrines from raising a stink. The Smokies had almost all been born in cities, however much they loved nature. They were products of a technological civilization, and didn't like bad smells.

This village was another matter altogether, almost like the mythical pre-Rusties who had existed before high technology. What sort of culture had these people descended from? In school, they taught that the Rusties had incorporated everyone into their economic framework, destroying every other way of life—and although it was never mentioned, Tally knew that the Specials did pretty much the same thing. So where had these people come from? Had they returned to this way of life after the Rusty civilization crashed? Or had they lived out in the wild even before then? And why had the Specials left them alone?

Whatever the answers to these questions, Tally realized that she couldn't face the latrine ditch—she was too much of a city girl for that. She wandered farther back into the forest. Although she knew this had been frowned on in the Smoke, she hoped young gods got special dispensations here.

When Tally waved to a pair of watchmen on duty at the edge of town, they nodded back a bit nervously, averting their eyes and clumsily hiding their clubs behind them. The hunters were still wary of her, as if wondering why they hadn't gotten in trouble yet for trying to cave her head in.

Only a few meters into the trees, the village disappeared from view, but Tally wasn't worried about getting lost. Gusts of wind still brought smells of staggering intensity from the latrine trench, and she was still close enough to yell to the watchmen if she wound up hopelessly turned around.

In the bright sun, the night frost was melting, falling in

a steady mist. The forest made soft shifting sounds, like her parents' old house when no one else was home. The shadows of leaves broke the outlines of the trees, making every shape indistinct, creating movement in the corner of her eye with every gust of wind. The feeling of being watched that she'd experienced the day before returned, and she found a spot and peed quickly.

But she didn't head straight back. It was pointless to let her imagination run away with her. A few moments of privacy were a luxury here. She wondered what lovers did when they wanted to be alone, and if anyone kept secrets for long in the village.

Over the last month, she'd gotten used to spending almost every minute with Zane. She could feel his absence right now; her body missed having his warmth next to her. But sharing sleeping quarters with a couple of dozen strangers was a strange and unexpected substitute.

Suddenly, Tally felt her nerves twitch, and she froze. Somewhere in her peripheral vision, something had shifted, not part of the natural play of sunlight and leaves and wind. Her eyes scanned the trees.

A laugh rolled from the forest.

It was Andrew Simpson Smith, crunching through the undergrowth with a big smile on his face.

"Were you spying on me?" she asked.

"Spying?" He said it as if he'd never heard the word, and Tally wondered if, with so little privacy, anyone here had even invented the concept of spying. "I woke when you left us, Young Blood. I thought maybe I would get to see you . . ."

She raised an eyebrow. "See me what?"

"Fly," he said sheepishly.

Tally had to laugh. The night before, no matter how

she'd tried to explain it, Andrew Simpson Smith had never quite grasped the concept of hoverboarding. She had explained that younger gods didn't use hovercars very much, but the idea that there were different kinds of flying vehicles seemed to befuddle him.

He looked hurt by her amusement. Perhaps he thought Tally was hiding her special powers just to vex him.

"Sorry, Andrew. But like I kept saying last night, I can't fly."

"But in your story, you said you were going to join your friends."

"Yeah. But like I told you, my board's busted. And underwater. I'm afraid I'm stuck walking."

He seemed confused for a moment, perhaps amazed that divine contraptions could get broken. Then suddenly he beamed, revealing a missing tooth that made him look like a littlie. "Then I'll help you. We will walk there together."

"Uh, really?"

He nodded. "The Smiths are holy men. I am a servant of the gods, like my father was."

His voice fell flat on the last few words. Tally was amazed again at how easy it was to read Andrew's face. All the villagers' emotions seemed to live right on the surface, as if they had no more invented privacy in their thoughts than they had in their sleeping arrangements. She wondered if they ever lied to one another.

Of course, some pretties had lied to them at some point. Gods, indeed.

"When did your father die, Andrew? Not long ago, right?"

He looked up at her in wonder, as if she'd magically read his thoughts. "It was only a month ago, just before the longest night."

Tally wondered what the longest night was, but didn't interrupt.

"He and I were searching for ruins. The elder gods like us to find old and Rusty places for them, for study. We came upon outsiders."

"Outsiders? Like you mistook me for?"

"Yes. But this was no young god we found. It was a raiding party looking for a kill. We spotted them first, but their dogs had our scent. And my father was old. Forty years, he had lived," he said proudly.

Tally let out a slow breath. All eight of her great-crumblies were still alive, and all in their hundred-teens.

"His bones had grown weak." Andrew's voice fell almost to a whisper. "Running in a stream, he turned his ankle. I had to leave him behind."

Tally swallowed, dizzy at the thought of someone dying from a sprained ankle. "Oh. I'm sorry."

"He gave me his knife before I left him." Andrew pulled it from his belt, and Tally got a closer look than the night before. It was a disposable kitchen knife with a notched, ragged blade. "Now I am the holy man."

She nodded slowly. The sight of the cheap knife in his hand reminded Tally of how her first encounter with these people had almost ended. She had almost met the same fate as Andrew's father. "But why?"

"Why, Young Blood? Because I was his son."

"No, not that," she said. "Why would the outsiders want to kill your father? Or anyone?"

Andrew frowned, as if this was an odd question. "It was their turn."

"Their what?"

He shrugged. "We had killed in the summer. The revenge was on them."

"You had killed . . . one of them?"

"Our revenge, for a killing in the early spring." He smiled coldly. "I was in that raiding party."

"So this is like payback? But when did the whole thing start?"

"Start?" He stared into the flat of the knife's blade, as if trying to read something in the mirror of its dull metal. "It has always been. They are outsiders." He smiled. "I was glad to see that it was you they brought home, and not a kill. So that it is still our turn, and I may still be there for my father's revenge."

Tally found herself speechless. In seconds, Andrew Simpson Smith had changed from a grieving son into some kind of . . . savage. His fingers had turned even paler, wrapped around the knife so tightly that the blood was forced from them.

She took her eyes from the weapon and shook her head. It wasn't fair to think of him as uncivilized. What Andrew was describing was as old as civilization itself. In school, they'd talked about this sort of blood feud. And the Rusties had only been worse, inventing mass warfare, creating more and more deadly technologies until they'd almost destroyed the world.

Still, Tally couldn't afford to forget how different these people were from anyone she'd ever known. She forced herself to stare at Andrew's grim expression, his weird delight in the heft of the knife in his hand.

Then she remembered Dr. Cable's words. Humanity is a cancer, and we are the cure. Violence was what the cities had been built to end, and part of what the operation switched off in pretties' brains. The whole world that Tally had grown up in was a firebreak against this awful cycle. But here was the natural state of the species, right in front of her. In running from the city, perhaps this was what Tally was running toward.

Unless Dr. Cable was wrong, and there was another way.

Andrew looked up from his knife and sheathed it, spreading his empty hands. "But not today. Today I will help you find your friends." He laughed, suddenly beaming again.

Tally breathed out slowly, for a moment wanting to reject his help. But she had no one else to turn to, and the forests between her and the Rusty Ruins were filled with hidden paths and natural dangers, and probably more than a few people who might think of her as an "outsider." Even if she wasn't being chased by a bloodthirsty raiding party, a sprained ankle alone in the freezing wilderness could prove fatal.

She needed Andrew Simpson Smith, it was that simple. And he had spent his life training to help people like her. Gods.

"Okay, Andrew. But let's leave today. I'm in a hurry."

"Of course. Today." He stroked the place where his slight beard was beginning to grow. "These ruins where your friends are waiting? Where are they?"

Tally glanced up at the sun, still low enough to indicate the eastern horizon. After a moment's calculation, she pointed off to the northwest, back toward the city and, beyond that, the Rusty Ruins. "About a week's walk that way."

"A week?"

"That means seven days."

"Yes, I know the gods' calendar," he said huffily. "But a whole week?"

"Yeah. That's not so far, is it?" The hunters had been tireless on their march the night before.

He shook his head, an awed expression on his face. "But that is beyond the edge of the world."

## FOOD OF THE GODS

They left at noon.

The whole village turned out to see them off, bringing offerings for the trip. Most of the gifts were too heavy to carry, and Tally and Andrew politely turned them down. He did fill his pack, however, with the scary-looking strips of dried meat that were offered them. When Tally realized that the grisly stuff was meant to be eaten, she tried to hide her horror, but didn't do a very good job. The only gift she accepted was a wooden and leather slingshot offered by one of the older members of her littlie fan club. Tally remembered being pretty handy with slingshots back in her own littlie days.

The headman publicly bestowed his blessing on the journey, adding one last apology—translated by Andrew—for almost cracking open the head of such a young and pretty god. Tally assured him that her elders would never be told about the misunderstanding, and the headman seemed guardedly relieved. He then presented Andrew with a beaten copper bracelet, a mark of gratitude to the young holy man for helping to make up for the hunters' error.

Andrew flushed with pride at the gift, and the crowd cheered as he held it aloft. Tally realized that she had caused trouble here. Like wearing semiformal dress to a costume bash, her unexpected visit had thrown things out of whack, but Andrew's helping her was making everyone relax a little. Apparently, placating the gods was a holy man's most important job, which made Tally wonder how much city pretties interfered with the villagers.

Once she and Andrew were past the town limits, and their entourage of littlies had been called back home by anxious mothers, she decided to ask some serious questions. "So, Andrew, how many gods do you know . . . uh, personally?"

He stroked his non-beard, looking thoughtful. "Since my father's death no gods have come but you. None knows me as holy man."

Tally nodded. As she'd guessed, he was still trying to fill his father's shoes. "Right. But your accent's so good. You didn't learn to speak my language only from your father, did you?"

His crooked grin was sly. "I was never supposed to speak to the gods, only listen as my father attended them. But sometimes when guiding a god to a ruin or the nest of some strange new bird, I would speak."

"Good for you. So . . . what did you guys talk about?"

He was quiet for a moment, as if choosing his words carefully. "We talked about animals. When they mate and what they eat."

"That makes sense." Any city zoologist would love a private army of pre-Rusties to help them with fieldwork. "Anything else?"

"Some gods wanted to know about ruins, as I told you. I would take them there."

Ditto for archeologists. "Sure."

"And there is the Doctor."

"Who? The Doctor?" Tally froze in her tracks. "Tell me, Andrew, is this Doctor really . . . scary-looking?"

Andrew frowned, then laughed. "Scary? No. Like you, he's beautiful, almost hard to look upon."

She shuddered with relief, then smiled and raised an eyebrow. "You don't seem to find it too hard to look upon me."

His eyes fell to the ground. "I am sorry, Young Blood."

"Come on, Andrew, I didn't mean it." She took his

shoulder lightly. "I was only kidding. Look upon me all you . . . um, whatever. And call me Tally, okay?"

"Tally," he said, trying out the name in his mouth. She dropped her hand from his shoulder, and Andrew looked at the place where she had touched him. "You are different from the other gods."

"I certainly hope so," she said. "So this Doctor guy looks normal? Or pretty, I mean? Or, anyway . . . godlike?"

"Yes. He is here more often than the others. But he does not care for animals or ruins. He asks only about the ways of the village. Who is courting, who is heavy with child. Which hunter might challenge the headman to a duel."

"Right." Tally tried to remember the word. "An anthro—"

"Anthropologist, they call him," Andrew said.

Tally raised an eyebrow.

He grinned. "I have good ears, my father always said. The other gods sometimes mock the Doctor."

"Huh." The villagers knew more about their divine visitors than the gods realized, it seemed. "So you've never met any gods who were really . . . scary-looking, have you?"

Andrew's eyes narrowed, and he started hiking again. Sometimes he took a long time to answer questions, as if being in a hurry was another thing the villagers hadn't bothered to invent. "No, I haven't. But my father's grandfather told stories about creatures with strange weapons and faces like hawks, who did the will of the gods. They took human form, but moved strangely."

"Kind of like insects? Fast and jerky?"

Andrew's eyes widened. "They are real, then? The Sayshal?"

"Sayshal? Oh. We call them Specials."

"They destroy any who challenge the gods."

She nodded. "That's them, all right."

"And when people disappear, they sometimes say it was the Sayshal who have taken them."

"Taken them?" Where? Tally wondered.

She fell silent, staring down at the forest path in front of her. If Andrew's great-grandfather had run into Special Circumstances, then the city had known about the village for decades, probably longer. The scientists who exploited these people had been doing so for a long time, and weren't above bringing in Specials to shore up their authority.

It seemed that challenging the gods was a risky business.

They hiked for a day, making good time across the hills. Tally was beginning to spot the trails of the villagers without Andrew's help, as if her eyes were learning how to see the forest better.

As night fell, they found a cave to make camp in. Tally started to collect firewood, but stopped when she noticed Andrew watching her with a mystified expression. "What's up?"

"A fire? Outsiders will see!"

"Oh, right. Sorry." She sighed, rubbing her hands together to drive the chill from her fingers. "So this revenge thing makes for some cold nights on the trail, doesn't it?"

"Being cold is better than being dead, Tally," he said, then shrugged. "And perhaps our journey will not last so long. We will reach the edge of the world tomorrow."

"Right, sure." During the day's hike, Andrew hadn't been convinced by Tally's description of the world: a planet 40,000 kilometers around, hanging in an airless void, with gravity making everyone stick to it. Of course, from his perspective it probably did sound pretty nutty. People used to get arrested for believing in a round world, they said in school—and it had usually been holy men doing the arresting.

Tally picked out two packages of SwedeBalls. "At least we don't have to build a fire to have hot food."

Andrew drew closer, watching her fill the purifier. He'd been chewing on dried meat all day, and was pretty excited about trying some "food of the gods." When the purifier pinged and Tally lifted the cover, his jaw dropped at the sight of steam rising from the reconstituted SwedeBalls. She handed it to him. "Go ahead. You first."

She didn't have to insist. Back in the village the men always ate first, and the women and littlies got leftovers. Tally was a god, of course, and in some ways they had treated her as an honorary man, but some habits died hard. Andrew took the purifier from her and stuck his hand in to grab a meatball. He yanked it out with a yelp.

"Hey, don't burn yourself," she said.

"But where is the fire?" he asked softly, sucking on his fingers as he held up the purifier to look for a flame underneath.

"It's electronic . . . a very small fire. Are you sure you don't want to try chopsticks?"

He experimented with the sticks hopelessly for a while, which allowed the SwedeBalls to cool, then finally dug in with his hands. A slightly disappointed expression crossed his face as he chewed. "Hmm."

"What's wrong?"

"I thought that food of the gods would be . . . better, somehow."

"Hey, this is dehydrated food of the gods, okay?"

Tally ate after he was done, but her CurryNoods were underwhelming after the feast of the night before. She remembered from her days in the Smoke how much better food could taste in the wild. Even fresh produce was never spectacular when it had been harvested from hydroponic tanks. And she had to agree with Andrew—dehydrated food was resolutely not divine.

The young holy man was surprised when Tally didn't want to sleep curled up with him—it was winter, after all. She explained that privacy was a god thing—he wouldn't understand—but he still moped at her as she chewed her toothpaste pill and found her own corner of the cave to sleep in.

It was the middle of the night when Tally awoke half-frozen, regretting her rudeness. After a long, silent session of self-recrimination, she sighed and crawled over to nestle against Andrew's back. He wasn't Zane, but the warmth of another person was better than lying on the stone floor shivering, miserable and alone.

When she awoke again at dawn, the smell of smoke filled the cave.

## THE EDGE OF THE WORLD

Tally tried to cry out, but a hand was planted firmly over her mouth.

She was about to thrash out with her fists in the semi-darkness, but some instinct told her not to—it was Andrew holding her. She could smell him, Tally realized. After two nights of sleeping next to each other, the back of her brain recognized his scent.

She relaxed, and he let go.

"What is it?" she whispered.

"Outsiders. Enough of them to build a fire."

She puzzled over this for a moment, then nodded:

Because of the blood feud, only a large party of armed men would dare build a fire outside the safety of their village.

Tally sniffed the smoky air, detecting the smell of searing meat. The sounds of raucous conversation reached her ears. They must have camped close by after Tally and Andrew had gone to sleep, and now they were cooking breakfast.

"What do we do?"

"You stay here. I will see if I can find one alone."

"You're doing what?" she hissed.

He drew his father's knife. "This is my chance to settle the score."

"Score? What is this, a soccer game?" Tally whispered. "You'll get killed! Like you said, there must be lots of them."

He scowled. "I will only take one who is alone. I'm not a fool."

"Forget it!" She took hold of Andrew, locking her fingers around his wrist. He tried to pull away, but his wiry strength was no match for her postoperation muscles.

He glared at her, then spoke in a loud voice. "If we fight, they'll hear us."

"No kidding. Shhh!"

"Let me go!" His voice raised in volume again, and Tally realized that he would gladly shout if he had to. Honor compelled him to hunt the enemy, even if it jeopardized both their lives. Of course, the outsiders probably wouldn't hurt Tally once they saw her pretty face, but Andrew would be killed if they were caught, which was going to happen if he didn't shut up. She had no choice but to release his wrist.

Andrew turned away without another word and crawled from the cave, knife in hand.

Tally sat in the darkness, stunned, replaying their fight in her mind. What could she have said to him? What whispered arguments could overcome decades of blood feud? It was hopeless.

Maybe it went deeper than that. Tally remembered again her conversation with Dr. Cable, who had claimed that human beings always rediscovered war, always became Rusties in the end—the species was a planetary plague, whether they knew what a planet was or not. So what was the cure for that, except the operation?

Maybe the Specials had the right idea.

Tally crouched in the cave, miserable, hungry, and thirsty. Andrew's waterskin was empty, and there was nothing to do except wait for him to come back. Unless he wasn't coming back.

How could he just leave her here?

Of course, he'd had to leave his own father lying in a cold stream, injured and certain to be killed. Maybe anybody would want revenge after going through a thing like that. But Andrew wasn't looking for the men who'd killed his father, he was just out to murder a random stranger—anyone would do. It didn't make any sense.

The smells of cooking eventually faded. Creeping up to the mouth of the cave, Tally no longer heard any sounds from the outsider camp, only wind in the leaves.

Then she saw someone coming through the trees. . . .

It was Andrew. He was covered in mud, as if he'd been crawling around on his belly, but the knife clutched in his hand looked clean. Tally didn't see any blood on his hands. As he grew closer, she saw with relief that he wore an expression of disappointment. "So, no luck?" she said.

He shook his head. "My father is not yet avenged."

"Tough. Let's get going."

He frowned. "No breakfast?"

Tally scowled. A moment ago he'd wanted nothing

more than to ambush and murder some random stranger, and now his face looked like a littlie's whose promised ice cream had been snatched away.

"Too late for breakfast," she said, and pulled her backpack up onto her shoulder. "Which way to the edge of the world?"

They walked in silence until well past noon, when Tally's grumbling stomach finally forced a stop. She prepared VegiRice for them both, not in the mood for the taste of pseudomeat.

Andrew was like an anxious-to-please puppy, gamely trying to use chopsticks and making jokes about his clumsiness. But Tally couldn't bring herself to smile. The chill that had seeped into her bones while he was out looking for revenge hadn't gone away.

Of course, it wasn't completely fair being upset with Andrew. Probably he couldn't understand Tally's aversion to casual murder. He'd grown up with the cycle of revenge. It was just a part of his pre-Rusty life, like sleeping in piles or cutting down trees. He didn't see it as wrong any more than he could understand how utterly the latrine ditch revolted her.

Tally was different from the villagers—at least that much had changed in the course of human history. Maybe there was hope after all.

But she didn't feel much like talking it over with Andrew, or even giving him a smile.

"So what's beyond the edge of the world?" she finally said.

He shrugged. "Nothing."

"There must be something."

"The world just ends."

"Have you been there?"

"Of course. Every boy goes, one year before you become a man."

Tally scowled—another boys-only club. "So what does it look like? A wide river? Some kind of cliff?"

Andrew shook his head. "No. It looks like the forest, like any other place. But it is the end. There are little men there, who make sure you go no farther."

"Little men, huh?" Tally remembered an old map on the library wall at her ugly school, the words "Here Be Dragons" written in flowery letters in all the blank spots. Maybe this world's edge was nothing more than the borderline of the villager's mental map of the world—like their need for revenge, they simply couldn't see beyond it. "Well, it won't be the end for me."

He shrugged again. "You are a god."

"Yeah, that's me. How far are we now?"

He glanced up at the sun. "We'll be there before nightfall."

"Good." Tally didn't want to spend another cold night huddled with Andrew Simpson Smith if she could help it.

They saw no more signs of outsiders over the next few hours, but the habit of silence had settled onto the journey. Even after Tally had decided she was no longer angry at Andrew, she found herself covering the kilometers without uttering a word. He looked dejected by her silent treatment, or maybe he was still moping about not getting his kill that morning.

A bad day all around.

Late afternoon shadows had begun to stretch behind them when he said, "We are close now."

Tally came to a halt for a drink of water, scanning the

horizon. It looked like every other bit of forest she'd seen since falling from the sky. Perhaps the trees were thinning a little here, the clearings growing larger and almost bare of grass in the growing cold of winter. But it hardly looked like someone's idea of the end of the world.

Andrew walked more slowly as they continued, as if looking for signs among the trees. He sometimes glanced at the faraway hills to point out landmarks. Finally, he halted, staring with wide eyes into the forest.

Tally took a moment to focus, then saw something hanging from a tree. It looked like a doll, a human-shaped bundle of twigs and dried flowers, no bigger than a fist. It swayed in the breeze, like a little person dancing. She could see more of them stretching into the distance.

Tally had to smile. "So those are the little men?"

"Yes."

"And this is your edge of the world?" It looked like more of the same to her: dense undergrowth and trees filled with squawking birds.

"The edge, not mine. No one has ever passed beyond it."

"Yeah, right." Tally shook her head. The dolls probably just marked the territory of the next tribe over. She noticed a bird perched close to one, regarding the doll curiously, possibly wondering if it was edible.

She sighed and adjusted her backpack on her shoulder, striding toward the nearest doll. Andrew didn't follow, but he would catch up with her once his superstitions were disproved. Centuries before, Tally remembered, sailors had been afraid to sail into the deep ocean, thinking that sooner or later they would fall off the edge. Until someone tried it, and it turned out there were more continents out there.

On the other hand, maybe it would be better if Andrew didn't follow her. The last thing she needed was a traveling companion who was bent on revenge at any cost. The people beyond of the edge of world certainly hadn't had anything to do with the death of his father, but one outsider would be as good as another to Andrew.

As she grew nearer, Tally saw more of the dolls. They hung every few meters, marking some kind of border, like misshapen ornaments for an outdoor party. Their heads were at funny angles, she saw—the dolls all hung from their necks, nooses of rough twine around every one. She could understand how the villagers might find the little men creepy, and a slow chill ran down her spine. . . .

Then the tingling sensation moved to her fingers.

At first, Tally thought her arm had fallen asleep, pins and needles spreading from her shoulders down. She adjusted the backpack, trying to restore her circulation, but the tingling continued.

A few steps later, Tally heard the sound. A rumble seemed to come up from the earth itself, a note so low that she could feel it in her bones. It played across her skin, the world trembling around her. Tally's vision blurred, as if her eyes were vibrating in sympathy with the sound. She took another step forward, and it grew louder, now like a swarm of insects inside her head.

Something was very wrong here.

Tally tried to turn around, but found that her muscles had melted into water. Her backpack felt suddenly filled with stone, and the ground had become mush under her feet. She managed a staggering step backward, the sound fading a little as she moved away.

Holding up a hand in front of her face, she saw it trembling; maybe her fever had returned.

Or was it this place?

Tally stretched her arm out farther, and the vibrations

in her fingertips increased, itching like an untended sunburn. The air itself was buzzing, growing worse with every centimeter her hand moved toward the dolls. It felt as if her flesh itself were repelled by them.

She gritted her teeth and took a defiant step forward, but the buzzing swarmed into her head, blurring her vision again. Her throat gagged on her next breath, as if the air were too electrified to breathe.

Tally staggered back from the dolls, sinking to her knees once the sound had faded. Tingles still ran across her skin, like a horde of ants swarming under her clothes. She tried to move farther, but her body refused.

Then she smelled Andrew again. His strong hands lifted her from the ground, and as he half-carried and half-dragged her away from the line of dolls, the riot of sensations slowly faded.

Tally shook her head, trying to clear the vibrating echoes. Her whole body was quivering inside. "That buzzing, Andrew . . . I feel like I swallowed a beehive."

"Yes. Buzzing, like bees." Andrew nodded, staring at his own hands.

"Why didn't you tell me?" she cried.

"But I did. I told you of the little men. I said you could not pass."

Tally scowled. "You could have been more specific."

He frowned, then shrugged. "It's the edge of the world. It has always been this way. How could you not know?"

She groaned in frustration, then sighed. Looking up at the closest doll, Tally finally noticed what she'd missed before. It seemed to be made of twigs and dried flowers—natural materials—but it showed no signs of weathering. All of the dolls Tally could see looked brand new, not like handmade things that had hung for days in a torrential downpour. Unless someone had replaced every single one of them since the rains, the dolls were made of something hardier than twigs.

Something like plastic, maybe.

And inside them was something far more sophisticated, a security system powerful enough to cripple human beings, but clever enough not to harm the trees or the birds. Something that attacked the human nervous system, drawing an impassable border around the villagers' world.

Tally saw it then, why the Specials could allow the village to exist. This wasn't just a few stray people living in the wilderness; it was someone's pet anthropology project, a preserve of some kind. Or . . . what had the Rusties called them?

This was a reservation.

And Tally was trapped inside.

## HOLY DAY

"You don't have a way across?" Andrew finally asked.

Tally sighed, shaking her head. Her outstretched fingers felt the tingling here, as they had every other spot she'd tried over the last hour. The line of dolls stretched unbroken as far as she could see, and all of them seemed to be in perfect working order.

She stepped back from the edge of the world, and the prickling in her hands subsided. After her first experience, Tally hadn't tested the barrier further than the tingling stage—once was enough for that—but she was fairly certain that all the other dolls had just as much punch as the one that had brought her to her knees. City machines could last a long time, and there was plenty of solar power up there in the trees.

"No. There's no way."

"I did not think so," Andrew said.

"You sound disappointed."

"I'd hoped you might show me . . . what is beyond."

She frowned. "I thought you didn't believe me, about there being more."

Andrew shook his head vigorously. "I believe you, Tally. Well, not about the airless void and gravity, but there must be something beyond. The city where you live must be real."

"Lived," she corrected him, sticking her fingers out again. The tingling traveled through them, feeling uncannily as if she'd sat on her hand for an hour or so. Tally stepped back and rubbed her arm. She had no idea what sort of technology the barrier was using, but it might not be very healthy to keep testing it. No point in risking permanent nerve damage.

The little dolls hung there, mocking her as they danced in the breeze. She was stuck here, inside Andrew's world.

Tally remembered all the tricks she'd pulled back in ugly days, sneaking out of dorms to cross the river at night, even crashing a party in Peris's mansion after he'd turned pretty. But her ugly skills didn't necessarily apply out here. As she'd learned in her conversation with Dr. Cable, the city was an easy place to trick. Security there was designed to stimulate uglies' creativity, not to fry anyone's nervous system.

But this barrier had been created to keep dangerous pre-Rusty villagers away from the city, to protect campers and hikers and anyone else who might have wandered out into nature. These dolls weren't likely to succumb to Tally's tinkering with the point of her knife.

The thought of ugly tricks sent Tally's hand to the slingshot in her back pocket. It seemed like an unlikely way to trick the edge of the world, but maybe the direct approach was worth a try.

She found a smooth, flat stone and loaded it up, the leather creaking as she drew it back. Tally let fly, but missed the nearest doll by a meter or so. "Guess I'm a little out of practice."

"Young Blood!" Andrew said. "Is that wise?"

She smiled. "Afraid I'll break the world?"

"The stories say that the gods put these here, to mark the edge of oblivion."

"Yeah, well. They're more like 'Keep Out' signs, or 'Keep In,' I guess—as in keeping you guys in your place. The world goes on for a whole lot farther, trust me. This is just a trick to keep you from knowing it."

Andrew looked away, and Tally thought he was going to argue some more, but instead he knelt and lifted a rock the size of his fist. He pulled back his arm, took aim, and hurled it. Tally saw from the moment it left his hand that the stone was dead on-target. It struck the nearest doll and sent it spinning, the noose tightening around its neck, then the doll spun the other way, unwinding like a top.

"That was brave of you," she remarked.

He shrugged. "As I said, Young Blood, I believe what you say. Maybe this isn't really the edge of the world. If that is true, I want to see beyond."

"Good for you." Tally stepped forward and thrust out a hand. No change: Her fingertips buzzed with the latent energy in the air, the ants crawling up her arm until she pulled away. Of course. Any system designed to last for decades in the wild—surviving hailstorms, hungry animals, and lightning strikes—was probably more than a match for a few rocks.

"The little men are still doing their thing." She rubbed life back into her fingers. "I don't know how to get past this place, Andrew. But nice try."

He was staring down at his empty hand, as if a little surprised at himself for challenging the gods' work. "It is a strange thing to want to go past the edge of the world. Isn't it?"

She laughed. "Welcome to my life. But I'm sorry to bring you all this way for nothing."

"No, Tally. It was good to see."

She tried to read his expression, a mix of puzzlement and intensity. "To see what? Me getting serious nerve damage?"

He shook his head. "No. Your slingshot."

"Excuse me?"

"When I came here as a boy, I felt the little men crawling inside me and wanted to run back home." He looked at her, still puzzled. "But you wanted to sling a rock at them. You don't know some things that every child knows, but you are so certain about the shape of this . . . planet. You act as if . . ." He trailed off, his knowledge of the city language failing him.

"As if I see the world differently?"

"Yes," he said softly, his intense expression deepening. Most likely, Tally thought, it had never occurred to him before now that people could see reality in completely different ways. Between surviving outsider attacks and getting enough food to live, villagers probably didn't have a lot of time for philosophical disagreements.

"That's the way it feels," she said, "once you get off the reservation, I mean, once you go beyond the edge of the world. Speaking of which, do you know for sure that no matter what direction we walk in, we'll run into these little guys?"

Andrew nodded. "My father taught that the world is a circle, seven days' walk across. This is the nearest edge to our village. But my father once walked around the entire compass of the world."

"Interesting. You think he was looking for a way out?"

Andrew frowned. "He never said."

"Well, I guess he didn't find one. So how am I going to escape this world of yours and get to the Rusty Ruins?"

Andrew was silent for a while, but Tally could tell he was thinking, taking one of his interminable delays to ponder her question. Finally, he said, "You must wait for the next holy day."

"The next what?"

"The holy days mark when the gods visit. And they will come in hovercars."

"Oh, yeah?" Tally sighed. "I don't know if you've figured this out yet, Andrew, but I'm not supposed to be here. If any elder gods see me, I'm busted."

He laughed. "Do you think I'm a fool, Tally Young Blood? I listened to your story about the tower. I understand that you have been cast out."

"Cast out?"

"Yes, Young Blood. You bear this mark." His fingers brushed her left brow.

"Mark? Oh, right . . ." For the first time since meeting the villagers, Tally remembered her flash tattoo. "So you think this means something?"

Andrew bit his lip, dropping his eyes from her brow. "I am not sure, of course. My father never taught me of such things. But in my village, we only mark those who have stolen."

"Yeah, sure. But you thought I was . . . marked somehow?" He looked up sheepishly, and Tally rolled her eyes.

No wonder the villagers had been so confused by her; they'd thought the flash tattoo was some kind of badge of shame. "Listen, it's just a fashion statement. Or, um, let me put that another way. It's just something me and my friends did to amuse ourselves. You notice how it moves sometimes?"

"Yes. When you are angry, or smiling, or thinking hard."

"Right. Well, that's called being 'bubbly.' Anyway, I ran away. I didn't get cast out."

"And they'll want to take you home, I understand. You see, when the gods come, they leave their hovercars behind when they walk in the forest. . . ."

Tally blinked, and then a smile spread across her face. "And you'd help me steal from the elder gods?"

He only shrugged.

"Won't they get cranky with you?"

Andrew sighed, stroking his non-beard as he considered this. "We must be careful. But I have noticed that the gods are not . . . perfect. You escaped their tower, after all."

"Well, well, imperfect gods." Tally allowed herself a chuckle. "What would your father say, Andrew?"

He shook his head. "I am not sure. But he isn't here. I am the holy man now."

That night, they camped near the barrier. Andrew said that no one—outsiders or otherwise—would be likely to venture this close to the dolls at night. It was a place of superstitious dread, on top of which, no one wanted to get their brains fried when they woke up and stumbled off into the darkness to pee.

The next morning they began a roundabout journey back to Andrew's village, taking their time, avoiding the outsiders' hunting grounds. It took three days, during which Andrew displayed his knowledge of the forest, mixing villager lore with scientific knowledge he'd picked up from the gods. He understood the water cycle, and a little about the food chain, but after a day of arguing about gravity, Tally gave up.

When they neared the village, it was still almost a week before the next holy day. Tally told Andrew to find her a cave to hide in, one near the clearing where the gods parked their hovercars. She had decided to stay out of sight. If none of the villagers knew she had returned, they couldn't give Tally away to the elder gods. And she didn't want anyone getting blamed for harboring a runaway.

Andrew headed back home, where he planned to tell how the Young Blood had passed through the edge of the world and to the beyond. Apparently, the villagers knew how to lie after all—at least the holy men did.

And his story would be true, once Tally got her hands on a hovercar. She was no expert at driving, but she'd taken the same safety course that every ugly took at fifteen: learning how to fly straight and level and how to land in an emergency. She knew that some uglies went trick-riding all the time, and said it was easy. Of course, they'd only stolen idiotproof cars that flew on the city grid.

Still, how much harder could it be than hoverboarding?

As Tally waited out the days in the cave, she couldn't stop wondering how the other Crims were. While her own survival had been an issue, it had been easy to forget them. But now that she had nothing to do all day but sit and watch the sky, Tally found herself slowly going crazy from worry. Had the Crims escaped the Specials' pursuit? Had they found the New Smokies yet? And, most important, how was Zane? She could only hope that Maddy had been able to fix whatever was wrong with him.

She remembered their last minutes before he'd jumped from the balloon—the last words he'd said. In all of Tally's tattered memories, she'd never experienced anything like that moment. It had felt beyond bubbly, beyond any trick, like the world would change forever.

And now she didn't even know whether he was still alive.

It didn't help Tally's state of mind that Zane and the other Crims had to be just as worried about her, wondering if she'd been recaptured or had fallen to her death. They would have expected to see her at the Rusty Ruins at least a week ago, and had to be thinking the worst by now.

How long would it be before even Zane gave up, deciding she was dead? What if she never made it out of the reservation? No one's faith could last forever.

When she wasn't driving herself crazy, Tally also spent the time wondering about Andrew's confined world. How had it come to exist? Why were the villagers allowed to live out here, when the Smoke had been ruthlessly destroyed? Maybe it was the fact that the villagers were trapped, believing old legends and stuck in ancient blood feuds, while the Smokies had known the truth about the cities and the operation. But why keep a brutal culture alive, when the whole point of civilization was to curb the violent, destructive tendencies of human beings?

Andrew visited her every day, bringing her nuts and a few root vegetables to go with her dehydrated god-food. He wouldn't give up on bringing strips of dried meat until she tried it. It tasted like it looked—as salty as seaweed and harder than an old shoe—but she gratefully accepted his other offerings.

In return, Tally told him stories about home, especially those that showed how the city of the gods wasn't all divine perfection. She explained about uglies and the operation, how the beauty of gods was just a technological trick. The difference between magic and technology was lost on Andrew, but he listened intently. He'd inherited a healthy skepticism from his father, whose experiences with the gods, it turned out, hadn't always left the old holy man full of respect.

Andrew could be frustrating company, though. He made some brilliant leaps of insight, but other times he was just as thick as could be expected from someone who thought the world was flat—especially when it came to the boys-in-charge thing, which she found particularly annoying. Tally knew she should be more understanding, but was only willing to cut Andrew so much slack; being born into a culture that assumed women were servants didn't make it okay to go along with the plan. After all, Tally had turned her back on everything she'd been raised to expect: an effortless life, perfect beauty, pretty-mindedness. It seemed like Andrew could learn to cook his own chickens.

Maybe the barriers around Tally's pretty world weren't as obvious as the little men hanging in the trees, but they were just as hard to escape. She remembered how Peris had chickened out as he'd looked down on the wild from the balloon, suddenly unwilling to jump and leave behind everything he'd known. Everyone in the world was programmed by the place they were born, hemmed in by their beliefs, but you had to at least try to grow your own brain. Otherwise, you might as well be living on a reservation, worshipping a bunch of bogus gods.

They arrived at dawn, right on schedule.

From overhead came the roar of two cars—the kind that Specials used, each with four lifting fans to carry it through the air. It was a noisy way to travel, the wind roiling the trees like a storm. From the mouth of her cave, Tally saw a huge cloud of dust rising up from the landing area, and then the whine of their rotors cycled down into a riot of frightened birdcalls. After almost two weeks of natural sounds, the powerful machines sounded strange to Tally's ears, like engines from another world.

She crept toward the clearing in the dawn light, moving in total silence. Rehearsing her approach every morning, Tally had become familiar with every tree along the way. For once, the elder gods were going to face someone who knew all their tricks, and a few of her own.

She watched from under cover at the clearing's edge. Four middle pretties were unpacking the cars' cargo holds, pulling out digging tools, hovercameras, and specimen cages, loading everything onto carts. The scientists looked like campers dressed in bulky winter gear, field glasses hanging around their necks, water bottles dangling from their belts. Andrew said they never stayed more than a day, but they looked ready for weeks in the wild. Tally wondered which one was the Doctor.

Andrew worked among the four pretties, lending a hand as they arranged their equipment, being a helpful holy man. When the carts were all packed with gear, he and the scientists pushed them into the forest, leaving Tally alone with the hovercars.

She hoisted her backpack and approached the clearing warily.

This was the trickiest part of the plan. Tally could only guess what sort of security the hovercars had on board. Hopefully the scientists hadn't thought to use more than childproof minders, the simple codes that kept littlies from flying off with a car. Surely the scientists wouldn't suspect the villagers of knowing the same tricks as a city kid like Tally.

Unless they'd been warned that there were runaways in the area . . .

That was nonsense, of course. No one knew Tally was stranded out here without a board, and she hadn't seen a hovercar since the night she'd left the city. If the Specials were looking for her, they weren't looking around here.

She reached one of the cars and peeked into its open cargo door, finding nothing but pieces of packing foam shifting in the soft breeze. A few more steps brought her to the window of the passenger cabin, also empty. She reached for the door handle.

A man's voice called from behind her.

Tally froze. After two weeks of sleeping rough, her clothes torn and dirty, she might pass for a villager from a distance. But once she turned around, her pretty face would give her away.

The voice called out again in the villagers' language, but it was inflected with a late pretty's gravelly air of authority. Footsteps were coming closer. Should she dive into the hovercar and try to make it away?

The words faded as the man grew closer. He had noticed her city clothes under all the dirt.

Tally turned around.

He was equipped like the others, with field glasses and a water bottle, his crumbly face a picture of surprise. He must have been sitting inside the other hovercar, moving a little slower than the rest of them—that's why he'd caught her.

"Good heavens!" he exclaimed, switching languages. "What are you doing out here?"

She blinked, pausing for a moment, a vacant look on her pretty face. "We were in a balloon."

"A balloon?"

"There was some kind of accident. But I don't remember exactly. . . ."

He took a step forward, then his nose wrinkled. Tally might look like a pretty, but she smelled like a savage. "I think I saw something on the feeds about balloons going wrong, but that was a couple of weeks ago! You couldn't have been here that . . ." He looked at her torn clothes, his nose wrinkling again. "But I suppose you have."

Tally shook her head. "I don't know how long it's been."

"You poor dear." Recovering from his surprise, he was now all late-pretty concern. "You're okay now. I'm Dr. Valen."

She smiled like a good pretty, realizing that this must be the Doctor. A bird-watcher probably wouldn't know the villagers' language, after all. This was the man in charge.

"It feels like I've been hiding out forever," she said. "There are all these crazy people out here."

"Yes, they can be quite dangerous." He shook his head, as if still not believing that a young city pretty had survived out here for so long. "You're lucky to have stayed clear of them."

"Who are they?"

"They're . . . part of a very important study."

"A study? Of what?"

He chuckled. "Now, that's all very complicated. Perhaps I should tell someone we've found you. I'm sure everyone's very anxious to know if you're okay. What's your name?"

"What are you studying out here?"

He blinked, perplexed that a new pretty was asking questions instead of whining about getting home. "Well, we're looking at certain fundamentals of . . . human nature."

"Of course. Like violence? Revenge."

He frowned. "Yes, in a manner of speaking. But how . . . ?"

"I thought so." All at once, it was becoming clear. "You're studying violence, so you'd need a violent, brutal group of people, wouldn't you? You're an anthropologist?"

Confusion still played across his face. "Yes, but I'm also a doctor. A medical doctor. Are you sure you're all right?"

A realization hit Tally. "You're a brain doctor."

"We're called neurologists, actually." Dr. Valen warily turned to reach for the hovercar door. "But perhaps I should make that call. I didn't get your name."

"I didn't give it."

Her tone stopped him cold.

"Don't touch that door," she said.

He turned to face her again, his late-pretty composure crumbling. "But you're . . ."

"Pretty? Think again." She smiled. "I'm Tally Youngblood. My mind is very ugly. And I'm taking your car."

The Doctor was quite afraid of savages, it seemed—even beautiful ones.

He meekly allowed himself be locked into the cargo container of one of the hovercars, and handed over the take-off codes to the other. The security was nothing Tally couldn't have tricked herself, but it saved time. And the expression on Dr. Valen's face as he gave her the codes was pretty indeed. He was used to dealing with villagers in awe of his godhood. But one look at Tally's knife and he'd realized who was giving the orders.

The man answered a few more of Tally's questions, until no doubt remained in her mind what this reservation was all about. This had been the place where the operation had been developed, from which the first test subjects had been drawn. The purpose of the brain lesions was to deter violence and conflict, so who better to experiment on than people caught up in an endless blood feud? Like rabid enemies in a locked room, the tribes trapped within the ring of little men would reveal anything you wanted to know about the very human origins of bloodshed.

She shook her head. Poor Andrew. His whole world was an experiment, and his father had died in a conflict that meant precisely nothing.

Tally paused a moment in the hovercar before taking off, familiarizing herself with the controls. They seemed about the same as a city car, but she had to remember that this one wasn't idiotproof—it would fly into a mountain if you told it to. She would have to be careful in the high spires of the ruins.

The first thing she did was put her boot through the communication system; she didn't want the car telling the city authorities where it was.

"Tally!"

She started at the shout, peering out through the front windows. But it was only Andrew, and he was alone. She slid out of the driver's door, waving for him to be silent and pointing at the other car. "I've got the Doctor locked up," she hissed. "Don't let him hear your voice. What are you doing back here?"

He looked at the other hovercar, eyes widening at the thought of a god imprisoned within, and whispered, "I was sent back to see where he was. He said he would be just behind us."

"Well, he's not coming. And I'm about to leave."

He nodded. "Of course. Good-bye, Young Blood."

"Good-bye." She smiled. "I won't forget all your help."

Andrew was staring into her eyes, the familiar pretty-awed expression coming over his face. "I'll not forget you, either."

"Don't look at me that way."

"What way, Tally?"

"Like a . . . god. We're just humans, Andrew."

He looked at the ground, nodding slowly. "I know."

"Not very perfect humans, some of us worse than you could imagine. We've done awful things to your people for a long time now. We've used you."

He shrugged. "What can we do? You are so powerful."

"Yeah, we are." She took his hand. "But keep trying to get past the little men. The real world is huge. Maybe you can get far enough away that the Specials will stop looking for you. And I'll try to . . ." She didn't finish the promise. Try to do what?

A smile broke across Andrew's face, and he reached out to touch her flash tattoo. "You are bubbly now."

She nodded, swallowing.

"We will wait for you, Young Blood."

Tally blinked, then hugged him wordlessly. She slid back into the hovercar and started the rotors. As the whine of its engines built, she watched the birds scatter from the clearing, terrified by the roar of the gods' machine. Andrew backed away.

The car rose at her first touch on the controls, its power shuddering through her bones. The rotors whipped the treetops around her into a frenzy, but the car rose steadily, under control.

Tally looked down as the car cleared the trees, and saw Andrew waving up at her, his crooked, gap-toothed smile still hopeful. Tally knew that she would have to return, just like he'd said; she no longer had a choice. Someone had to help the people here escape the reservation, and they had no one else but Tally.

She sighed. At least one thing was consistent about her life: It just kept on getting more complicated.

## THE RUINS

Tally reached the sea while the sun was still rising, painting the water pink through the low clouds out on the horizon.

She angled the machine northward in a slow, even turn. As she'd expected, this out-of-city car had a scary tendency to do whatever Tally asked of it. Her first turn had been sharp enough to bang her head against the driver's side window. This time, she was taking it easy.

As the car gradually climbed, she soon spotted the outskirts of the Rusty Ruins. A distance that would have taken a week on foot had shot by in a blur below Tally in less than an hour. When the sinuous shape of the ancient roller coaster came into view, she began to bank the craft inland.

Landing was the easy part. Tally pulled the emergency bar, the one they taught littlies to use if their driver had a heart attack or passed out. The car brought itself to a halt and began to descend. Tally had picked a flat spot, one of the many giant concrete fields that the Rusties built to park their groundcars in.

The vehicle settled onto the weed-choked ground, and Tally opened her door the moment the car bumped to a stop. If the other scientists had found the Doctor and made some sort of emergency call, the Specials would already be looking for her. The more distance she put between herself and the stolen hovercar, the better.

The spires of the ruins rose up before Tally, the tallest about an hour away on foot. She was, of course, arriving almost two weeks after the others. But hopefully they hadn't given up on her, or maybe they'd left a message of some kind.

Surely Zane would have stayed, waiting in the tallest building, unwilling to leave while there was still a chance she would show up.

Unless, of course, their escape had come too late for him.

Tally shouldered her backpack and started to walk.

The ruined streets were full of ghosts.

Tally had hardly ever walked in the city before. She had always cruised around on a hoverboard—ten meters up, at least—avoiding the burned-out cars down at ground level. In the last days of Rusty civilization, an artificial plague had spread across the world. It didn't infect human beings or animals, just petroleum, reproducing itself in the gas tanks of groundcars and jet aircraft, slowly making the infected oil unstable. Plague-transformed petroleum burst into flame when it came into contact with oxygen, and the oily smoke from the sudden fires spread the bacterial spores on the wind, into more gas tanks, more oil fields, until it had reached every Rusty machine across the globe.

The Rusties really hadn't liked walking, it turned out. Even after they'd figured out what the plague was doing, panicked citizens still jumped into their funny, rubber-wheeled groundcars, thinking to escape into the wild. If Tally looked hard enough, she could see crumbling skeletons through the smeared windows of the cars jammed onto the ruins' streets. Only a few of the people back then had been smart enough to walk out, and strong enough to survive the death of their world. Whoever had engineered the plague had definitely understood the Rusties' weakness.

"Boy, you guys were stupid," Tally muttered at the car windows, but calling them names didn't make the dead Rusties any less ominous. The few intact skulls just stared back at her with empty expressions.

Farther into the dead city, the buildings grew taller and taller, their steel frameworks rising up like the skeletons of giant and extinct creatures. Tally took a winding path through the narrow streets, looking for the tallest building in the ruins. The huge spire was easy to spot from a hoverboard, but from the ground the city was a tangled maze.

Then she turned a corner and saw it, chunks of old concrete clinging to the towering matrix of steel beams, the empty windows gazing down at her, jagged shapes of bright sky showing through. This was definitely the place—Tally remembered when Shay had taken her up to its top the first time she'd come out to the Rusty Ruins. There was only one problem.

How was she going to get up?

The innards of the building had long since rotted away. There were no stairs, and hardly any floors to speak of. The steel frame made it perfect for a hoverboard's magnetic lifters, but there was no way for a person to climb it without serious mountaineering gear. If Zane or the New Smokies had left a message for Tally, it would be up there, but she had no way of reaching it.

Tally sat down, suddenly exhausted. It was like the tower in her dream, without stairs or elevator, and she'd lost the key, which in this case was her hoverboard. All she could think of was to hike back to the stolen car and fly it up there. Maybe she could bring it close enough beside the building . . . but who would hold it in a steady hover while she climbed out onto the ancient steel frame?

For the thousandth time, Tally wished that her board hadn't been wrecked.

She stared up at the tower. What if no one was up there? What if, after traveling all this way, Tally Youngblood was still alone?

She got to her feet and yelled as loud as she could, "Heeeey!"

The sound echoed through the ruins, sending a flock of birds into flight from a distant rooftop.

"Hey! It's me!"

Once the echoes faded, there was no sound in answer. Tally's throat felt sore from yelling. She knelt to dig a safety flare out of her backpack. A fire would be pretty obvious down here in the shadows of the cavernous buildings.

She cracked the flare open, holding its hissing flame away from her face, then cried out again. "It's meeeee . . . Tally Youngblood!"

Something shifted in the sky above.

Tally blinked away the spots that the flare had left in her eyes and stared into the bright blue sky. A shape drifted away from the towering building, a tiny oval that began to grow slowly. . . .

The underside of a hoverboard. Someone was coming down!

Tally tossed the flare onto a pile of rocks, her heart pounding, suddenly realizing she had no idea who was descending to meet her. How had she been so dimwitted? It could be anyone up there on the board. If the Specials had caught the other Crims and made them talk, they would know this was the planned meeting place, and Tally's latest escape was about to come to a sudden end.

She told herself to calm down. It was a hoverboard, after all, and only one. Surely if Specials had been lying in wait, they would have rushed out from every direction in a bunch of hovercars.

In any case, there was no point in panicking. She wasn't likely to escape on foot now. The only thing to do was wait. The safety flare sizzled out to a sputtering death while the hoverboard descended slowly, hugging the metal frame of the building. Once or twice, Tally thought she saw a face peering over the edge, but against the bright sky it could have been anyone.

When it was only ten meters overhead, Tally found the nerve to cry out again. "Hello?" Her voice sounded shaky in her ears.

"Tally . . . ," someone called back, the voice familiar.

The hoverboard settled beside her, and Tally found herself staring into a thoroughly ugly face: the forehead too high, the smile crooked, a small scar cutting a white line through one eyebrow. She stared at him, blinking in the gloom of the broken city.

"David?" she said softly.

## FACES

He stared at her, of course.

Even if she hadn't shouted out her name, David knew her voice. And he had been waiting for Tally, after all, so he must have known from the first cry who was down here. But the way he stared at her, it was as if he were seeing someone else.

"David," she said again. "It's me."

He nodded, still speechless. But it wasn't pretty-awe that had caught his tongue—that much Tally realized. His gaze seemed to be searching for something, trying to recognize what the operation had left of her old face, but his expression remained unsure . . . and a bit sad.

David was uglier than she remembered. In Tally's ugly-prince dreams, his imbalanced features had never been so disjointed, his unsurged teeth never so crooked or discolored. His blemishes weren't as bad as Andrew's, of course. He looked no worse than Sussy or Dex, city kids who'd grown up with toothpaste pills and sunblock patches.

But this was David, after all.

Even after her time with the villagers, many of them toothless and scarred, his face sent a shock through her. Not because he was hideous—he wasn't—but because he was simply . . . unimpressive.

Not an ugly prince. Just ugly.

And the weird thing was, even as she had these thoughts, her long-suppressed memories were finally flooding back. This was David, who had taught her how to make a fire, how to clean and cook fish, how to navigate by the stars. They had worked side by side, traveled together for weeks on end, and Tally had given up her city life to stay with him in the Smoke—she'd wanted to live with him forever.

All those memories had survived the operation, hidden somewhere inside her brain. But her life among the pretties must have changed something even more profound: the way she saw him, as if this wasn't the same David in front of her anymore.

Neither of them said anything for a while.

Finally, he cleared his throat. "We should probably get moving. They sometimes send patrols out around this time of day."

She looked at the ground. "Okay."

"I've got to do this first." He pulled a wandlike device from one pocket and swept it over her. It stayed silent.

"No bugs on me?" she said.

He shrugged. "Can't be too careful. You don't have a board?"

Tally shook her head. "It got damaged in the escape."

"Wow. Takes a lot to break a hoverboard."

"It was a long fall."

He smiled. "Same old Tally. I knew you'd show up, though. Mom said you'd probably . . ." He didn't finish.

"I'm fine." She looked up at him, unsure of how much to say. "Thanks for waiting."

They rode his board. Tally was taller than David now, so she stood behind him, hands around his waist. She'd abandoned her heavy crash bracelets before her long trek with Andrew Simpson Smith, but her sensor was still clipped to her belly ring, so the board could feel her center of gravity and compensate for the extra weight. Still, they went slowly at first.

The feel of David's body, the way he leaned into the turns, was so familiar—even the smell of him set her memories spinning. (Tally didn't want to think about how she smelled, but he didn't seem to have noticed.) She was amazed at how much was coming back; her memories of him seemed to have been ready and waiting, and were all flooding in now that he stood next to her. Here on the board, with David turned away from her, Tally's body cried out to hold him tight. She wanted to take back all the stupid, pretty-minded thoughts she'd had at her first glimpse of his face.

But was it just that he was ugly? Everything else had changed as well.

Tally knew she should be asking about the others, especially Zane. But she couldn't bring the name to her lips, couldn't speak at all. Just standing on the board with David was almost too much.

She kept wondering why it had been Croy who'd brought her the cure. In Tally's letter to herself, she had been so certain that David would be the one to rescue her. He was the prince of her dreams, after all.

Was he still angry that she had betrayed the Smoke? Did he blame her for his father's death? The same night she'd confessed everything to David, Tally had gone back to the city to give herself up, to become pretty so she could test the cure. She'd never had a chance to explain how sorry she was. They hadn't even said good-bye to each other.

But if David hated her, why had he been the one waiting in the ruins? Not Croy, not Zane—David. Her head was spinning, almost like being pretty-minded again, but without the happy part.

"It's not far," David said. "Maybe three hours, traveling tandem like this."

She didn't answer.

"I didn't think to bring another board. Should have known you wouldn't have one, since it took you so long to get here."

"I'm sorry."

"No big deal. We just have to fly a little slower."

"No. I'm sorry. For what I did." She fell silent. The words had exhausted her.

He let the board coast to a stop between two towering husks of metal and concrete, and they stood there for a long moment, David still facing away. She rested one cheek on his shoulder, her eyes beginning to burn.

Finally, he said, "I thought I would know what to say. Once I saw you."

"Forgot about the new face, didn't you?"

"I didn't forget, exactly. But I didn't think it would be so . . . not you."

"Me either," Tally said, then realized her words wouldn't make sense to him. David's face hadn't changed, after all.

He turned around carefully on the board and touched her brow. Tally tried to look at him, but couldn't. She felt her flash tattoo pulsing under his fingers.

Tally smiled. "Oh, is that freaking you out? It's just a Crim thing, to see who's bubbly."

"Yeah, a tattoo keyed to your heartbeat. They told me. But I hadn't imagined one on you. It's so . . . weird."

"It's still me inside, though."

"It feels that way, flying together." He turned away, tilting the hoverboard forward and into motion.

Tally held him tighter now, not wanting him to turn around again. This was hard enough without the confused feelings that rose up every time she looked at him. He probably didn't want to look at her city-made face either, with its huge eyes and animated tattoo. One thing at a time. "Just tell me, David, why did Croy bring me the cure instead of you?"

"Things got messed up. I was going to come for you when I got back."

"Got back? From where?"

"I was away scouting another city, looking for more uglies to join us, when the Specials came in force. They started to make huge sweeps of the ruins, looking for us."

He took her hand and pressed it to his chest. "My mom decided to get out of town for a while. We've been holed up in the wild."

"Leaving me stuck in the city," she said, and sighed. "Maddy wouldn't have much problem with that, I guess." Tally had little doubt that David's mother still blamed her for everything—the end of the Smoke, Az's death.

"She didn't have a choice," David protested. "There's never been so many Specials before. It was too dangerous to stay here."

Tally took a deep breath, remembering her little chat with Dr. Cable. "I guess Special Circumstances has been recruiting lately."

"But I hadn't forgotten about you, Tally. I'd made Croy promise to bring you the pills and your letter if anything happened to me, just to make sure you had a chance of escaping. When they started to pack up the New Smoke, he figured we might not be back for a while, so he snuck into the city."

"You told him to come?"

"Of course. He was my backup. I never would have left you alone in there, Tally."

"Oh." Dizziness swept over her again, as if the board were a feather spinning toward the ground. She closed her eyes and held David tighter, finally grasping the solidness and reality of him, more powerful than any memory. Tally felt something inside herself depart, a disquiet that she'd hardly known was there. The torment in her dreams, the worry that David had forsaken her, had all been over a mix-up, just plans that had gone wrong, like in old stories when a letter arrived too late or was sent to the wrong person, and the trick was not killing yourself over it.

David had wanted to come for her himself, it turned out.

"Of course, you weren't alone," he said softly.

Tally's body stiffened. By now he knew about Zane, of course. How was she supposed to explain that she'd simply forgotten David? It wouldn't sound like much of an excuse to most people, but he knew all about the lesions—his parents had raised him knowing what being pretty-minded meant. He had to understand.

Of course, in reality it wasn't as simple as that. Tally hadn't forgotten Zane, after all. She could see his beautiful face right now, gaunt and vulnerable, the way his golden eyes had flashed just before he jumped from the balloon. His kiss had given her the strength to find the pills; he had shared the cure with her. So what was she supposed to say?

The easiest thing was, "How is he?"

David shrugged. "Not great. But not too bad, considering. You're lucky it wasn't you, Tally."

"The cure is dangerous, isn't it? It doesn't work for some people."

"It works perfectly. Your pals have already all had it, and they're fine."

"But Zane's headaches . . ."

"More than just headaches." He sighed. "I'll let my mother explain it to you."

"But what . . ." Tally let her question fade into silence. She couldn't blame David for not wanting to talk about Zane. At least her unasked questions had all been answered. The other Crims had made it here and had hooked up with the Smokies; Maddy had been able to help Zane; the escape had worked perfectly. And now that Tally had made it to the ruins herself, everything was just fine and dandy. "Thank you for waiting for me," she said again, softly.

He didn't answer, and they flew the rest of the way without looking at each other once.

## DAMAGE CONTROL

The path to the New Smokies' hiding place wound along streams and ancient railway beds, wherever there was enough metal to keep the hoverboard aloft. Finally, they climbed a small mountain far outside the Rusty Ruins, the board's lifters clinging to the fallen remains of an old cable car track, up to where a huge concrete dome, cracked open by the centuries, stood against the sky.

"What was this place?" Tally asked, her voice dry after three hours in silence.

"An observatory. There used to be a big telescope in that dome. But the Rusties took it out once the pollution from the city got too bad."

Tally had seen pictures of the sky filled with dirt and smoke—they showed those a lot in school—but it was hard to imagine that the Rusties had really managed to change the color of the air itself. She shook her head. Everything that she thought her teachers had exaggerated about the Rusties always turned out to be true. The temperature had dropped steadily as they'd climbed the mountain, and the afternoon sky looked crystal clear to her.

"After the scientists couldn't see the stars anymore, the dome was just for tourists," David said. "That's what all these cable cars were for. Lots of ways down by hoverboard, if we ever need to get out of here fast, and we can see for miles in every direction."

"Fort Smokey, huh?"

"I guess. If the Specials ever find us, at least we've got a chance."

A lookout had evidently spotted them on the way up—people were spilling from the broken observatory as the hoverboard settled to the earth. Tally spotted the New Smokies—Croy, Ryde, and Maddy, along with a few uglies she didn't recognize—and the two dozen or so Crims who'd come along on the escape.

Tally searched for Zane's face among the crowd, but he wasn't there.

She jumped from the board, running to hug Fausto. He grinned at her, and she could see from his sharpened expression that he'd taken the pills. He wasn't just bubbly anymore; he was cured.

"Tally, you smell," he said, still grinning.

"Oh, yeah. Long trip. Long story."

"I knew you'd make it. But where's Peris?"

She took a deep breath of the cold mountain air.

"Chickened out, huh?" Fausto said before she could answer. When she nodded, he added, "Always thought he would."

"Take me to Zane."

Fausto turned, gesturing toward the observatory. The others were hovering close, but looked a little put off by her bedraggled appearance and ripe smell. The Crims called out hellos, and she could see the uglies reacting to a new pretty face, their eyes widening even though she was a mess. Worked every time, even when they didn't think you were a god.

Tally paused to nod at Croy. "I haven't had a chance to thank you yet."

He raised an eyebrow. "Don't thank me. You did it yourself."

She frowned, noticing that Maddy was staring strangely at her. Tally ignored the look, not interested in what David's mother thought, and followed Fausto into the broken dome.

It was dark inside—a few lanterns were strung up around the edge of the huge, open hemisphere, and a narrow shaft of blinding sunlight streamed through the dome's great fissure. An open fire cast jittering shadows through the space, its smoke climbing lazily up through the crack overhead.

Zane lay on a pile of blankets by the fire, his eyes closed. He looked even thinner than when they'd been trying to starve the cuffs off, his eyes sunken into his head. The covers rose and fell softly with his breathing.

Tally swallowed. "But David said he was okay. . . ."

"He's stable," Fausto said, "which is good, considering."

"Considering what?"

Fausto spread his hands helplessly. "His brain."

A chill moved through Tally, the shadows in the corners of her eyes rippling for a moment. "What about it?" she said softly.

"You had to experiment, didn't you, Tally?" came a voice from the darkness. Maddy stepped into the light, David at her side.

Tally held her steely glare. "What are you talking about?"

"The pills I gave you were meant to be taken together."

"I know. But there were two of us . . ." Tally trailed off at David's expression. And I was too scared to do it alone, she added to herself, remembering the panic of those moments in Valentino 317.

"I suppose I should have known," Maddy said, shaking her head. "This was always a risk, letting a pretty-head treat herself."

"What was?"

"I never explained how the cure worked, did I?" Maddy said. "How the nanos remove the lesions from your brain? They break them down, like the pills that cure cancer."

"So what went wrong?"

"The nanos didn't stop. They went on reproducing, breaking down Zane's brain."

Tally turned to look at the form on the bed. His breathing seemed so shallow, the movement of his chest at the edge of perception.

She faced David. "But you said the cure worked perfectly."

He nodded. "It does. Your other friends are fine. But the two pills were different. The second pill, the one you took, is the cure for the cure. It makes the nanos self-destruct after they finish with the lesions. Without it, Zane's nanos kept reproducing, kept eating away at him. Mom said they stopped at some point, but not before they did a . . . certain amount of damage."

The sickening feeling in Tally's stomach redoubled as the realization sunk home: This was her fault. She had swallowed the pill that would have kept Zane from this, the cure for the cure. "How much damage?"

"We don't know yet," Maddy said. "I had enough stem tissue to regenerate the destroyed areas of his brain, but the connections that Zane had built up among those cells are gone. Those connections are where memories and motor skills are stored, and where cognition happens. Some parts of his mind are almost a blank slate."

"A blank slate? You mean . . . he's gone?"

"No, just a few places are damaged," Fausto spoke up. "And his brain can rewire itself, Tally. His neurons are making new connections. That's what he's doing right now. Zane had been doing it all along; he hoverboarded all the way here on his own before he collapsed."

"Rather amazing that he lasted so long," Maddy said, shaking her head slowly. "I think not eating is what saved him. By starving himself, he eventually starved the nanos. They appear to be gone."

"He can still talk and everything," Fausto said. He looked down at Zane. "He's just a little . . . tired right now."

"It could have been you in that bed, Tally." Maddy shook her head. "A fifty-fifty chance. You just got lucky."

"That's me. Little Miss Lucky," Tally said softly.

Of course, she had to admit to herself that it was true. They'd split the two pills randomly, assuming they were the same. The nanos could have been eating away at Tally's brain all this time instead of Zane's. Lucky her.

She let her eyes close, realizing at last how hard Zane must have worked to hide what was happening to him. All those long silences when they'd been wearing the cuffs, he'd been fighting, struggling to keep his mind together, unsure of exactly what was happening, but risking everything to escape becoming pretty-minded again.

Tally gazed down at him, wishing for a moment it had been the other way around. Anything was better than seeing him like this. If only she'd taken the nano pill, and he had taken the one that . . . had done what? "Wait a second. If Zane got the nanos, how did my pill cure me?"

"It didn't," Maddy said. "Without the other pill, the anti-nanos you took would have no effect whatsoever."

"But . . ."

"It was you, Tally," came a soft voice from the bed. Zane's eyes had opened a slit, catching the sunlight like the edges of gold coins. He gave her a weary smile. "You got bubbly on your own."

"But I felt so different after we . . ." She fell silent, remembering that day—their kiss, sneaking into Valentino Mansion, climbing the tower. But, of course, all those things had happened before they'd taken the pills. Being with Zane had changed her from the beginning, from that first kiss.

Tally remembered how her "cure" always seemed to come and go. She'd had to work to stay bubbly, more like the other Crims than Zane.

"He's right, Tally," Maddy said. "Somehow, you cured yourself."

## COLD WATER

Tally stayed at Zane's bedside. He was awake and talking now, and it was easier to be here than dealing with everything that she and David still had to work out. The others left them alone.

"Did you know what was happening to you?"

Zane took a moment before answering. His speech was full of long silences now, almost like Andrew's epic pauses. "I knew that everything was getting harder. Sometimes I had to concentrate just to walk. But I hadn't felt so alive since I'd turned pretty; it was worth it, being bubbly with you. I figured once we found the New Smoke, they could help me."

"They are helping. Maddy said that she put in some new . . ." Tally swallowed.

"Brain tissue?" he supplied, and smiled. "Sure, blank neurons fresh out of the oven. Just got to fill them up now."

"We will. We'll do bubbly-making things," Tally said, but the promise felt strange in her mouth—"we" meant she and Zane, as if David didn't exist.

"If there's enough left of me to be bubbly," he said tiredly. "It's not like all my memories are gone. It was mostly my cognition centers that were affected, and some motor skills."

"Cognition? You mean like thinking?" Tally said.

"Yeah, and motor skills, like walking." He shrugged. "But the brain's built to take damage, Tally. It's wired so that everything is stored everywhere, sort of. When a part of it gets damaged, things don't get lost, just fuzzier. Like a hangover." He laughed. "A really bad one. On top of which, I'm sore from lying in bed all day. And it feels like I've got a toothache from all this Smokey food. It's just phantom pains from brain damage, Maddy says." He rubbed one cheek with a scowl.

She took his hand. "I can't believe you're so brave about this. It's incredible."

"You should talk, Tally." He struggled to sit up, his movements shaky and infirm. "You managed to cure yourself without getting your brain chewed up. That's what I'd call incredible."

Tally looked down at their clasped hands. She didn't feel very incredible. She felt smelly and dirty, and horrible that she hadn't had the guts to take both pills, which would have prevented all of this from happening. She didn't even have the guts to talk to Zane about David, or vice versa. Which was just pathetic.

"Is it strange, seeing him?" he asked.

She looked at Zane, and he chuckled at her surprise. "Come on, Tally. It's not like I'm reading your mind. I had plenty of warning about this. You told me about the guy the first time we kissed, remember?"

"Oh, yeah." So Zane had been expecting this all along. Tally should have foreseen it herself. Maybe she simply hadn't wanted to face the obvious. "Yeah, it is strange seeing him. I definitely didn't expect to find him waiting for me in the ruins. Just me and him alone."

Zane nodded. "It was interesting, waiting for you. His mother said you wouldn't come at all. That you must have chickened out, because you hadn't really been cured. Like you were just playing along with me, imitating my bubbliness."

Tally rolled her eyes. "She doesn't much like me."

"You don't say?" He grinned. "But David and me figured you'd show up sooner or later. We figured that—"

Tally groaned. "So are you guys like friends now?"

Zane took one of his excruciatingly long pauses. "I guess so. He asked me a lot about you when we first got here. I think he wanted to know how being pretty has changed you."

"Really?"

"Really. He was the one who met us when we arrived in the ruins. Him and Croy, camping out and watching for flares. It turns out that those two left the magazines for the city uglies to find, so they'd know the ruins were being visited again." Zane's voice had gotten dreamy, as if he was falling asleep. "At least I finally got to see him again, after chickening out all those months ago." He turned to her. "David really missed you, you know."

"I ruined his life," Tally said softly.

"You didn't do anything on purpose; David understands that now. I told him how when you'd planned to betray the Smoke, it was because the Specials threatened to keep you ugly for life."

"You told him that?" Tally let out a slow breath.

"Thanks. I never really had a chance to explain why I'd come to the Smoke, how they'd forced me. Maddy made me leave the same night I confessed everything."

"Yeah. David wasn't happy with her about that. He wanted to talk to you again."

"Oh," she said. There was so much that she and David hadn't gotten straight between them. Of course, the thought of Zane and him discussing her history in great detail didn't exactly thrill Tally, but at least David knew the whole story now. She sighed. "Thanks for telling me all this. It must be weird."

"A little. But you shouldn't feel so bad. About what happened back then."

"Why not? I destroyed the Smoke, and David's father died because of me."

"Tally, everyone in the city is manipulated. The purpose of everything we're taught is to make us afraid of change. I've been trying to explain it to David, how from the day we're born, the whole place is a machine for keeping us under control."

She shook her head. "That doesn't make it right to betray your friends."

"Yeah, well, I did, long before you even met Shay. When it comes to the Smoke, I'm just as much at fault as you."

She looked at him in disbelief. "You? How?"

"Did I ever tell you how I met Dr. Cable?"

Tally looked at him, realizing that this was one conversation they'd never had a chance to finish. "No. You didn't."

"After the night that Shay and I chickened out, most of my friends were gone away to the Smoke. The dorm minders knew I was the leader, so they asked me where everyone had run off to. I played tough, and didn't say a word. So Special Circumstances came for me." His voice grew softer, as if the cuff were still around his wrist. "They took me to that headquarters of theirs out in the factory belt, same as you. I tried to be strong, but they threatened me. Said they'd make me into one of them."

"One of them? A Special?" Tally swallowed.

"Yeah. After that, being a pretty-head didn't seem so bad anymore. So I told them everything I knew. I told them that Shay had planned to run away, but also chickened out, and that's why they knew about her. And that's probably why they started watching . . ." His voice trailed off.

Tally blinked. "Watching me, when she and I became friends."

He nodded tiredly. "So, you see? I started the whole thing, by not leaving when I was supposed to. I'll never judge you for what happened to the Smoke, Tally. It was my fault as much as yours."

She took his hand, shaking her head. He couldn't accept blame, not after everything he'd gone through. "Zane, no. It can't be your fault. That was a long time ago." She sighed. "Maybe neither of us is to blame."

They were silent for a while, Tally's own words echoing in her head. With Zane lying here in front of her, his mind half-missing, what was the point of wallowing in old guilt—his, or hers, or anyone's? Maybe the bad blood between her and Maddy was as meaningless as the feud between Andrew's village and the outsiders. If they were all going to live together here in the New Smoke, they would have to let the past go.

Of course, things were still complicated.

Tally took a slow breath, then said, "So what do you think of David?"

Zane looked at the arched ceiling dreamily. "He's very intense. Really serious. Not as bubbly as us. You know?"

Tally smiled, and squeezed his hand. "Yeah, I do."

"And kind of . . . ugly."

She nodded, remembering how back in the Smoke, David had always looked at her as if she was pretty. And at times, looking at him had felt the same as looking into a pretty's face. Maybe when she'd had the real cure, those feelings would come back. Or maybe they were really gone for good, not because of any operation, but just because time had passed, and because of what she'd had with Zane.

When Zane had finally fallen asleep, Tally decided to take a bath. Fausto told her how to get to a spring on the far side of the mountain, choked with icicles at this time of year, but deep enough to submerge your whole body. "Just take a heated jacket," he said. "Or you'll freeze to death before you make it back."

Tally figured death was better than being this filthy, and she needed more than a rubdown with a wet cloth to feel clean again. She also wanted to be alone for a while, and maybe the shock from some freezing water would help her get up the nerve to talk to David.

Hoverboarding down the mountain in the crisp, late afternoon air, Tally was amazed at how clear and bright everything looked. She still found it hard to believe that she hadn't really taken the cure; she felt as bubbly as ever. Maddy had muttered something about a "placebo effect," as if believing you were cured would be enough to fix your brain. But Tally knew it was more than that.

Zane had changed her. From their very first kiss, even before he'd had the cure himself, being with him had made her bubbly. Tally wondered if she even needed the cure now, or if she could stay this way forever on her own. The thought of swallowing the same pill that had eaten away

Zane's brain didn't thrill her, even with the anti-nanos as a chaser. Maybe she could skip it altogether, and rely on Zane's magic. They could help each other now, rewiring his brain at the same time Tally fought becoming pretty-minded.

They had come this far together, after all. Even before the pills, they had changed each other.

Of course, David had changed Tally too. Back in the Smoke, he'd been the one who'd convinced her to stay in the wild, even to stay ugly, giving up her future in the city. Her reality had been transformed by those two weeks in the Smoke, starting . . . when? That first time David and she had kissed.

"How lucky is that?" Tally muttered to herself. "Sleeping Beauty with two princes."

What was she supposed to do? Choose between David and Zane? Especially now that all three of them were living together here at Fort Smokey? Somehow it didn't seem fair that she found herself in this position. Tally had barely remembered David when she'd met Zane—but she hadn't wanted to have her memories erased, after all.

"Thanks again, Dr. Cable," she said.

The water looked really cold.

Tally had easily kicked through the layer of ice on top, and was now staring down with dread into the gurgling spring. Maybe smelling bad wasn't the worst thing in the world. Spring would come in only three or four months, after all. . . .

She shivered, turning the heat up in her borrowed jacket, then sighed and started to take off her clothes. This little bath would be very bubbly-making, at least.

Tally smeared a soap packet onto herself before jumping in, rubbing some into her hair, guessing she would last about ten seconds in the half-frozen spring. She knew she'd have to jump—no dangling of the foot or lowering herself in slowly. Only the laws of gravity would keep her going once her naked flesh hit cold water.

Tally took a breath, held it . . . and leaped into the spring.

The icy water crushed her like a vice, forcing the breath from her lungs, locking every muscle tight. She hugged herself with her arms, rolling into a ball in the shallow pool, but the cold seemed to cut through her flesh and straight into her bones.

Tally fought to take a breath, but managed only shallow little gasps of air, her entire body shaking as if it would break apart. With a titanic act of will she dunked her head in, erasing all sound, the rasp of her breath and gurgle of the spring replaced by the rumble of roiling water. She rubbed furiously at her hair with trembling hands.

When her head burst into the air again, Tally drew in great breaths and found herself laughing—everything had turned strangely clear, the world more bubbly than a cup of coffee or a glass of champagne could make it, the sensation more intense than falling toward the earth on her hoverboard. She lay there for a moment in the water, amazed at it all—the clarity of the sky and the perfection of a leafless tree nearby.

Tally remembered her first bath in a cold stream on the way to the Smoke, all those months ago. How it had shifted the way she saw the world—even before the operation had put the lesions on her brain, before she'd met David, much less Zane. Even then, her mind had started to change, realizing that nature didn't need an operation to make it beautiful, it just was.

Maybe she didn't need a handsome prince to stay awake—or an ugly one, for that matter. After all, Tally had cured herself without the pill and had made it all the way here on her own. No one else she'd ever heard of had escaped the city twice.

Maybe she'd always been bubbly, somewhere inside. It

only took loving someone—or being in the wild, or maybe just a plunge into freezing water—to bring it out.

Tally was still in the pond when she heard the cry: a hoarse shout that came from the air.

She climbed out hurriedly, and the wind cutting through her felt colder than the water. The towels Tally had brought were brittle in the chill air, and she was still drying herself when a hoverboard streaked into view, banking to a halt a few meters away.

David hardly seemed to register that she was naked. He jumped from the board and ran toward her, clutching something in his hand. Skidding to a halt by her pack, he waved the device across it—scanning it for bugs, she realized.

"It's not you," he said. "I knew it wasn't."

Tally was pulling on her clothes. "But you already—"

"A signal just started up out of nowhere, broadcasting our location. We picked it up on the radio, but haven't localized it yet." He looked down at her pack, the relieved expression still on his face. "But you didn't bring it."

"Of course I didn't." Tally sat down to yank on her boots. Her pounding heart began to drive the cold from her body. "Don't you scan everyone who joins you?"

"Yeah. But the bug must have been dormant—it only started sending when someone activated it, or maybe it was set to go off at a certain time." His eyes scanned the horizon. "The Specials will be here soon."

She stood. "So we run."

He shook his head. "We can't go anywhere until we find it."

"Why not?" She pulled on crash bracelets.

"It's taken us months to build up the supplies we've got, Tally. We can't leave them all behind, not with all you Crims having just joined us. But we won't know what's safe to take until we figure out where the signal's coming from. It's not showing up anywhere."

Tally hoisted her pack and snapped her fingers, her board rising into the air. As she stepped on, her mind still racing from the freezing bath, she recalled something from earlier that day. "Toothache," she said.

"What?"

"Zane was in the hospital two weeks ago. It's inside him."

## TRACKER

They swept back up the mountain, banking hard against the high gravities of their turns. Tally stayed in the lead, positive that she was right. The doctors had made Zane unconscious for a few minutes in the hospital while they'd repaired his broken hand. They must have hidden a tracker in his teeth at the same time. Of course, regular city doctors wouldn't have done something like that on their own—it had to be the work of Special Circumstances.

The camp was bedlam when they arrived. New Smokies and Crims ran in and out of the observatory door with equipment, clothing, and food, making two piles beside Croy and Maddy, who stood waving scanners over everything wildly. Others hurriedly repacked the scanned gear, getting ready to flee once the bug was found.

Tally tipped back her hoverboard and forced it up as high as it would go, launching herself over the chaos, directly at the broken dome. When the board reached its maximum height the lifters shuddered, then firmed up as the magnets found the steel frame of the observatory. The crack in the dome was wide enough to glide through, and Tally dropped straight down through the rising smoke, jumping off next to Zane's makeshift bed.

He looked up at her with a soft smile. "Nice entrance, Tally."

She knelt beside him. "Which tooth hurts?"

"What's going on? Everyone's freaking out."

"Which tooth hurts, Zane? You have to show me."

He frowned, but stuck a trembling finger into his mouth, tenderly probing the right side. Tally pulled his hand away and opened his mouth wider, and he made a whimper of protest.

"Shush. I'll explain in a second."

Even in the dim firelight, she could see it: One tooth stood out from the others, its shade of white imperfectly matched—a rushed bit of dentistry, of course.

The signal was coming from Zane.

The wheep of a scanner booting up sounded beside her ear; David had followed her down the hole into the dome. He waved the scanner past Zane's face, and it buzzed angrily. "It's in his mouth?" David asked.

"In his tooth! Get your mother."

"But, Tally—"

"Get her! You and I can't take out a tooth!"

He put a hand on her shoulder. "Neither can she. Not in a few minutes."

She stood, staring into his ugly face. "What are you saying, David?"

"We'll have to leave him behind. They'll be here soon."

"No!" she shouted. "Go get her!"

David swore and turned away, running toward the door

of the observatory. Tally looked down at Zane again.

"What's happening?" he asked.

"They put a tracker in you, Zane. At the hospital."

"Oh," he said, rubbing his face. "I didn't know, Tally, honest. I thought my toothache was from all this wild food."

"Of course you didn't know. You were unconscious for those minutes at the hospital, remember?"

"Are they really going to leave me?"

"I won't let them. I promise."

"I can't go back," he said weakly. "I don't want to be pretty-minded again."

Tally swallowed. If Zane was returned to the city now, the doctors would put the lesions back in, right on top of his blank new tissue. His brain would rewire around them. . . . What chance would he have of staying bubbly?

She couldn't let this happen.

"I'll take you on my hoverboard, Zane—we'll escape on our own if we have to." Her mind raced. She'd still have to get rid of the tracker somehow. She couldn't just bash it out with a rock. . . . Tally looked around for some sort of tool, but the New Smokies had taken everything useful outside to be scanned.

Voices came from the darkness. It was Maddy, David, and Croy. Tally saw that Maddy was carrying some sort of forceps in her hand, and her heart skipped a beat.

Maddy knelt beside Zane and forced open his mouth. He whimpered in pain again as the metal tool probed his teeth.

"Be careful," Tally pleaded softly.

"Hold this." Maddy handed her a flashlight. When Tally pointed it into Zane's mouth, the discolored tooth was obvious.

After a moment, Maddy said, "This isn't good." She

released Zane's head, and he fell back onto the blankets with a groan, his eyes closing.

"Just take it out!"

"They've rooted it to the bone." She turned to Croy. "Finish packing up. We have to run."

"Do something for him!" Tally cried.

Maddy took the light from her. "Tally, it's bonded to the bone. I'd have to shatter his jaw to remove it."

"So don't take it out, just make it stop sending! Smash the tooth! He can take it!"

Maddy shook her head. "Pretty teeth are made of the same stuff they use in aircraft wings. You can't just smash them. I'd need special dental nanos to break it down." She turned the flashlight on Tally, reaching for her mouth.

Tally twisted away. "What are you doing?"

"Just making sure about you."

"But I didn't go into the hos—," Tally began, but Maddy wrenched open her mouth. Tally growled at the back of her throat, but let the woman poke around for a moment; it was quicker than arguing. When she grunted and let go, Tally said, "Satisfied?"

"For now. But we have to leave Zane behind."

"Forget it!" Tally shouted.

"They'll be here in another ten minutes," David said.

"Less." Maddy stood.

Tally's vision swam with spots from the little flashlight. She could hardly see their faces in the firelight. Didn't they understand what Zane had gone through to get here, what he had sacrificed for the cure? "I won't leave him."

"Tally—," David began.

"It doesn't matter," Maddy interrupted. "Technically, she's still a pretty-head."

"I am not!"

"You didn't even take the right pill." Maddy put a hand on David's shoulder. "Tally's still got the lesions. Once they scan her brain, they won't even put her under the knife. They'll think she just came along for the ride."

"Mom!" David shouted. "We are not leaving her!"

"And I'm not coming," Tally said.

Maddy shook her head. "Perhaps the lesions aren't as important as we thought. Your father always suspected that being pretty-minded is simply the natural state for most people. They want to be vapid and lazy and vain"—Maddy glanced at Tally—"and selfish. It only takes a twist to lock in that part of their personalities. He always thought that some people could think their way out of it."

"Az was right," Tally said softly. "I'm cured now."

David let out a pained growl. "Cured or not, Tally, you can't stay here. I don't want to lose you again! Mom! Do something!"

"You want to argue with her? Go ahead." Maddy spun on one heel and strode toward the observatory entrance. "We're leaving in two minutes," she said without turning around. "With or without you."

David and Tally were silent for a few moments. It was like when they'd first seen each other in the ruins that morning, neither knowing what to say. Though now, Tally realized, David's face no longer shocked her. Maybe the panic of the moment or the freezing bath had stripped her remaining pretty thoughts away. Or maybe it had simply taken a few hours to align her memories and dreams with the truth. . . .

David wasn't a prince—handsome or otherwise. He was the first boy she'd fallen in love with, but not the last. Time and experiences apart had changed what had been between them.

More important, she had someone else now. However unfair it was that her memories of David had been erased, Tally had built a whole new set of memories, and she couldn't just trade them in for the old ones. Zane and she had helped each other become bubbly, had been imprisoned by the cuffs together, and escaped the city together. She couldn't abandon him now, just because he had been robbed of part of his mind.

Tally knew too well what that was like, being handed over to the city all alone.

Zane was the one person in her life she had never betrayed, and she wasn't about to start now. She took his hand. "I'm not leaving him."

"Think logically, Tally." David spoke slowly, talking to her like she was a littlie. "You can't help Zane if you stay here. You'll both be captured."

"Your mother's right. They won't do anything more to my brain, and I can help him from inside the city."

"We can smuggle Zane the cure, like we did for you."

"I didn't need the cure, David. Maybe Zane won't either. I'll keep him bubbly, I can help him rewire his brain. But he won't stand a chance without me."

David started to speak, but froze for a moment. Then his voice changed, his eyes narrowing. "You're just staying with him because he's pretty."

Tally's eyes widened. "I'm what?"

"Don't you see it? It's like you always used to say: It's evolution. Since your Crim friends got here, Mom's been explaining to me how prettiness works." He pointed at Zane. "He's got those big, vulnerable eyes, that childlike perfect skin. He looks like a baby to you, a needy child, which makes you want to help him. You're not thinking rationally. You're giving yourself up just because he's pretty!"

Tally stared back at David in disbelief. How dare he say this to her? The mere fact that she was standing here proved that Tally could think for herself.

Then she realized what was going on: David was only repeating Maddy's words. She must have warned him not to trust his feelings when he saw the new Tally. Maddy didn't want her son turning into some awestruck ugly, worshipping the ground Tally walked on. So now David thought that all that Tally could see was Zane's pretty face.

David still thought she was just some city kid. Maybe he didn't even really believe that she was cured. Maybe he'd never really forgiven her.

"It's not the way Zane looks, David," she said, her voice trembling with anger. "It's because he makes me bubbly, and because we took a lot of risks together. It could just as easily be me lying there, and he would stay with me if it was."

"It's just programming!"

"No. It's because I love him."

David started to speak again, but the sound choked off.

She sighed. "Go on, David. Whatever your mother said a second ago, she won't really leave without you. They'll all get caught if you don't start moving now."

"Tally—"

"Go!" she cried. David had to start running, or the New Smoke would die, and it would be her fault again.

"But you can—"

"Get your ugly face out of here!" Tally screamed.

The echoes shuddered back at her from the observatory walls for a moment, and Tally tore her gaze away from David. She cradled Zane's face in one hand and kissed him.

The shouted insult had the effect she'd wanted, but Tally couldn't bring herself to look up as she heard David's footsteps retreating into the darkness, first walking, then at a run.

She saw shapes pulsing in the corners of her vision. It wasn't shadows cast by the flickering fire—it was her heart, pounding so hard that she could see the rushing blood beating against her eyes, like something trying to escape.

She had called David ugly. He would never forget that, nor would she.

But she'd had to use that word, Tally told herself. Every second counted, and nothing else would have pushed him away so powerfully. She'd made her choice.

"I'll take care of you, Zane," she said.

He opened his eyes into slits and smiled weakly. "Um, I hope you don't mind if I pretended to pass out for that."

Tally let out a strangled laugh. "Good idea."

"We really can't run? I think I can stand up."

"No. They'd just find us."

He probed at his tooth with his tongue. "Oh, yeah. That sucks. And I almost got everyone else caught too."

She shrugged. "Been there. Done that."

"Are you sure you want to stay with me?"

"I can escape the city again, Zane, anytime I want. I can save you and Shay, and everyone else we left behind. I'm cured for good now." Tally looked at the entrance, saw hoverboards lifting into the air. They were leaving, all of them. She shrugged again. "Besides, I think it's pretty much a done deal. Running after David now would kind of spoil my brilliant breakup line."

"Yeah, I suppose that's true. " Zane chuckled softly. "Do me a favor, Tally? If you ever break up with me, just leave a note."

She smiled back at him. "Okay. As long as you promise never to put your hand in a crusher again."

"Agreed." Zane looked at his fingers, then made a fist. "I'm scared. I want to stay bubbly."

"You'll be bubbly again. I'll help you."

He nodded, grasping her hand. His voice shook as he said, "Do you think David was right? My big beautiful eyes are why you chose me?"

"No. I think it was . . . what I said. And what you said, before you jumped off the balloon." She swallowed. "What's your opinion?"

Zane lay back and closed his eyes, and was silent so long that Tally thought he had fallen asleep again. But then he said softly, "You and David could both be right. Maybe humans beings are programmed . . . to help one another, even to fall in love. But just because it's human nature doesn't make it bad, Tally. Besides, we had a whole city of pretties to choose from, and we chose each other."

She took his hand and murmured, "I'm glad we did."

Zane smiled, then closed his eyes again. A moment later, she saw his breathing slow, and realized that he had managed to pass out again. At least brain damage had some advantages.

Tally felt the last scraps of energy leave her body, and wished she could sleep too, just spend the next few hours unconscious and wake up in the city—an imprisoned princess again, as if this had all been a dream. She laid her head onto Zane's chest and closed her eyes.

Five minutes later, Special Circumstances arrived.

# SPECIALS

The scream of hovercars filled the observatory, echoing like the cries of predatory birds. Whirlwinds from their rotors swept through the crack in the dome, sending the fire into a sudden blaze. Dust choked the air, and gray forms charged through the entrance, taking up positions in the shadows.

"I need a doctor here," Tally announced in a tentative, pretty voice. "Something's wrong with my friend."

A Special appeared beside her out of the darkness. He held a weapon. "Don't move. We don't want to hurt you, but we will if we have to."

"Just help my friend," she said. "He's sick." The sooner city doctors looked at Zane, the better. Maybe they could do more than Maddy had.

The Special said something into a handphone, and Tally glanced down at Zane. Fear showed through his slitted eyes.

"It's okay," she said. "They'll help you."

Zane swallowed, and Tally saw his hands trembling, the last of his brave front crumbling now that their captors had arrived.

"I'll make sure you're cured, one way or another," she said.

"A medical team is coming," the Special said, and Tally smiled prettily at him. The city doctors might mistake Zane's condition for some kind of brain disease, or maybe they would figure out that someone had attempted a cure for the lesions, but they would never recognize how Tally had transformed herself. She could pretend that she'd just come along for the ride, as Maddy had put it. Tally was safe from the operation now.

Maybe Zane could be cured again without more pills.

Maybe everyone in the city could be changed. After their balloon escape and another "rescue" by the Specials, Tally and Zane would be even more famous. They could start something huge, something the Specials couldn't stop.

A razor-edged voice came through the shadows, and Tally flinched.

"I thought I might find you here, Tally." Dr. Cable came into the light, stretching her fingers toward the fire as though she'd stepped inside to get warm.

"Hi, Dr. Cable. Can you help my friend?"

The woman's wolflike smile gleamed in the dark. "Toothache?"

"Something worse." Tally shook her head. "He can't move, can hardly talk. Something's wrong with him."

More Specials streamed into the observatory, including three carrying a stretcher, wearing blue silk instead of gray. They pushed Tally out of the way and laid the litter down next to Zane. He closed his eyes.

"Don't worry," Dr. Cable said. "He'll be fine. We know all about his condition from your little trip to the hospital. It seems that someone slipped Zane some brain nanos. Very bad for his pretty head."

"You knew he was sick?" Tally stood up. "Why didn't you fix him?"

Dr. Cable patted her shoulder. "We brought the nanos to a halt. But the little implant in his tooth was programmed to give him headaches—false symptoms to keep you motivated."

"You were playing with us . . . ," Tally said, watching as the Specials took Zane away.

Dr. Cable was looking around the observatory. "I wanted to see what you were up to and where you would go. I thought you might lead us to those responsible for young Zane's illness." She frowned. "I was going to wait a bit longer to activate the tracker, but after you were so rude to my good friend Dr. Valen this morning, I thought we should come out and bring you home. You certainly know how to cause trouble."

Tally stayed silent, her mind racing. The tracker in Zane's tooth had been activated remotely, but not until the other scientists had discovered Dr. Valen. Once again, Tally had brought Specials along with her.

"We wanted a car to get away," she said, trying to sound pretty. "But we got lost."

"Yes, we found it in the ruins. But I don't think you made it all the way here on foot. Who helped you, Tally?"

She shook her head. "No one."

A Special in gray silk appeared beside Cable and gave a quick report. His razored voice made Tally's flesh crawl, but she couldn't make out any of the muttered words.

"Send the youngsters after them," Dr. Cable ordered, then turned to Tally. "No one, you say? What about the cooking fires and hunting snares and latrines? Quite a few people were camped here, it seems, and they left not long ago." She shook her head. "Pity we didn't get here quicker."

"You won't catch them," Tally said with a pretty smile.

"Won't we?" Dr. Cable's teeth gleamed red in the firelight. "We've got a few new tricks ourselves, Tally."

The doctor turned and strode toward the entrance. When Tally tried to follow, a Special took her shoulder in a grip of iron and sat her down by the fire. Shouted orders and the sounds of more hovercars landing filtered into the dome, but Tally gave up trying to see what was going on through the entrance, and stared at the flames unhappily.

Now that Zane had been taken away, Tally only felt defeated. She'd been played perfectly by Dr. Cable again, tricked into finding the New Smoke, almost betraying everyone one more time. And after her last words, David probably hated her now.

But at least Fausto and the other Crims had escaped the city, hopefully for good. They and the New Smokies had the benefit of a few minutes' head start. They couldn't outrun the Specials' cars in a straight line, but their hoverboards were more nimble. Without Zane's tracker to give them away, they could simply disappear into the surrounding forest. Tally and Zane's rebellion had swelled the ranks of the New Smokies by a couple of dozen members. And now that the cure had been tested, they could bring it to the city, and to other cities, and eventually everyone would be free.

Maybe the city hadn't won, this time.

And being caught might be the best thing for Zane. The city doctors would be better able to treat him than a band of outlaws on the run. Tally focused her mind on how she would help him recover, making him bubbly all over again if she had to.

Maybe she would start with a kiss. . . .

An hour or so after the Specials had first arrived, the fire had burned low, and Tally began to feel the cold again. As she turned up her jacket's heater, a shadow moved in the red shaft of sunset that slanted through the dome's opening.

Tally started. It was someone coming down on a hoverboard. Was it David returning to save her? She shook her head. Maddy would never let him.

"We got a couple of them," a harsh voice called from the board. The gray silk of Special uniforms fluttered in the gloom—two more figures descending through the crack in the dome. The hoverboards were longer than normal, with lifting fans built into their front and back ends. Their rotors stirred the embers of the fire.

So this was their new trick, Tally thought. Specials on hoverboards, perfect for tracking the New Smokies. She wondered who they'd caught.

"Uglies or pretties?" Dr. Cable called. Tally looked up and saw that the doctor had rejoined her by the fire.

"Just a couple of the Crims. The uglies all got away," came the answer. Tally realized that beneath its razor sharpness, she recognized the sound of the Special's voice.

"Oh, no," she said softly.

"Oh, yes, Tally-wa." The figure hopped off her board and strode into the firelight. "New surge! Do you like it?"

It was Shay. She was Special.

"Dr. C let me get more tattoos. Aren't they totally dizzying?"

Tally looked at her old friend, awestruck by the transformation. The spinning lines of flash tattoos covered her, as if Shay's skin were wrapped in a pulsing black net. Her face was lean and cruel, her upper teeth filed down to sharp, triangular points. She was taller, with hard new muscles in her bare arms. The line of the scars where she had cut herself stood out prominently, outlined with swirling tattoos. Shay's eyes flashed in the firelight like a predator's, shifting between red and violet as the flames danced.

She was still pretty, of course, but her cruel, inhuman grace sent shivers through Tally, like watching a colorful spider traverse its web.

Behind her, the other hoverboards descended. Ho and Tachs, Shay's fellow Cutters, each held a limp form. Tally grimaced when she saw that they'd caught Fausto, who'd never been on a hoverboard in his life before a few days ago. But most of the others had escaped, at least . . . and David had made it to safety.

The New Smoke still lived.

"Think my new surge is pretty-making, Tally-wa?" Shay said. "Not too much for you?"

Tally shook her head tiredly. "No. It's bubbly, Shay-la."

A broad, cruel smile filled Shay's face. "About a zillion milli-Helens, huh?"

"At least." Tally turned from her old friend and stared into the fire.

Shay sat down beside her. "Being Special is more bubbly than you can imagine, Tally-wa. Every second is totally spinning. Like, I can hear your heartbeat, can feel the electric buzz of that jacket trying to keep you warm. I can smell your fear."

"I'm not afraid of you, Shay."

"You are a little bit, Tally-wa. You can't lie to me anymore." Shay put her arm around Tally. "Hey, remember the crazy faces I used to design back when we were uglies? Dr. C will let me do them now. Cutters can surge however we want. Even the Pretty Committee can't tell us what we can and can't look like."

"That must be great for you, Shay-la."

"Me and my Cutters are the bubbly new thing in Circumstances. Like special Specials. Isn't that totally happy-making?"

Tally turned to face her, trying to see what was behind the flashing violet-red eyes. Despite the pretty-talk, she heard a cold, serene intelligence in Shay's voice, a pitiless joy in having snared her old betrayer.

Shay was a new kind of cruel pretty, Tally could see. Something even worse than Dr. Cable. Less human.

"Are you really happy, Shay?"

Shay's mouth quivered, her sharp teeth running along her lower lip for a moment, and she nodded. "I am, now that I've got you back, Tally-wa. It wasn't very nice, all of you running off like that without me. Totally sad-making."

"We wanted you along, Shay, I swear. I left you all those pings."

"I was busy." Shay kicked at the dying fire with one boot. "Cutting myself. Searching for a cure." She snorted. "Besides, I've had enough of the camping thing. And, anyway, we're together now, you and me."

"We're against each other." Tally barely whispered the words.

"No way, Tally-wa." Shay's hand squeezed her shoulder roughly. "I'm sick of all the mix-ups and bad blood between us. From now on, you and I are going to be best friends forever."

Tally closed her eyes; so this was Shay's revenge.

"I need you in the Cutters, Tally. It's so bubbly-making!"

"You can't do this to me," Tally whispered, trying to pull away.

Shay held her firmly. "That's the thing, Tally-wa. I can."

"No!" Tally cried, lashing out and trying to struggle to her feet.

Quick as lightning, Shay's hand shot forward, and Tally felt a sharp sting on her neck. Seconds later, a thick fog began to settle over her. She managed to pull away and take a few stumbling steps, but her limbs seemed to fill with liquid lead, and she fell to the ground. A shroud of gray descended across the fire in front of her, the world growing dark.

Words tumbled at her through the void, carried on a razor voice: "Face it, Tally-wa, you're . . ."

## BOGUS DREAMS

Over the next few weeks, Tally never quite awoke. She would stir sometimes, and realize from the feel of sheets and pillows that she was in bed, but mostly her mind floated free of her body, drifting in and out of disjointed versions of the same dream. . . .

There was this beautiful princess locked in a high tower, one with mirrored walls that wouldn't shut up. There was no elevator or any other way down, but when the princess grew bored of staring at her own pretty face in the mirrors, she decided to jump. She invited all her friends to come along, and they all followed her down—except her best friend, whose invitation had been lost.

The tower was guarded by a gray dragon with jeweled eyes and a hungry maw. It had many legs and moved almost too fast to see, but it pretended to be asleep, and let the princess and her friends sneak past.

And you couldn't have this dream without a prince.

He was both handsome and ugly, bubbly and serious, cautious and brave. In the beginning he lived with the princess in the tower, but later in the dream he seemed to have been outside all along, waiting for her. And in a dream-logic way he was often two princes, which she had to choose between. Sometimes the princess chose the handsome prince, and sometimes the ugly one. Either way, her heart was broken.

And whomever she picked, the dream's ending never changed. The best friend, the one whose invitation had been lost, always tried to follow the princess. But the gray dragon woke up and swallowed her, and liked her taste so much that it came after the rest of them, hungry for more. From inside its stomach, the best friend looked out through the dragon's eyes, and spoke with its mouth, swearing it would find the princess and punish her for leaving a friend behind.

And over all those sleepy weeks, the dream always ended the same way, with the dragon coming for the princess, saying the same words every time. . . .

"Face it, Tally-wa, you're Special."

**Scott Westerfeld** is the acclaimed author of numerous best-selling novels for teens, including the UGLIES sequence; *Uglies*, *Pretties*, *Specials* and *Extras* published by Simon and Schuster. His other teen novels include *The Midnighters Trilogy*, *Parasite Positive*, *Last Days* and *So Yesterday* which was named an ALA Best Book for Young Adults.

Scott was born in Texas and now he and his wife, Justine, alternate summers between Sydney, Australia and New York City. Visit Scott's website at www.scottwesterfeld.com.